Divided Loyalties

STEVEN VEERAPEN

First published in 2019 by Sharpe Books.

CONTENTS

DIVIDED LOYALTIES

Prologue

The North, Summer, 1570

He rapped a gloved hand against the door. Nothing. Tried again, a little louder. Eventually, the hollow sound of boots on wood came from somewhere inside. He chanced a look behind him, away from the mean little shack. The street was deserted, the only sound some pigs grunting down an alley. The lock clicked and light spilled out.

'Please, father,' he said. 'Please, I would speak with you.' The man who answered hesitated, his hand on the door. But he opened it a little wider.

'Who are you?'

'My name's Owen, father. I heard tell there were a priest here, of the old faith.'

'Keep your voice down, please.'

You wouldn't take the man for a priest, thought Owen. He could not have been more than twenty-one, his face beardless and his hair an untidy mop. Rather than vestments, he was wearing a plain, buff-coloured pair of breeches and a stained white shirt. He might have been an apprentice boy. That was probably how they hoped to survive in England. The youthful priest looked over his visitor's shoulder, his eyes wide. His voice trembled when he spoke. 'Were you seen?'

'No, father. I were right careful none should see. But better it were that I come in. It's advice I need, that these bloody 'eretics can't give.'

Another hesitation. 'Yes. Yes, come in, Goodman Owen.'

'Just Owen.'

'Just so.' He threw the door open and stood back, a nervous, friendly smile exposing good teeth. A fair lad, thought Owen, probably from a good family. Still smiling, the priest closed the door as soon as his guest was inside, before leaning over to turn the key. 'Pray call me Father John. Speak freely, please. I have time until–'

His words were cut off. Whilst his back was turned, the man calling himself Owen had pulled out a thin loop of cord and brought it down over his head. He yanked hard.

Father John went down easily. He was not to die – not quite yet – but it was a delicate matter choking someone just to the point of unconsciousness. Mistime it and they would die or come around too quickly. Owen gritted his teeth as he gripped the cord. The young man's hands flailed at first, scrabbling uselessly at his throat, but as his face reddened, he went limp. Owen let him slide to the floor, a small and weightless bundle. Not that it mattered: take even a giant's throat by surprise and he'll drop like a stone.

There was not much time; the other one would return soon, and things had to be made ready. The little hovel was a depressing place. Two mattresses lay against the far wall, a broom stood in a corner, and a couple of upturned crates were doing duty as tables, stubs of candles glowing on them. It would not take long to search. He moved the candles in their cheap holders onto one of the boxes and lifted the lid of the other. Nothing. He reversed the process and found what he was looking for. Typical, he thought – you never got it on the first try. He pulled out the robes, crucifix, and beads. The searchers who came would have found them in the box, of course, but one could never underestimate the stupidity of northerners. They had proven that with their hare-brained rebellion. Better to ensure the baubles were found, and found quickly and publicly. He took them to one of the mattresses and half-hid them underneath, the crucifix poking out like a broken finger.

'Now, young man,' he mumbled, turning back to the unconscious John. 'This will not be pleasant.' He lifted him under the armpits and dropped him face-down on one of the makeshift beds. The young man grunted in his throat. Owen retrieved the broomstick, returned to the mattress, and pulled down the man's breeches. He looked away before doing what he did next, his face an impassive slate. Yet his heart began to race, as it always did before he was about to kill, no matter how much discipline he tried to impose on himself. As he had expected, the pain of defilement roused life back into the priest, and it was only then that his captor did him the service of finishing him off with the cord. There was no resistance. He pulled out the bloodied broom and left the corpse, retreating to a corner of the room.

Time seemed to spin out as he waited. He knew that the priest who shared the shack, an older mentor to the dead man, did his rounds amongst the local papists until late into the night. He had been studying their pattern for over a week, and had even managed to purloin one of the elder fellow's letters of introduction to sympathisers, the better to learn his handwriting. It was an ugly business and he did not like it. Not the murders – that was simply part of the job – but the instructions he had been given to leave the bodies posed just so. There were rules to murder, whether it were done for sport, business, or necessity. He had come to learn them all, he fancied, and the first was that, whenever possible, bodies must disappear. That risked questions, of course – people loved a mystery – but it prevented any accidental evidence. No carelessly dropped gloves, no buttons or locks of hair clasped in dead men's fingers. If the bodies had to be found, though, then the only thing to do was to make the whole thing look explicable. The diamond plot, however, would require display. It would require artistry. On the wings of the musing he reached under his coat and pulled out the scribbled note he had tucked into his belt.

'I cannot live with the burthen of these my great sins and commit myself to one last. May God forgive me.' Would a priest write such a thing? he wondered for the hundredth time. The knave would know, but he could not gain passage to England until the job was done. So, also for the hundredth time, he assured himself that it did not matter. People would believe it of them. He dropped the note next to the dead man and reached under his coat again, this time retrieving a coiled length of rope. With one end tied in a noose, he slung the other over a roof beam and secured it. All was ready now. He inspected the end of the broom handle and silently urged the other priest to hurry up, to return whilst the blood was still wet. Then he blew out all but one candle and moved the box well away from the body.

When Old Father Time returned, he would see nothing amiss until it was too late. Perhaps he would be gone out of the world before seeing anything at all.

The man who had called himself Owen stationed himself against the wall next to the door, his garrotte held tight in his hands, and waited. He allowed himself a little time to think. Did his northern accent need work? Possibly. He would work it on it. And no more 'Owen' – a stupid Welsh name.

Would he be well rewarded? A ghost of a smile passed his face at that. Men who excelled at their profession always were, and few could touch him. He was the ace of diamonds, and those above him would have further use for him. Would killing priests damn him to the fires of Hell? He grinned. If there were a such a place, he had bought passage to it long ago, and at least now he would be a prince of it. His finger wandered under his coat, to the little diamond-topped pin that they had each been given. Satan himself would probably build him a throne made of the fools he had sent before him. Before long it would be a throne to rival the Queen of England's and the Pope's combined.

He shook his head free of thoughts of Hell.

Since childhood, he had been told that only God had the right to kill. In childhood he had learnt that man has spent every year on earth rejecting that foolish notion. He visualised ancient Egyptians burying men and women alive, and Moors swinging strange blades from atop huge Barbary horses, heads flying from spurting necks. It passed the time.

Before ten minutes had gone by, the sound of a key turning in the lock signalled the night's last job of work.

Part One: The Rules of the Game

1

Old Aberdeen, August 1570

The child's cry pierced the air, shrill and insistent. At any other time, in any other place, it might have been a welcome sound, joyful, proclaiming new life. 'Hush, Maria,' said Anne. 'Kat, you must hush her.' The little Scottish girl, round-faced and wide-eyed, lifted the baby from her cradle and rocked her. Instantly the cries ceased. 'Bless you, Kat.'

'She smiles, my lady. She looks for you. Come see.'

Anne Percy, countess of Northumberland, turned away. In truth, she found it difficult to look upon the little girl she had brought into the world only months before. Since fleeing England after the Northern Rising and becoming separated from her husband, her life had been one of uncertainty and continual movement. It seemed a cruel act to bring a child into such a life. Rather than taking her daughter in her arms, she paced the room, her shoes making dull thumps on the bare boards. It was a miserable place, Old Aberdeen – the town had no great house to coddle and protect her. Even the building she was in, the Chancellor's Manse, she was told, was far from even a good-sized townhouse. With longing, she thought of Strathbogie, the magnificent castle cradled in the hills northwest of the burgh. She might have been safe there, she and Maria. Safe for a while but cut off from the world.

She moved to the whitewashed stone wall and cracked open a shutter, letting morning sunshine spill in. The house looked down on an empty alley, but the breeze was welcome. Breathing deeply, she closed her eyes. The late-summer sun was deceptive; unless you stood directly in its gaze, the North Sea wind groped its way under clothing. She was shaken from her thoughts not by the baby or the weather, but by the sound of footsteps coming upstairs. Tensing, she opened her eyes, flashed a warning look at Kat, and turned towards the door. It opened slowly.

George, Lord Seton, stepped over the threshold, a travelling cloak pinned over his shoulder. The hard face, which seldom saw a smile, lit up. Anne returned it, though not without a trace of anxiety. 'What news? All is well?'

'Passing well, my lady. It's a fine ship I've had made ready for you – *The Port of Leith*. We maun make haste, though.' He crossed to her and then, hesitantly, took her hands in his. She smiled again, more fully, tossing her head back and showing her teeth. Rather than letting her hands go limp in his, she traced a finger over his knuckle.

'There is nothing from Lennox? Morton? From any of them?' Her voice dropped to a whisper. 'No whispers in the wind of this diamond league?'

'Nothing,' he replied. His voice, she noticed, was a little cracked. Satisfying. A man in love was a man who could be trusted – even a stern-faced older man. Not for the first time she wondered if he was even aware that he had fallen for her. Probably not – his wife was equally eager to embrace her in friendship.

'Then we are free to leave.' She laid emphasis on the 'we'. No harm in reminding him that he was coming with her. Since coming into Scotland with nothing she had drawn a team of adherents to her side: refugees from the north of England, Catholics from Europe eager to pledge their support, and the many who supported Queen Mary, though she still languished in confinement in England. No man, she supposed, could have done better.

The people of northern Scotland, especially, had adopted her, despite the regent Lennox and his bulldog Morton proclaiming her to be of the northern English stock that had long bedevilled their country. A hollow attack, given the world knew that Scotland's new rulers, the rebels against the rightful queen, were Queen Elizabeth's lapdogs.

Yet little could be achieved in war-torn Scotland, not whilst the Protestant rebels held the reins of power. They could be dealt with later, as could the bastard queen of England. First, she needed to secure her country's future in Europe – the heart of the world. She was undertaking no midnight flight from hazard, but a triumphant entry on to a stage larger and more splendid than the island Elizabeth had poisoned with heresy and blood.

'Aye, my lady,' said Seton. 'Aye. I'll be by your side. You shan't be alone.' A furrow deepened his brow. 'I'll do the queen service winning her friends and freedom in Europe. Not fighting her rebels here. And,' he added, averting his eyes, 'your husband's too. Of course.' She pursed her lips at the justification. Reluctantly, she thought, he released her hands. 'If you could get your servants in order, we'll march through the town and take ship. We'll be flittin' this day.' Her lip twitched at the word 'march'. A show of defiance indeed, for a group of people scurrying out of the country in secret.

'I shall see to it. Bless you, my lord.' She averted her own eyes to the ground in a sham of innocent helplessness. 'I just cannot think what I should have done without your friendship. Without your protection. I should be lost, in faith. Truly lost.'

'Aye,' he repeated, inclining his head. And then, a little awkwardly, 'I'll see to the menfolk. Downstairs.'

When he had gone, Anne folded her arms over her chest and exhaled. 'Kat, see to the child. I shall send others up for my things.' Her things, such as they were, had already been packed into rough wooden coffers. Now that she knew they were going she was desperate to be gone. Before she could crouch down under the low lintel to follow Seton out of the room and down the stairs, a frenzied tumble of steps announced another visitor. In the doorway appeared a young girl, her mousy hair pinned up under a mob cap. Anne looked at her blankly for a few seconds, and then registered the face, but not the name: one of the English girls who had come into her service only a few weeks before. A northerner, she recalled.

'My lady,' said the girl, almost out of breath.

'Ah, bless you, girl – see to these coffer-'

'No time, no time – they are coming for you!'

Anne did not need to know who they were, only which colours they wore. 'Morton or Lennox?' Her voice was business-like.

'Morton.'

'They are in the town?'

'No, but they are making for it.'

'My Lord Seton, he knew of no surprise. Has he just discovered this?'

The girl, Anne thought, looked suddenly evasive, and yet seemed to draw taller in stature. 'I can't speak for the Lord Seton.'

'Then for whom do you speak?'

'My husband.'

'You hus-' Anne looked towards Kat, who had given up wrapping the baby in blankets and was watching the two other women in rapt silence. 'Kat, do you know this girl? Or her husband?'

'No, madam, I've no' spoke with her.'

The countess turned her gaze again to the intruder, this time with narrowed eyes. The name came back to her. 'Margery, isn't it?'

'Yes. No. I mean …' The girl seemed to deflate. 'My name is Amy, my lady. Amy Cole.'

'You have lied to me. Who are you? Do you serve my enemies, do you mean to stay my passage? I can have men in here before you can touch us.' Anne moved in front of Kat and the baby, her dress sweeping the floorboards.

'I … I did lie, but I don't – my husband – we don't serve any Scotch lords. Not truly. Please, my lady, I speak honestly. My husband has been in with the Scotch Protestants, but he-'

'A heretic!'

'No!' The girl's voice had rose in pitch and a look of angry determination passed her face. 'No, madam, no heretic. My husband is a Catholic and he is sworn to see you across the seas. Yet he knows people and knows that the rebel Scots are coming for you. He has fled them and raced ahead to warn you. Please, you must trust us.'

Anne put a hand to her head and rubbed at her temple. 'I shall trust you now, in trust that you shall explain yourself later, girl.'

'Amy,' replied the servant, and put out her lip. Anne glowered back at the insolence. 'My husband is Jack Cole, and we are to be your saviours today. Please, bring the child. No time for the chests.'

9

With little choice, Anne nodded. Amidst protests of, 'but the kists, yer things' from Kat, the women moved downstairs.

The courtyard of the house was a tumult of conversation, servants' voices raised in a jangle of languages. A young man, his hair falling in a fringe over one eye, was moving from group to group, waving his arms in the air. He was splattered with mud and steam rose from the horse he had presumably rode in on. Anne shielded her eyes from the sun and raised her voice. 'We must go, now. Bless you, my good people – I hear we are to be surprised.'

Stunned silence fell across the courtyard and then the voices again began tearing at one another. 'Where is my Lord Seton?' Anne shouted. The frantic chattering stilled again. The young man stepped forward and bowed.

'He has gone for the docks, my lady. I missed him.'

'You are, I think, that impetuous young whippet's husband?' At this, the young man grinned broadly, and the girl, Amy, moved to stand beside him.

'I am.'

'A fine pair of creeping folk you are. Is it true? Are the rebels marching on us? Have you had eyes in their camp?'

Before he could answer, a hooting sound passed over their heads. A hunting horn, Anne thought, and her heart began a deep, hammering thump. Yet her mind remained calm, analytical. It was excitement that powered it. This strange new life, still dreamlike, was a world away from the library and closets of Topcliffe. The horn flattened and died out. Still some distance away but carrying low on the wind. 'Them?'

'Yes, madam. Please, take my horse – I'll take another.'

'You are coming?'

'I am to see you safe to the continent.'

'On whose orders?' cut in a new voice. At Anne's elbow had appeared her secretary, a sallow-faced man called Cottam. Anne looked down at him.

'Yes,' she said. 'Who is your master, young sirrah?'

Jack Cole glanced at his wife and both took on the evasive look Amy had worn earlier. 'It is hard to explain, my lady. And not the time. Please, take my horse.'

10

'Lady Northumberland shall sit on my horse,' sniffed Cottam. 'And her girl shall take the baby on yours. Madam, I do not trust this pair. They mean to stop you and hand you over to those heretics.' The horn sounded again, louder. Anne thought she could hear hoofbeats echoing from somewhere to the south of the burgh. They seemed to be outpacing her heart.

'Fight them later, Will. Help me and Kat mount and take us from here.'

Within a few minutes all were mounted, including the disagreeable young couple, and Anne shouted across the heads of her remaining servants, 'my good people – we are attacked by enemies who would stop our passage. For the love you bear God and myself, go out into the streets and hold them.' Then, turning to her companions, she said in a lower voice, 'let us be off!' Riding alone, she led Cottam and Kat out of the courtyard, and, turning, saw Jack and Amy Cole bringing up the rear. A group of male servants, armed with knives, saws, and, in one case, a broom, marched out after them, turning in the opposite direction. A stable boy with a bucket on his head and a riding crop in his hand ran to join them.

They rode pell-mell through the streets, passing wattle-and-daub houses, sending up clouds of dusty mud. A huddle of women scattered as they passed by the cathedral and into another maze of alleyway-like streets, buildings overhanging like curious old judges.

'Stop!'

'No – no!'

Rounding a corner, Anne heard the cries behind her and reined in. She twisted her neck to see what was happening. A man in the austere black of the Protestants was grappling at the Coles' horse with one hand. In the other, he held a club. 'What is this?' she shouted.

'A ballie,' said Cottam, drawing up alongside her. 'Must think he has more to gain by selling us to the heretics. Probably one himself. Leave them, my lady, before we are all taken.'

Anne remained, irresolute, watching the scene unfold. Amy, she saw, had taken hold of the end of the bat as the baillie had tried to swing it and would not let go. 'Let us go, you fat turd!'

11

she screeched. 'Let go!' Her husband was kicking out with one leg. All of this seemed to frighten the horse, who reared up, nearly toppling them both. The hunting horn, definitely within the town walls now, bleated, and the baillie half-turned to it. Jack leant forward and seemed to whisper to the horse, calming it. When their attacker returned his attention to them, the pair were once again firmly seated, and their mount had swung around. Fear erupted on the baillie's face, his triumphant expression wiped away by sudden realisation. The horse bounded over him, throwing him to the ground and trampling him underfoot. Not content, it kicked its back legs out, throwing the unfortunate man. Blood sprayed against the wall of the house he had come from. A hoof had caught the side of his head. Jack Cole's eyes met hers, his grin fixed and nervous. Amy's did too, but those were full of angry glee. She nodded at them and the whole party continued its flight.

The smell of the sea, fresh and invigorating, rose towards them as they reached the shore. Thundering over clumps of beach grass, they made for the stone-built harbour. Once there, Seton's party was not difficult to find. He stood on the docks, directing men and goods onto one of the ships that stood amongst the forest of masts. Before they could get within speaking distance, he had spotted them and apparently begun hurrying his orders.

'We are surprised,' Anne called, without preamble.

'Board, my lady. You and your people. Now.'

Immediately, Seton hopped away from the landing board and helped her dismount, the rest of the group tossing themselves to the ground. 'Hellfire with the horses,' snapped Seton. 'Shift yourselves aboard and leave them.' Needing no further encouragement, Kat, Cottam, and the Coles followed him and Anne up the planked ramp and onto the deck, crouching low to avoid the rigging and the half-furled sails. As soon as they were all safely aboard, he was barking orders down to a surly group of sailors still on dry land.

As soon as she was on deck, Anne moved to the ropes that formed a low railing and looked back towards the burgh. Smoke had begun issuing from somewhere. Men's cries carried on the wind. She stood transfixed, watching as a colourful cloud emerged from between the nearest houses. She recognised a standard – the arms of the house of Morton – and cursed under her breath. They were coming for her, just as the Cole girl had said. Behind them were visible the tiny figures of her own folk, their arms rising and falling as they appeared to be hurling rocks.

'We are moving, my lady.' She turned to face Cottam. 'Your things, though, I think are lost. No doubt to be worn by some fat common heretics' wives.'

'I have lost more precious things,' she said.

'What was that?'

She did not respond. Instead, she looked over his shoulder for her daughter, who was in Kat's arms. One child would be coming with her at least, she thought, cuffing away a tear and hoping it would look only like the sting of saltwater had got to her. Goodbye sensible Elizabeth. Goodbye flighty Lucy. Goodbye darling Jane. And goodbye, Thomas – God be with you. One day, if He was good, little Maria might meet her sisters, who were safe with friends in England; would meet her father, who languished in the evil Morton's custody.

Farewell, old life.

She had heard or read somewhere that every ending was a beginning, for as long as the world endured. As her eyes roved over the strange crew who were sailing with her, she prayed it were true. Amy Cole was offering the baby one of her fingers. Jack Cole was staring down at them both, a lopsided smile on his face. Neither seemed upset by the fact that they had almost certainly killed a man. 'Who are they?' Cottam asked, 'who are they to be coming with us?'. Again, Anne ignored him. She returned her gaze to the shore. Morton's men were drawing closer, mostly on foot as they crossed the sand-grass. Anne's stomach lurched as *The Port of Leith* seemed to settle in the water. Looking down, she saw a group of sweating, shirtless men pushing at the hull with long planks. Then the ship seemed to detach itself from the dockside, as though cut loose by a knife. She felt her legs waver.

'Will you come down?' It was not Cottam this time, but

Seton.

'You have saved us all, my lord,' Anne said, remembering to smile. 'Bless you.'

'Aye,' he said, looking down and shuffling his feet, a forty-year-old boy of sixteen. 'Those soldiers will turn tail back to Lochleven, lest your … your husband … attempts escape. Westmorland's friends will see that he follows us from the town in some days. The Low Countries will see the rebirth of the true faith on this benichted island. It'll be a lang space before I see Scotland again.' The things men do for love and loyalty, she thought.

Anne nodded. The angry shrieking on the shore rose, as the dockyard workers threw themselves into a melee with the attackers. Then it began to fall, as the ship put out to sea. 'A farewell to Scotland,' she said. 'And a good morrow to that strange pair.'

2

Jack stood with his hands behind his back and a nervous smile stretching his features. The countess did not invite him to sit, though there was a cushioned stool opposite the narrow cot on which she sat. A tall, handsome woman, with soft, refined features, somewhere in her thirties. It was a nonsense, he knew, that women's faces betrayed their breeding – many noblewomen he had seen looked like decorated draymen – but this lady's eyes reflected an educated and razor-sharp mind. She let silence spin out between them and he stood, content to be watched, hoping that simple honesty showed on his face.

'What is your true name?' she said at length, not taking her eyes from his face.

'Jack Cole, my lady.'

She continued to stare awhile, before blinking and speaking. 'And for whom do you work, Jack Cole?'

'I …' she was not going to make things easy for him. He had had a speech prepared, but it had been for a stupid, grateful woman, not a sharp one. 'I am paid by the ambassador to France. England's ambassador, Sir Henry Norris.'

'Then you are paid by Elizabeth,' she said. The ship rolled a little and she sucked in her cheeks, her prominent cheekbones catching the light from a tiny window. 'You are not my friend.'

'Madam, I … it is true I've been employed by the English queen. I had no choice, nor my wife. We were constrained to it. We were made to flee England. Yet I am a true Catholic. I have betrayed my orders and …. In truth I've risked my life to see you out of Scotland. Because it was the right thing to do.'

'Then,' she said, her voice cold, 'you are an ambidexter.' Jack opened his mouth to speak and then closed it. To his shame, the countess half-smiled. 'I mean that you play on both hands, sirrah. You are a man who will sell himself to any who care to pay and betray them afterwards. A man not to be trusted. A man without loyalty.'

He balled his hands into fists. There it was. Loyalty. Everyone expected it, and condemned others for lacking it, even when their own was questionable. Had Lady Northumberland not betrayed her queen, heretic though Elizabeth was? Was loyalty not inferior to faith? A heavy, clunking word, loyalty, even the sound of it: an anvil wrapped in purple velvet. In the past he had had no loyalties to ideas or men, preferring instead to espouse whatever he thought others expected. No more. 'I am no such thing. I mean, I do what I think right, not what pays.'

'What are you,' she said over him, 'a young gentleman deprived of his fortune? Your voice speaks the north to me, yet you have been in league with the southern pretender and her minions. A knight, perhaps, selling his sword and secrets?'

'I am,' said Jack, raising his chin, 'formerly a groom in the household of the duke of Norfolk. Son to a yeoman now dead.'

'A yeoman's son?' For the first time, surprise registered on her face, and was quickly smoothed away. 'You betrayed Norfolk to the she-wolf?'

'No, madam. I ...' He faltered, shaking his head. 'Can I tell you my story from the beginning?'

Jack thought he detected interest from the countess at the mention of Norfolk's name, and he tilted his head as he asked his question. She did not answer immediately, but again let silence fall between them. Outside, two sailors were hurling oaths and curses about each other's mothers. Others were egging them on to deeper channels of vulgarity and cheering and sucking their teeth loudly at every insult. Eventually, she glanced towards the window. 'I gather it will be some days before we reach our destination. Speak, then, if you will, Cole.'

'Call me Jack, my lady, please. My masters have always done so,' he said, before launching into the catalogue of dramas which had set him on the strange path he had followed since leaving Norfolk's employ.

***

Amy did not like being at sea. She liked it even less that her husband seemed to be unaffected by the interminable rolling and pitching. Most of the women aboard – she and a few other

16

sour serving women – had been confined in a tiny, unlit cargo hold deep in the ship's bowels, so small one could not even stand fully. Only the countess, her baby, and the young nurse, Kat, had been given the luxury of a small, velvet-lined cabin on a deck above.

The Port of Leith pitched deeper in the water and rose like a cork, and Amy's stomach went with it. She huddled her knees up to her chin and braced her back against the bulwark. No matter how often she sailed, she would never get used to it. It was like being buried alive, the weight of the upper decks pressing down on you. 'I need air,' she said to no one in particular, rising on wobbly legs and feeling her way along the bulwark to the patch of light that deigned to intrude from above. A short rope ladder hung down from it.

Emerging from the darkness, she clutched her way out into daylight, timing her steps with the movements of the ship, and made her way to the upper deck, desiring only to have nothing hanging over her head. As she got closer to the more habitable areas, she felt eyes on her and, turning, saw a sailor staring. He did not break his gaze. Instead, he grinned, and deliberately looked her up and down. A drawn-faced devil with a neatly clipped moustache – but a cocky one. Of course she would be getting peeped at when she looked like a drab. Without a word, she raised her middle finger, turned her hand, and jabbed it at him, pulling a face and moving on. His booming laughter followed her.

Without realising it, she had reached the deck on which the countess' cabin lay. Curious to see the kind of luxury the little maid Kat was enjoying so that she might complain about the unfairness, she moved towards it. Outside the door, she saw the clerk, Cottam, standing with his ear to it.

'Listening at doors, sir?' she asked, a note of triumph in her voice. He started and turned, anger further darkening his features.

'You … how dare you speak to me like that. I shall tell the countess to tell your husband what a sharp little creature you are.'

'Tell her you were listening at her door, you mean?'

Discomfort always made her bold. Boldness, she knew, could sometimes make her behave stupidly.

'Hold your tongue, wench. As it happens, I was on the point of seeking you. Your man's in there now, and the countess would have you go in and corroborate the wild tales he tells. Without speaking to him first.'

Amy looked him squarely in the eye. She had never heard the word 'corroborate' before, and suspected he knew it. 'I'll be glad to speak before her. If you'll kindly get out of my way. Shall I keep my voice loud enough for you to hear?' She made to shove past him, but he gripped her arm just as her fingers brushed the iron door handle.

'I trust neither you nor the man you call husband,' he hissed. 'I shall be watching you both. Traitors never prosper.'

'I've no need to care what you think,' she snapped. 'Only what the countess thinks.' There, she thought. No friends won. It was a curious thing, but given what her life had become, she truly seldom cared what people thought. Only Jack mattered – if they could be safe somewhere together, they could overcome anything. He had proven it by coming back from the dead the previous year. 'Now let go of my arm.' He did. She opened the door without knocking or giving Cottam a second glance.

Inside, the small chamber was a study in opulence compared to her own quarters. Dominating the room was a bunk on which the countess sat, an empty, blanketed coffer next to it. Beside a stool stood Lord Seton, his arms folded, and just in front of her was Jack. He turned and smiled. She was unsure whether it was nervous, habitual, or a sign that things were going well.

'Amy Cole,' said the countess. 'The woman I wished to see.' Amy inclined her head. The older woman had a Yorkshire edge to her speech. It was an accent she had always found straightforward and sensible, quite unlike the affected style of English spoken in the south. 'Your husband has been telling us a strange tale. So strange I had to call his lordship in to hear it. Do you believe it, my lord, or should we have the wife verify it? I trust to your shrewd opinion as in all things.'

'No harm having the lass speak,' said Seton, deepening his voice.

'I agree. Wise. Where were you living a year ago?'

'In the Shrewsburys' household, my lady.'

'And whom did you serve?'

'The Scotch queen. Queen Mary. And the Shrewsburys, of course.'

Seton and the countess exchanged glances. 'Describe her to me,' he said.

'Queen Mary ... is a tall lady. Like yourself, madam.' She frowned a little. 'Pretty. Gracious. Liked to walk and embroider.'

'Who visited her?'

'Many. I recall a man from Scotland. Bog. Or Bock. Sandy was the first name, I think.'

Seton nodded, satisfied. 'They match.'

'Now,' said the countess, clapping her hands together, 'we come to the stranger parts of the tale. Plots upon plots and Queen Elizabeth's minions. Tell us what happened.' Amy looked at Jack, who nodded encouragement. She inclined her head and spilled out the story.

'And thereafter you came to live where?'

'France,' said Amy. 'A strange land. We have lived there nearly this whole year. Until a few weeks ago, when Sir Henry Norris said we were to go to Scotland.' She balked at saying the man's name. As far as she was concerned, she and Jack had gone as paupers to Norris, begging for work and aid from England's ambassador. Not that she would ever admit that publicly. It would mean admitting that Jack could not provide for them without resorting to spiery.

'Why you? Why should two watching sort of servants living in France be sent to Scotland?'

Amy shrugged. 'We were told to ensure that you were returned to England, my lady. To be investigated for your ... um ... for your crimes.' Seton bristled at the word, but the countess pressed on, her face stony.

'But why you?'

'I can't say. Can't speak for the men of power in England. Maybe ... maybe, perhaps they knew we shouldn't betray one another. A man sent as friend to the Scotch Protestant rebels and a woman sent into your service. I can't say.'

'And yet here I sit, on a ship bound for the Low Countries. Like your husband, you betray your masters. Tell me, which faith do you profess?'

'I'm a Catholic, madam,' said Amy. That was true. She had converted in France. She did not particularly care about the intricacies of theological debate and argument, but it made for a quiet life. Besides, it seemed a fair enough religion. It left God and Godly matters largely in the hands of priests, as one would leave matters of the law to lawyers and medical matters to physicians and apothecaries. Catholicism meant not having to concern yourself with deep and troubling things in which you were not expert.

The countess sighed. 'And so true faith has led you to deliver me from Scotland. I imagine you expect me to thank you.'

'No, my lady. My husband does what he thinks is right. In his heart. I do as he does.' She felt him beam at her, and then felt a little stab of resistance rise. 'I will protect him. Always.'

'As a wife should,' said Seton. He did not smile, but Amy felt she had won a minor victory.

'And I suppose you are none of the diamond league? Either of you?' This time her words came out like a torrent of hailstones. Amy looked at her blankly and, turning, saw the same confusion written on Jack's face.

'What's the diamond league?' he asked.

Again, the countess sighed. 'From what I understand, a group of hot Protestants. Lord Seton?'

'My eyes in Scotland,' the older man began, 'tell me that folk calling themselves the house of diamonds made entreaties to the rebels. Morton's rebels and the false regent Lennox's. If your tale stands true, you have had dealings with the hard sort of heretics.'

'Those men never mentioned diamonds,' said Jack. Amy noticed his face had paled at the mention of the men who had tried to kill them the previous year. His voice had lowered too. 'No. Never said anything about diamonds. Who are they?'

'In truth, we do not know. Perhaps no one of any importance. It is only that we heard that they offered themselves to the

Scotch heretics. Offered to help do harm to the true faith. If the Scots would give assurance – or money – to their league and help spread their great hatred.'

'Claimed to be working against the Roman church across Europe,' put in Seton. 'My ears in the rebel camps heard whispers that there were diamond agents infecting the continent. One headed for the true faithful in the north of England, one somewhere about the French queen, and others reaching across the seas.'

'And then you two appear. From England, sailing to the Low Countries, and bragging of living in France this past several months.'

'We know no diamonds,' said Jack, firmly. Amy shook her head in support.

'Very well,' said the countess. 'As I say, it is perhaps nothing. Another crop of heretics. Pray leave us, both of you. You might do me service by finding Kat and my daughter and sending them back here. Lord Seton and I shall discuss whether or not to repose trust in you. Whether your tale is true or not, I cannot help but think you bring trouble on all our heads.' Jack and Amy bowed, and turned to leave. 'Wait,' she added. 'I am curious. If you have betrayed your masters, how do you expect to live? I cannot imagine that demon Burghley will allow Norris to let you do so for long.'

'My lady, we … we will find a way,' said Jack.

'Together,' added Amy.

They stepped out onto the deck. The sun had disappeared behind a blanket of clouds. Cottam had apparently given up listening at the door. Jack took her hand. 'Did you think about it?' he asked.

'About what?'

'About what next. For us.'

'No,' she said. 'What does it matter?'

'You don't care where we fetch up?'

'No.' Her lip twitched. A desire to be light came over her, and to share that lightness with him. 'Do you know, with each day that passes, I reckon I hate everyone just the same, no matter where they are or where they come from.' Jack laughed. 'To the

21

devil with it,' she said. 'A new life in the Low Countries. We'll find work somewhere. Work our way up. If the countess won't have us, I mean.'

'I really love you, Amy Cole.'

'Well, that's why I stick with you, isn't it?' She smiled and let his arms enfold her, and for a moment they were the innocents they had once been, embracing in their own tiny chamber in the duke of Norfolk's house.

'Your hands are cold,' he said, letting go of her, and drawing them up to his lips. He kissed warmth into them. She felt her stomach twist.

A crack of thunder rent the sky, and the ship began to roll on an enormous swell. The pair stumbled towards a rope-railing and gripped it. Amy cried out as the water rushed up to meet them in a spray of salt mist. They hung there, at a sharp angle between sea and sky, for what seemed like an eternity. Then slowly, interminably, the deck beneath them began to right itself and the sea to retreat. All around them, sailors' shouts began to fill the air.

'I thought we'd had it there,' said Jack. Astonishingly, he was grinning again. 'I thought we were gone in the sea for sure.'

'Jesus, Jack.' She turned her face skywards. Rain had begun to fall, and she blinked it away. In every direction the horizon blurred into slate.

'The next yin'll be worse,' said a sailor, pushing by them. 'Better get oot o' it if you dinnae want tae be washed oot tae sea. Storm's comin'. Bad yin. Next yin'll be worse.'

3

'Why have we stopped? Where are we? I mean, we have stopped, haven't we?' asked Jack.

'You should know these waters as well as anyone,' said Cottam.

They were closed in the room that was serving as the countess' male servants' quarters, a room in which the windows did not close properly, and misty air hissed in in clouds. Jack judged it had been ten minutes since the ship had stopped its plunging progress. Instead it had settled to a surprisingly gentle bob. It was their second day at sea.

'I know that we're passing England,' he said.

'Then perchance you have some scheme afoot,' snapped Cottam, throwing off the blanket that lay over him and getting to his feet. 'I shall warn her ladyship of it, mark you.' Before Jack could respond, the surly clerk had tilted his chin and crossed towards the door. It flew open at his touch and he was gone.

Jack sighed and lay on his back, rocking with the gentler movement of the ship at rest. Every so often another jet of water spurted in and sank into the stained floorboards. It had crept into his own blanket. It was no good, sitting around. He was beginning to think about the man in black in Old Aberdeen – the one who had tried to stop their horse. Very probably he was dead – or worse, his mind might be whilst his body lived. Neither possibility was attractive, and both threatened to paint pictures in his dreams.

The problem was that he had nothing to do, and that was always apt to set his teeth on edge. Even during their exile in Paris he had managed to keep himself occupied, acting as an ostler at an inn in the Quartier Latin whilst Amy mended clothes. That had been their front at least, as secretly he had passed on to Sir Henry Norris the comings and goings of English Catholics. Only, though, when he judged those Catholic men to be conspicuous enough that it would look odd to his

23

master if he did not reveal their presence. And never, never, did he reveal exactly where they had come from or where they were going, even when he knew.

It was an odd sort of compromise – an intelligencer who sympathised with the enemy. Each day he expected that one of Norris' men would clap him in irons, or that he might even take a knife in the gut from a Catholic who knew only that once a month he visited the Faubourg Saint-Germain, a cap pulled low over his head, and slipped into the stables to pass over a list of names. If his conscience ever ached, the knowledge that the names on the list were of men who had a head start of days eased it. If he worried about betraying his master, the pompous Sir Henry Norris, who never deigned to meet him personally, he told himself that at least he did not share with the Catholics any of the names he heard whispered amongst the staff of the big house – 'Captain Sassetti', or 'Captain Franchiotto'. He was an invisible spy to both sides, blending in, not important enough to be noticed. Even the language had come to him easily; he was not word-perfect, but having to speak it every day, month after month, had provided the basics, and the accent was enjoyable mimicry.

The game was up now, though. It had been since the day that one of Norris' servants had arrived at the inn with written instructions. He could still recall the sudden beat of his heart at the sight of the man – who never came to the inn – with the paper in his gloved hand. An arrest warrant, he had thought, not even sure that ambassadors in foreign countries could issue such things. Instead, it had been a letter from Norris himself, commanding that he and his wife should leave the city and take ship for Scotland, there to insert themselves into the service of Queen Elizabeth's friends, and the treacherous countess of Northumberland's household. On no account was the traitor to be allowed to find succour with papists abroad, and if the Scotch lords needed aid in detecting her and handing her over to England, every courtesy was to be extended to them. Jack knew as soon as he had read it that he could not put the woman, wherever she was hiding in Scotland, in the hands of her enemies, English or Scottish. Yet one did not refuse instructions signed by the master. Instead, he decided to enjoy the sight of a new country and let God guide his actions.

Amy, he knew, would not be content to let God do anything without giving Him fifty answers back. Still, she was loyal. He smiled at the thought of her, shuttered somewhere beneath him in the creaking ship. There was that word again. It was something Amy had never struggled with. If he had learnt one thing about her, it was that she was loyal to a fault. Those she loved – and she really only had him – she would kill for, as she had proven. Everyone else could go to the devil. If he had learnt something else, it was that she spoke French like an English mastiff with a mouthful of marbles. He smiled to himself. A sudden urge to see her washed over him, to rest his head in her lap and lie together as man and wife. The least he could do was see if the malady that affected her on the sea had passed with the stopping of the ship. He sprang to his feet and moved towards the door. Cracking it open, he saw that the sky had darkened. It must be late, or the days were getting shorter already. A figure loomed out of the darkness and he squinted to see if it was Cottam.

'Cole,' snapped Lord Seton. Jack stepped back, bowing his head but keeping the door open. Seton did not step inside. 'Do you ken Briddleston?'

'I dinnae ken it, my lord.' Seton gave a half-smirk at the Scots Jack had picked up during his weeks posing as an English messenger amongst the Protestants there.

'Somewhere a ways from York.'

'We're not stopping?' Fear briefly clutched at Jack's heart. Yet Seton did not have the air of a panicked man.

'No, no, no. Dinnae fash yourself, lad. It is this storm, the captain says. A north-eastern wind attacks us. The countess shall be feart. We have had to take shelter in a bay in Briddleton, or Briddleston.'

'Bridlington?'

'Aye,' he said, an eyebrow raised. 'Possibly that. You do ken it?'

'It's in the north,' offered Jack. 'I know that. The north would be safe awhile for the countess. Do we have to go ashore?' His forehead wrinkled. She would not be safe for long, not anywhere in England.

'No, no, no,' Seton said, wiping rain from his brow. 'We drop anchor here until God grants us safe passage. Already it is blowing itself out, the captain says. We are not alone. Other boats have hailed us.'

'Others? Do they know who we carry?'

'They do not. They cannot. We are a merchant vessel out of Scotland is all they know.'

Jack exhaled relief and smiled broadly. It was not the old smile he used to use, the one that sometimes unsettled people, but one of genuine joy. 'Then we're safe.'

'Aye, we are that. A fine vessel this. Yet I shall speak to the countess just the same. It might be she is worried at this sudden delay. So close to England.' He turned his head back to the misty rain before returning his gaze to Jack. 'I did not like to yap in front of the lady,' he said, moving into the doorway. 'But when she called me yesterday to hear your spiel, you said that you were in the household of my queen. I feared you might still your tongue for fear of drawing her tears. A good, soft-hearted lady is the countess.' Jack noticed that he stared off towards his cot as he said it. 'Tell me, laddie, is Queen Mary in chains? Is she held fast by that damned bastard-queen and her imps?'

'Her Majesty … her Majesty is full of spirit, I think,' said Jack. The image of Mary of Scotland came into his mind, tall and smiling, touching his hand as she climbed down from her horse, her breath hot in his ear.

'A lass of spirit, aye, she is that,' smiled Seton.

'And not liking to be caged.'

'She was never one to be confined for long. And she won't be, not as long as her friends have breath in our bodies. You are for my queen, over the pretender?'

Jack looked directly at Seton and nodded. 'If I can be. In my conscience.'

'Hmm. Cannae see into a man's conscience, more's the pity.' Neither spoke for a moment, letting the sound of water, from above and below, splash and patter. Seton shook his head, as though clearing cobwebs. 'God's foot, but it is damp in here, boy. Can you not shut those windows?' Jack glanced behind him. Seton shared the room at night, albeit he had a bunk fastened to a corner rather than a pile of raggedy blankets on the floor. 'See to it. I'm not minding hard living on this voyage. I am minded not to be drowned in my own bed without her even going down.'

Jack nodded his head again and, once Seton had gone, went over to the window which hung loosely on its frame. Window, he thought, was the wrong word on two levels. Portholes, they were called at sea. And, given that it was a jagged wooden shutter on a rusted hinge, even that seemed extravagant. He pulled his sleeve down over his hand, wary of splinters, and pushed it shut, as he had done dozens of times. It fell back inwards. With another hand he jiggled the hinge and then closed it again. When that didn't work, he tried both at the same time, holding it shut awhile. As soon as his hands left it, it flew open. 'Fucking stupid piece of shit!' he shouted, ripping the whole thing, hinge and all, from the bulwark. He threw it to the floor where it lay dejected. His face crimsoned. Now you've done it, he thought. Hardly worth the satisfaction of a moment of temper. He could not even blame anyone else – Seton had put him to the task directly, and there were no children aboard capable of such damage. He picked up the pieces and tried to slot them back in. The wind, maybe, could have done it.

'Tssk,' said a cool voice behind him. He spun around, his mouth already forming an apology. A gloved hand clamped over it. 'You are a troubled lad.' He was staring into the eyes of a moustachioed sailor he had spotted about the ship, and he tried to mumble inarticulate swear words. He stopped when he saw the glint of metal in the fellow's other hand. 'You and I are to take a trip, Mr Cole. Not a long one. I don't want to have to cut you first, but I will deliver you to old Neptune in ribbons if you cry out.' From the hard look he was given, Jack could tell that he meant it.

***

Movement stirred Amy from her dreams. For a few moments

she was tucked up in her cot over the stables of the inn on the Place de la Contrescarpe where Jack looked after horses. Dimly, she wondered why the cot was rocking, and even in the blackness the bitter sting of salt, sweat, and musky wood filled her nostrils and reminded her where she was. Her stomach instinctively sought to cartwheel, and she lay still, willing it to pass, as it had the evening before when they had stopped. She had considered going up and seeking out Jack then, but had instead found herself sharing stories in the dark with her neighbours, the washerwomen who thought her quite exotic for having been resident in Paris. As unpleasant as the coffin-like, slimy chamber was, being cut off from the sight of the waves and avoiding using your legs seemed to stave off the butterflies. Somewhat, anyway.

Her companions were still asleep, and she clambered to her feet, planting them far apart and walking crab-like to where her hands told her the rope-ladder was. She climbed it and emerged into dazzling sunlight. She tiptoed along a corridor, up a tiny flight of wooden stairs, and then another, until she reached the upper deck. In the wash of the ship she could see dozens of others, of all sizes, and realised that they must have spent the night cheek by jowl in a company of boats sheltering from the squall. A good thing, she thought, that she had stayed inside. Women wandering about the deck might have attracted attention from the lusty sailors within spitting distance of the ship. Looking up at the clouds, she put her fists to the small of her back and arched it until it cracked, wondering what time it was. She had not learnt to read the sun and missed the regular chiming of church bells. Late enough for breakfast, anyway. Stale bread, she thought, and warm, watered-down ale with unidentifiable flecks of God-only-knew-what floating in it. Hurrah. She would be as thin as a ghost by the time they made land. Well, it was only for a few days, and she would have to see if Jack wanted anything, or any of the other menfolk.

Maintaining her unsteady gait, she made towards the men's quarters. When she reached them, she stood hesitantly, and then shivered it away and knocked. The door opened and Cottam's gaunt face stared out. 'You,' he said, leering. 'Returning your husband after a night spent in lust? Do not think I shan't tell Lady Northumberland that you spent your time in pleasure, both of you.'

Amy gaped stupidly, and then anger rose. 'Go to the devil,' she said. His eyes flared.

'You common-tongued whelp, how dare you!' Amy recovered her wit, stifling the urge to claw at him.

'Wait! What do you say, Jack's not here? Where is he?'

'As if you do not know, after he–'

'I don't know. I haven't seen him since yesterday afternoon.' Panic bubbled. 'I haven't seen him,' she repeated. Cottam sneered and made to shut the door. 'Please!' She stuck her foot in. 'I'm sorry,' she said, her teeth clenched. 'I'm sorry, Mr Cottam, for speaking so. I swear before God I haven't seen my husband since yesterday.' Cottam's eyes narrowed as he read her face. 'He didn't sleep with you last night?'

'No. Haven't seen the fool since he broke a window. We've been all night swimming in foul airs from the sea. No doubt he has ranged away to hide from his crime.'

'But where is he?' A note of hysteria had crept into her voice. Cottam shrugged, but she thought she read curiosity in his face, if not suspicion.

'Perhaps the sailors favour his company, beardless young whelp.'

'To hell with you,' snapped Amy, unable to contain herself. 'Lord Seton!' she shouted. 'Are you there, my lord?' Cottam's eyes popped and he tried again to wrestle the door, but the rumble of Seton's voice interrupted him.

'Who is there? Kat?'

'Amy Cole, my lord. Please, please come. Please.' Irritated murmuring filled the air, and Amy had time to look at Cottam in triumph before he was forced to step back and make way for Seton. The older man stood, grumpy-looking and unshaven, his fine doublet unbuttoned.

'What do you mean by this, coming to the men's quarters?'

'I can't find my husband!'

'Ha! Young Cole. If he's a thimble of sense he'll be hiding from me, so he will. Asked him to fix a window in here and he breaks it and is gone.'

'I can't find him!'

'Have you looked, girl?' Amy bit her lip, turning on the spot and blinking at the sun. 'Don't you be turning your back on your betters, lass, when I'm having words with you.' Amy barely heard him, but when he spoke again, the softness that had come into his voice brought her back. 'Ach, listen, lass, he's not grown a fish-tail and taken to the sea, has he? Like as not he's supping breakfast. Now you go a wee wander and come to me when I'm dress– when you've found him. Tell him not to fash about the window. We'll be home and dry in but a day or two. You find him and bring him to me and don't be bothering my lady. She needs her rest, her and the bairn.'

Amy stared at the door as it closed, her mind racing. He broke a window and hid. Breakfast, she thought – he'll be having breakfast somewhere in the sun.

He wasn't. Nor was he in the galley. Or the deck. Amy wandered everywhere she could, stopping only to vomit over a rope-railing. Then she tried again, less wildly, more methodically, supposing that they might just have missed each other somewhere, despite how small the ship was. It was no good. The sailors at first ignored her, and then began laughing at her and calling her names, to which she did not even bother to respond with insults. When she returned to Seton, her panic had risen to such a height that he and Cottam had to take an arm each and march her to the countess. If they did not escort her, she insisted, she would burst in herself and demand the lady order the ship to turn around. 'He's gone in the sea,' she said, tears beginning to run from her eyes. 'He's fallen, he's fallen in, and we've just been sailing away and leaving him, leaving him drowning.' It had become fixed in her mind; she could see him, groping in the dark for the rope, hoping to relieve himself over the side, only for the deck to pitch, slope, and deposit him into the depths

'Cottam,' Seton snapped when they stood before the door to the countess's cabin. 'Take her in and explain matters. I shall speak to the captain. Gang, now.' He released Amy's arm and stamped off, allowing the clerk to roughly drag her inside. Out of the corner of his mouth he hissed, 'keep quiet, woman. Do not forget yourself.'

'My lady,' Amy cried, as soon as they were in. The little scene, rather than Cottam's furious look, shut her mouth. Lady Northumberland was lying supine on the bed, one arm over her eyes. Kat, the nursemaid, was sitting on the stool, the baby in her arms. The countess rose, her expression more curious than otherwise. 'What is this?' she asked. Something of her calmness communicated itself to Amy, and she let her arm slip from Cottam's grip.

'This wench says her husband has run off, my lady,' he said.

'Run off, at sea?'

'He's not aboard, my lady,' Amy said. The passion had drained from her voice. 'He's not anywhere. I can't find him, not anywhere.' It rose again. 'He's gone over the side, he's gone overboard in the night, I know it!'

'Calm yourself,' said the countess.

'She's insensible,' Cottam sniffed. 'Mad.' Amy turned furious eyes on him, ready and eager to begin shouting. A lifetime of being spoken down to and spoken over had taught her exactly how best to make her voice heard.

'Is it true the husband is gone, Mr Cottam?' The countess seemed to sense a fracas brewing and sought to forestall it.

'So she says. His lordship is making some enquiry of the captain. Yet I think there is some dark business afoot. I said, my lady, that the pair could not be trusted, man or wife. I thank God we are put to sea again before they could work their design.'

'We've no design, you pompous goat,' spat Amy, before looking again to the countess. 'He's fallen in, I know it. And we've been sailing on while he drowned.' She began sobbing, anger, frustration, and shock reddening her face. The sound woke the baby, who began to match it.

'Kat, take her out. Walk with her, feed her, anything,' said Lady Northumberland. She screwed her eyes shut briefly, and kneaded her forehead, before smoothing her features. As Kat bustled out, holding the screaming child in a close embrace, Lord Seton opened the door and stood back for her. 'My lord, I hope you have some solution to this madness which overtakes us. We are making for Bruges still, are we not?'

'Aye, my lady.'

'What news of the boy?'

'Jack,' mumbled Amy.

'None. Yet …' he trailed off, biting his lip as though deciding whether to speak further in company. He shrugged. 'The captain says another loon has gone. Lad who joined as a sailor not a day before we left Scotland. From the Low Countries, he said, looking for passage home. Spoke little. Looks like he made off during the night. Skiff's missing.'

'What?' This was Amy, wild hope drying her eyes. 'What's a skiff? Did Jack go with him?'

'A skiff,' said the countess, raising a knuckle to her lips, 'it is a small craft, is it not?'

'Aye, madam, a wee thing. For passage between larger vessels. Or to make for shore. The captain reckons if it carried the two men, one other maun have been aboard *The Port of Leith* for to lower it. He's asking the rest of the lads now. If any has helped a robbery in the taking of it, he'll be flogged for it.'

'So he's alive? He went off on a boat? Why? He wouldn't go on a boat without telling me!'

'Mrs Cole …' The countess started to rise, and Seton ploughed past the two servants to give her his arm. 'Bless you, my lord. You are sweet to me.' He smiled. 'Mrs Cole, I cannot speak for your husband. I do not know him. I have said before I have my cares regarding you and him both.' A head taller than Amy, she looked down and drew in her cheeks. 'Yet I think he would not dare to leave you without word.' Amy shook her head, trying to make sense of it all. 'In the strange circles in which you have moved, are there any who would wish him harm?' Again, Amy only shook her head. 'His past employers, perhaps.' This brought her round, and her mouth dried. She tried to speak, but it seemed full of sawdust. She licked her lips.

'We must go back,' she said eventually. 'For this skiff. We must go back and discover it.'

'We shall do no such thing,' said Cottam, and all eyes turned to him. 'There, my lady, my lord – there's the game. Back to England, eh? To deliver us all into the English queen's hands!'

'Hang the English queen. I'm going back, and I'll kill anyone who tries to stop me, I swear I will, I'll go over the side and swim.'

'You see? Insensible!'

'Enough!' The countess's voice had turned to iron. 'Mrs Cole, if you persist I shall have you tied down.' Seton looked at her, amazed, and her face quickly softened back into its usual patrician lines. 'My lord, I am feeling quite unwell.' She took a tighter grip on his arm. 'If you would take me out to hear what the captain says out of his own mouth, I should be right grateful.' Amy was momentarily pulled out of her hysteria as she saw Lady Northumberland demurely turn her eyes to the floor, and Seton visibly melt. Silly old fools, she thought – the lady past thirty and Seton about forty. They left, Cottam scurrying after them, and she collapsed to the cabin floor. An urge came upon to smash up the room, upend the cot, the cradle. What other remedy was there for frustrated helplessness? She sat awhile, gripping and releasing the folds of her dress, sweat beading her forehead. After a while, she rose and walked unsteadily out into the sunlight. Staring out to her left, across the sea, their wake made a white v-shape. A rainbow sprung from the horizon, petering out into nothingness. She had no idea how far they had travelled since dawn had broken.

A tug at her elbow turned her, and she found herself staring at a boy of about fourteen. 'Mrs Cole? Urh ye Mrs Cole?' She said nothing. 'It wiz me.' Colour rose in his cheeks, making him look even younger. 'It wiz me helped yon man wi' the moustaches get the skiff aff. Yer husband wiz wi' him. Hands tied.'

'What?' Amy grabbed the boy's jerkin and shook, bringing a look of fear to his face. 'Man with the moustache?'

'He sailed wi' us. Told me to get you telt after they were gone.'

'You let him steal my husband? I'll get you flogged! The captain's asking questions now – I'll see you whipped bloody!'

'Naw,' said the boy, shaking his head. Her mania had put fear into him. She could tell. 'He said you widnae get me intae trouble. Said to get only you telt. Say nothin' tae the captain.'

'What?' she asked again. 'What's going on? I'm telling on

you.' Only when the words were out did she realise how childish and petulant they sounded. 'Where is Jack? What has this knave done with him?'

'Said to tell you Mr Cole was going back to England. Tae make answer for himself. Said if you told … the lady …' Sudden confusion overtook him. 'Lady …'

'Northumberland.'

'Aye, her. If you told her, you'd no' be seein' your husband again.'

'But why? Why? What am I to do?'

'Said you've jist tae stay by the lady. Watch her. And Mr Cole will be safe. Meet you later. And I've tae remind you who you work for. That wiz all.'

Only then did Amy realise she was still holding the boy's coat, and her hands had turned white. She released him. 'Why?' she asked, but this time to no one. As soon as he was free, he turned and scuttled up a rope ladder that went up the side of the cabin. She put her head in her hands. Jack had been taken back to England, probably to be tortured and interrogated. Punished, even. She was the hostage for his life, expected to spy on the countess and report her movements to … well, to whomever would contact her with news of Jack. When that might be, she had no idea. She had no option, either. If it came to either betraying the countess or saving her husband, she would see Lady Northumberland thrown to the sharks. She had killed for him before, and she would see the whole ship rotting on the bed of the Narrow Sea before letting him die.

Turning to grip the rope, Amy again tossed bile into the ocean.

4

The Reverend Henry Lansing of Gilling East hated the north and every papistical savage in it. His dispatch north, designed to ensure uniformity amongst the recalcitrant Catholics, had been a sentence rather than a sinecure. When the northern rebellion had failed and its participants sentenced to hang, he had ensured that his parish followed the letter of the law. So it was that the remains continued to hang from trees – there had not been gallows enough to accommodate all two-hundred-and-twenty-five of them – when the softer ministers and justices had ordered the bodies discreetly cut down and claimed by their families. It did not make East Gilling the most fragrant part of Yorkshire, but then the entire north smelt of rotting meat anyway. The summer heat had done little to improve matters. The corpses, which had been stripped naked by opportunistic vagabonds the night of the executions, had since been picked clean by birds, and what fell from them carried off by rats. Only skeletal remains were still visible, some suspended and some littering the ground.

It was, he reflected, of little consequence to the rabble, save to sear their hatred of the reformed faith and the queen who led it into their hearts. He doubted if even the news that reached Gilling East from farther north would wipe the scales from their eyes: two filthy priests out of Douai, one having sodomised the other to death before taking his own life, blood still smeared around his privy member. He smacked his lips at the scandal, trumpeted by all good Protestants and studiously ignored or dismissed as a lie by the papists. There was nothing quite as effective at bringing a body into hatred as its sins and corruptions being held up to the world.

The only good thing about the north was the money that was free for the taking from the attainted rebels. Reverend Lansing sat in a good chair with his feet to his fire and a board across his capacious lap. He put aside the sermon he had been working on. He smiled. Isaiah 44. To the verses, he had added his own flourishes: rebellion was a sin; disobedience to the queen was disobedience to God; rebels deserved their shameful deaths, to be hanged in chains, their bodies fit for carrion. Every man, woman, and child who harboured Catholic thoughts was a traitor – all who believed the Pope's false doctrines and bulls still were traitors, and they too should be hung in chains, for no gentleness could ever hope to win papist hearts.

He could imagine the look on his flock's face at the condemnation of their beloved idolatry and the denunciation of their dead fathers and brothers and sons. They were out of luck. If they did not attend, did not listen to their false religion debunked, they would be fined. In place of the pages, he laid out a bag of gold. He knew how much he had accumulated already, but it had become a ritual to count it out each night. There was no finer sight than neat little piles of coins, each the same height. He lifted one between his thumb and forefinger. An angel, with the queen's bust in profile, she looking rather flat-faced. It caught the light of the fire. He placed it down and was about to reach for another when someone knocked at the door.

'Damn and blast it,' he hissed. His housekeeper had left and his wife was visiting her sister down south, and not due to return until the following day. He paused, hoping that the visitor would go away. The knocking repeated, more insistently. Cursing again, he replaced the coins in their velvet bag and hoisted himself up, taking the board to a cabinet which lay against the wall. He shut it away, turning the key in the lock. Still the hammering persisted, and he grunted his way to it.

Opening the door, Lansing found himself looking at a thin-faced, dark fellow. 'Yes? What news, neighbour?' He assumed that the man was of his parish. Seldom did he bother looking at their faces.

'Begging your pardon, sir,' said the stranger, turning his hat in his hand, 'my name is Acre, sir.' Pleasantly unprepossessing, thought Lansing.

'Yes, and how might I help you, Mr Acre?'

'I'm but Goodman Acre, sir, no more.'

'I see.' He stood, the forced smile on his florid features

starting to wane.

'I've come to beg a favour, father, about the next sitting of the church courts. My brother's to be examined. He's been right poorly of late, you see. Missed services.' Lansing tutted. His brow had already furrowed at the word 'father'. Acceptable, of course, but stinking of Rome.

'A serious matter, goodman. Services must be attended. He shall have to pay his fines.' He waved a fat finger in the young man's face. Warm air blew in, carrying on it the sweet smell of the herb garden. 'Unless, of course, you have something else to discuss?'

'I do, sir.' Acre coughed discreetly. 'My mam and I – it's just the two of us – we don't have much. But we thought we could come to … oh, what was it mam said? A private arrangement.' He reached down and tapped a purse that hung from his belt. Coins tinkled. 'Save going through the courts, see, and us not able to pay the fines, and even if we could, you know, it going away to London.'

Lansing smiled and threw the door wide. It was not the first time he had made such arrangements. 'Well, young man, I should be glad to hear your case privately. Come in, come in. Don't want to be advertising your business for all the world to see.' He stood back and let Acre inside, smiling to himself.

Lansing returned to his seat before the fire. He did not ask his guest to sit, though the bare box on which his wife usually sat was vacant. 'Well then. How many weeks of church has he missed?'

'What's that, sir?' Lansing turned to the young man, who was standing with his hands behind his back, surveying the room as though he had never set foot in a decent house before. Probably he had not, thought the reverend. Savages, all.

'How many weeks of church?'

'Three, sir.'

'Three,' said Lansing, clucking his tongue. 'That's a grave matter.' He leant forward, half-swivelling to pull the box before his chair. He coughed, and then tapped a finger on it.

'Oh, yes, father.' Acre pulled loose his purse and emptied it out on the wooden surface. Lansing leaned in, surprised at the

37

amount. Instinctively, he began sorting it into piles, his lips moving as he counted.

'Is it enough?'

'Hm?' The fool was throwing him off. 'Yes, yes, enough.'

'And your wife shall return on the morrow?'

'My wife?'

'Mrs Lansing, sir.'

Lansing paused. 'How the devil did you know?' He shook his head. It must be known in the parish that Anna had gone south. He bent again to the pile of money. He did not have time to finish counting. Before he could, he sensed his visitor behind him. He made to turn, and the man's arm was around his neck, snaking from his left side. His mouth fell open. Acre's hand slid across his throat. The pain was so sudden, sharp, and intense, that his eyes bulged. Blood spurted, drenching the coins. Lansing slumped forward, hitting the box with a muted thud.

'Don't be spending it all in one shop, sir.'

It had been a busy few weeks for the man who had once called himself Owen. Acre, he decided, was more fitting – it was as close as he felt he could get away with to 'ace', and he was, after all, the ace in the suit of diamonds. Yet a slit throat would not do. His instructions had been to make a greater display. The deaths of the priests had not had the effect that had been hoped for, and his friends were disappointed. The whole matter had been largely hushed up – an embarrassing disgrace to the Catholics and a pair of names scored off the government's list of covert priests to the Protestants. The death of a minister could not be so ignored. It would not be enough, of course – no single event ever was – but it was not his job to make strategy. It was his job to dispatch those who deserved it for the greater glory, and to do it with whatever spectacle might be necessary. He set to work, knowing that he would have to be gone from Gilling East before dawn broke.

***

Mrs Taylor found the reverend's front door unlocked when she called the next morning. She had served him as she had served his far more loveable predecessor, but it was not her place to like or dislike those who paid her. She stepped inside and found that the fire was still burning, fresh logs having been thrown on. It was not the good smell of woody smoke that filled her nostrils, however, but something coppery, something raw and savage. It smelled vaguely like the shambles on which she purchased fresh meat. She stepped inside.

And screamed.

Mrs Taylor's screams were heard by neighbours, who found her in the garden of the house. When they ventured inside themselves, they found the Revered Henry Lansing crucified on the timber beams which criss-crossed the whitewashed plaster. On his body, which had been stripped to the waist, were carved the five wounds of Christ. His money and valuables had been untouched; in fact, the door of his cabinet stood open, gold spilling from it. More sat on a box before his chair, dried blood flaking off of it. Still more lay on some pages of paper – transcribed Bible verses – on the floor.

On one wall was daubed, in the reverend's blood, the words, 'Ye North Ys Catholique'. When the local justices arrived, along with the dead man's mystified wife, no one could testify as to having seen anyone come or go from the place. The message, though, spread like wildfire, changing according to the teller. To some, Catholic assassins charged by the Pope had done murder, intent on sinking England in blood. To others, a corrupt and tyrannical southerner had met a fitting end.

To Mr Acre – and the name had really come to sound good in his ears – the confusion, hatred, and suspicion were like music. England would be at war with itself before long.

Part Two: Splitting the Deck

1

Jack was losing track of the days. Since being stolen from *The Port of Leith*, he had been shifted across the country, his hands bound. Where he was he had no sure idea – the sailor, who had introduced himself as Edward Polmear, had rowed them both to what he assumed was Bridlington, and thereafter they had gone deeper into Yorkshire. He had said little, attending instead to handling the skiff and securing a horse in the village; Jack had said nothing. At first relief had flooded him. After passing through the huddle of great ships in the bay, Polmear had rowed steadily for land. It was then Jack realised that he was not going to be tossed overboard.

After a night sailing and riding, Polmear had deposited him in an inn and released his hands. Then he had spoken. 'Always pay bills, my young friend – a great rule of the game we play. No man of intelligence should attract the law. Observe,' he had added, producing a purse. 'I'll pay your lodging this night and the next.' He had then provided some food and locked Jack in, disappearing. The day and night passed without further word from him. It would have been an easy matter to escape – the door did not look sturdy. The problem was what Polmear had said after volunteering his words of wisdom. 'Now you sit tight here, Cole. If you run, your wife will bear the scars of it. Our friends will have eyes on her too.' With Amy bound for Europe amongst strangers, he could not risk causing trouble.

He lay on his cot, chewing on a chunk of manchet. There was some cheese on the floor beside it, but he had developed a distaste for cheese in Paris. Even the smell of it turned his stomach. *The Port of Leith*, he thought, must be drawing close to Bruges by now. He could imagine Amy's reaction to his disappearance. Had there been another skiff on the ship, undoubtedly she would have freed it herself to hunt him down. On the heels of the thought rose questions about Polmear. It was not hard to guess who he worked for – Elizabeth, Cecil, Walsingham: they were all the part of the same thing. He had betrayed them and would now have to pay the piper. The Tower, perhaps? If they had wanted him dead, the sea would have taken care of him; they must want to interrogate him. He did, after all, know things – about Lady Northumberland and her husband, imprisoned at Lochleven's water-castle, about the Scotch lords; he had even heard that the earl of Westmorland, also an exile in Scotland under Catholic protection, was planning flight to Europe. How much of it should he give up? It all depended what their plans were for Amy. Or perhaps how much torture they applied to him.

He was stirred by the click of the lock. Polmear strode in, and he was not alone. Behind him stood a stout girl, her bosom daringly exposed by a low-cut neckline. He put an arm around her. 'Mr Cole, or Jack, may I call you?' Jack said nothing. 'Good lad. Clever. You have done as I said.'

'Where,' Jack asked, his voice heavy with reluctance, 'have you been?'

'On business.' Polmear ran a finger over his bare upper lip. 'Rule of the game, lad – alter your appearance.' Jack relapsed into silence, crossing his arms moodily, frowning, and putting his feet on the floor. It did not take days to shave off a moustache. 'Look here – I have a gift for you.' He nudged the girl forward with the crook of his elbow. 'You like her? What's your name, love?'

'Holwice, sir.'

'Eurgh. So it is. You like her, Cole?' Jack stared at the wall.

'Still not a talker, eh? Don't need to talk though, does he, Hol?' The girl giggled. 'You cut along, now. I'm afraid the lad is not for sporting.' She gave a little bow and left.

'Not very gallant of you. She's the finest whore I could find. They're cleaner here than in the cities. Fewer sailors to pox them. And I do love the yellow-hairs.' Polmear closed the door and bounded forward, swinging an arm up and over a low roof beam. Jack started at the sudden burst of frenetic energy. 'But I daresay you get sport aplenty with that wife of yours.' This got a reaction, as Jack sprung up himself. 'I had a good peep at her on that ship. Spirit in her, eh? I would lay money that she is fire itself between the sheets. What does she like, being bent over a barrel?'

Jack's hand flew out and hit Polmear in the gut. He made to hit him again, but the taller man grabbed his wrist. Rather than hitting him back, he threw his head back as laughter rang out. 'So you have a little of her spirit yourself, eh? Calm yourself, boy.' His voice hardened. 'I mean it. Sit.' He forced Jack back towards the bed. 'I jest with you. I am a great lover of women. Less guile in them than most men. I like that.'

'Why am I here?'

'Why?' echoed Polmear, bounding across the room. The man seemed unable to keep still. 'Because you've been a naughty boy. Ah, I can see from your face that you know it. Rule of the game – never let your face betray you. Now, if you are not to take sport before we go, we had best just be off. A shame – I always think a journey is more pleasant with a good memory to push it on.'

'Where are you taking me?'

'Ugh, is our entire journey to be thus? Questions and questions? If we are to travel together, I would that we were friends, Jack.' He sat down on the bed beside him. Jack edged away. The man's display of friendliness did not fool him. If anything, he had grown to distrust shows of it. There was little worse than being stabbed in the back by someone who feigned friendship.

'Travelling where?'

'South. A long road, but you'll know that already, eh? I have a task ahead of me. It is to make you my fast friend before we reach … oh, let us say Norwich. After that, it might not matter.' The levity decreased again. 'You're going to need friends, Jack Cole. Where you're going you will. If you play your part well, I might even be tempted to speak up for you. Say as you were a good little boy who did as he was told.'

'The Tower?' It came out in a whisper. Again, Polmear barked laughter.

'Hark at it – the Tower! Who do you think you are, son – Sir Jack Cole of Fancy-thorpe? The Tower. The Tower's for people the world cares for. You'd no more be at home with the ghost of the queen's mother than I would be dining at table in Windsor

Castle. The Tower. You're precious.'

Jack's cheeks turned scarlet and he half turned away, working the rough blanket with one hand. As foolish at it was, he was still capable of embarrassment, even sitting next to a man who was holding him prisoner and very likely leading him to torture. 'Where then?' he mumbled.

'What's that?'

'Where?'

'London. A great man wishes to see you there.'

'Cecil?' It came out in a whisper. He had met the chief secretary, wispy-bearded and serious, only once. It had been enough. The old man had been quiet, courteous, and somehow the more threatening for it. He had had the air of a schoolmaster and the eyes of a tiger.

'Hell's teeth, you do think high of yourself, don't you? No. Not him.' Polmear bounced up. 'Not touched your cheese? I'll give that a fair home.' He scooped it up and began shovelling it in. Through mouthfuls, he said, 'you had best sleep. We leave on the morrow, early. I've sent word of your coming ahead. He'll be ready for you. No more questions, Sir Questioner. I'll even let you have the bed. Don't fancy sharing with a girl-faced boy when you've left a real lass begging. What a name, eh? Holwice. Fine pair of ducks, though.' He burped, letting cheese crumbs fly, and left. At the door, he paused, and said, 'friends yet?' Jack turned away and lay back on the bed as the door closed. The lock snapped.

Polmear seemed an unlikely sort to be working for one of Cecil's minions. But then, he was an unlikely sort to be in the pay of the English government himself. And the name, Polmear – from the west of the country, perhaps?

Animal-like grunting sounded from a room somewhere else in the little building, followed by exaggerated squeals. Holwice had apparently offered her services. Jack pulled the blankets up over his head and thought of Amy. What, he wondered, would she make of his captor? He'd receive the rough edge of her tongue rather than stony silence – that much he knew. He would find his way back to her somehow, if he had to lie, kill, or betray to do it. It was what she would do for him.

When Polmear came for him the next morning, he was already up and booted. 'Good night? Not so fine as mine, I imagine. You missed yourself with that young bawd. Country girls, eh? They know country tricks. Well, come on then, Sir Silent. As a mark of true trust, I've your very own horse for you this time.' He led Jack unprotestingly out of the room and down the flight of wooden steps. They left the inn for the courtyard in front of it, where two horses were tethered. 'These will take us part of the way. Though God knows I've ridden enough this past night.' Jack moved over to one of the pair, an old grey mare, and put his hand out. 'Nothing?' asked Polmear. 'Not even a smile? You're a hard man, Jack Cole. See, this is why I prefer the company of jades. For a penny they'll laugh at a poor jest, and at least will pretend to be your friend.'

The ostler came out to help them mount and they set off, Jack maintaining what he had come to think of as a dignified silence and Polmear offering a repertoire of tired and increasingly bawdy jokes. It would be a long journey.

***

'Well, there she is. A fine old bitch, London. Started up by the Trojans – did you know that?'

Jack reined in. Over the course of the journey he had begun to talk, careful to reveal nothing. It was easy enough. It was difficult not to occasionally laugh at some of the things his strange captor said, and the fellow had been right in saying that journeys seemed to go more quickly if you had someone to talk to. Thankfully, Polmear did not ask questions either, about Jack's activities or his personal life. The closest he got was asking how he had come to marry Amy. It had almost been possible to forget why the journey was necessary. That was, at least, until the smoke smudging the horizon announced London's brash presence.

Jack had never thought to see London again. As always, the place refused to be ignored. They were entering by Aldersgate, passing the old Charterhouse that had been the duke of Norfolk's London home and, only a couple of years before, Jack and Amy's. The sight of the building's walls sent a chill through him. Despite all that had happened, it was possible to imagine just wandering in and heading to the stables, as though such a strange act could turn back time; the duke of Norfolk would be at court, Amy in the laundry, and he with nothing on his mind but obeying old Tom the horse master's orders. Instead it would put him in the Bedlam. Or worse.

Polmear led him through the Aldersgate and onto Newgate Street, turning left onto Cheapside. Here, merchants called out their wares and a stomach-churning combination of odours attacked the nostrils. Horse dung gave a sharp edge to fish, meat, and spices. The wealthier shoppers – the merchants' wives and gentlemen – held pomanders against their faces as they browsed, and cast dark looks up at the riders as their horses kicked up filth. When they passed the Mercers' Hall and came to the junction of Three Needle, Cornhill, and Lombard, they were forced to pull in to the side of the road. A small parade was coming their way.

Two city constables were dragging a younger man, who came reluctantly, kicking, screaming, and skidding through the muck. Behind the trio followed a mob of about ten, hurling handfuls of mud and straw. 'Thief!' went the chant. 'Thief! Thief!'

'He'll not have a good end to his day, poor bastard,' said Polmear. 'Hope it's his first time caught.'

As they passed, something of the mob's anger rippled up and through Jack. 'Thief!' he cried, raising a fist in the air.

'No sympathy for the condemned?'

'Not for thieves.' He twisted in the saddle, spitting after the mob. The gob sent ripples through his own image reflected in a puddle. Once, living in Norfolk's household, someone had stolen a ring from under his mattress. It had been the only thing he had ever owned that had belonged to the mother he had never known – even his father did not know he had it; it had come from another servant who remembered her fondly when he was a little boy. One day it had simply been gone, taken from his room. He could raise no fuss – his father was still alive at the time and would not take well to his hated son making any kind of tumult. Since then, though, he had harboured a severe antipathy towards thieves of any stripe. They should all, as far as he was concerned, be hanged – and preferably quartered too. As it was, the chap being dragged off to his doom would likely get away with a whipping. He looked reasonably well-groomed enough to have come from a good family.

Polmear shrugged and, in the wake of the mob heading for Newgate, led them up Thread Needle Street and along the Bishopsgate, turning them right. Away from the markets, the air freshened, but not by much. Here were finer homes. Not far from Camomile Street, Polmear reined in.

'Here we are – Aldgate parish. The Papey. You know it? Home to Mr Francis Walsingham and family.'

Jack's mouth ran dry.

The house in Aldgate was fronted by a small, ornate garden. It was a modest brick building – well-kept and tidy, but not the kind of place he imagined Francis Walsingham to inhabit. They skirted it and entered through a small archway that led to an inner quadrangle, leaving behind the heavy, choking city air. The courtyard was cooler, fresher, smelling only of horses and the delicate perfume of ornamental shrubs. After they had dismounted, Polmear went into a small covered walkway running parallel to one side of the yard and lowered his head in conversation with a cluster of men in black. Jack looked up and around the building bearing down on him from all sides. It was quiet, the windows shuttered against the late summer heat. No servants bustled about the courtyard; the whole place had the sad, waiting atmosphere of desertion. When Polmear returned from conversing with the small murder of crows, his face was like thunder. For all his bonhomie, Jack recalled that the man had threated to cut him to ribbons.

'You, my young lord of Silent-tongue, have just won a great prize.'

Jack gave him a sour look, intending to say nothing. 'Freedom from your company?' he offered instead.

'Ha! You'll be missing my company in a few weeks, I reckon. No, a far greater prize. A reprieve. A stay of execution, you might say.' Jack's eyebrows lifted. 'My master is still from home. And so you are to wait. Make yourself useful. I

47

understand you are a fine fellow with horses – old Norfolk's stable-lad, were you not?' Looking at the horses in confusion, Jack's mind whirled.

'Execution?'

'I jest,' Polmear said mildly. 'Yet without the master, nor any instructions from him direct, you must attend upon his return.'

'Walsingham,' he whispered.

'Mr Walsingham, indeed.' Polmear waved a hand around. Jack shrugged. 'Mr Walsingham, secretary to the queen and friend to Sir William Cecil, chief of the secretaries. An up and coming man, highly spoken of at court, I hear. Will be across the world, some day. There's been your mistake – being tied to sinking ships, not fresh-launched ones. Always remember: your fate and your master's are bound. You sink or swim together. Until you have a new master, of course.'

Jack paled. Walsingham was Cecil's creature. He was one of the men who had held him prisoner the previous year, drawing his story out, demanding his loyalty and sending him out of the country. 'Where is he?'

'He …' Polmear hesitated, then seemed to make a decision. 'France. Paris. The French court.' It was his turn to shrug. 'Matters of state, not concerning you.'

'Paris,' echoed Jack dully. No doubt the secretary was busy with Sir Henry Norris, his old master, discussing his betrayal and what ought to be done with him.

'I doubt,' said Polmear, as though reading his thoughts, 'you're foremost in their minds. I am sorry to have to pluck you from your ideas of pomp.'

'Well,' Jack replied, recovering, 'I can see that you're not so great either. You didn't know he was away.'

Anger flared Polmear's nostrils. 'I knew – I didn't know the length – I –' The passion faded, and he smoothed back his dark hair. 'Clever boy. Sharper than you look. Mind you don't cut yourself, lad. Or your wife's throat, for that matter. It's a poor intelligencer who lets his mouth run off with him. Now, see, if you were truly clever, you'd have made your observation and locked it away in your mind, safe.' He tutted. 'Never try to score points against men stronger than you. Not with your tongue.'

'So what am I to do?' Jack was eager to divert Polmear's attention from talk of Walsingham.

'You were a servant, weren't you? Serve. Until the master returns. Look at the place – it's in want of care. Mrs Walsingham is in the country. Help make the place ready for the return of the rich folks.'

'Wait, you mean – wait until I'm put on the end of a rope?'

'Temporise.' Polmear smiled at his Jack's expression and repeated the word. 'A lesson for you. 'You've been told to do something. Say yes. Agree. No one cares what you think of it, whether you desire to do it. Whether you mean it. It buys you time.'

'You should have gone for a schoolmaster if you like giving lessons so much. Is it your masters teach you big words and what to do?'

'Ha! It's my own errors've taught me what to do and what not to do. Now I can tell you. And maybe help you keep breathing a bit longer. It's by not listening to men like me that I'm only good for watching ports and giving lessons.' As he spoke, Polmear caught Jack looking around. 'Heh. Fine place, isn't it? The kind you might fancy for yourself one day? Me, I wouldn't have it, not for gold. A grand house with a crew of listening servants wanting fed and watered.' He spat at the ground. 'Give me a steady bed and a steady woman any day of the week. A nice barren one with big ducks. No sons troubling me nor wishing me dead for my money.'

'Amy,' said Jack. Then, louder, 'I can't just stay here. My wife, she must know where I am. I have to go to her, get word to her.'

'Cole, I'm sorry again. I see my error. I've given you the fool idea that this is an offer. It's not. The master's friends and I have decided. This is no negotiation. You stay here to await the master's pleasure. If you run, if you try and get word to your wife, it will not go well for either of you.' Jack clenched his jaw. 'Ah, don't let that temper run away with you. I like you, Mr Cole, and I'm a fair fellow. Your wife knows that you've been taken and that you will be quite safe as long as she plays her part. She does not share in your treachery. She might yet have

49

her uses.'

'If any of you harm her …'

'Don't make threats, Cole. Don't do it.' Jack relapsed into silence. 'Good lad. Ugh.' Polmear looked up at the sky. Little spots of rain had started. 'Tend the horses, will you? Back where you started, eh? Well, there's another lesson for you. Life's like that. One day up, the next down.'

2

The smell of the sea, fresh and salty, blew in on oppressive gusts. Like the harbour at Old Aberdeen, the mouth of the canal was a jungle of masts, albeit on a smaller scale. Before coming to the inland city, Amy had lost no time in enquiring of *The Port of Leith*'s sailors whether they or any others would be returning to British waters. They would. Would they take her? If she could pay, which she could always find means of doing, even if she had to cut purses. Yet her questions were more born of a desire to take some kind of action. It was intolerable to think that the means of rescuing her husband were there, solid, timbered and seaworthy, and yet she had been commanded by his captor to remain tethered to Lady Northumberland.

She stood by a stall in the town square, chewing on her nails and trying to work out what to do: plot out her own wild path, beating a retreat to England and searching for Jack herself, or doing as she had been instructed, spying on the countess and hoping that the English government would keep him safe in payment for her cooperation. There had to be some third way, some safer course. It did not suggest itself, and so she trudged towards the lodging house were Seton had boarded the penniless countess.

As she walked, a jumble of harsh and strange languages rose into the air around her: Flemish, German, Dutch, she supposed. It infuriated her that people were living their lives quite heedless of her plight and powerless to do anything about it. She could probably go to whoever the local authorities were in Bruges, pleading for aid, and be met with either laughter or confused apologies. Yet she could not quite bring herself to hate the place. Each city, she thought, had a distinct colour that gave it its character. Aberdeen had been a devoutly austere slate grey – fitting for the countess, who had heard Mass every day. London was an upturned palette, like the mix of people who filled it, ultimately making it loud and messy. Paris was sandy and pale blue, like the faded page of an illuminated manuscript: just right for such an old place. Bruges' buildings were warm and brown, hearth-like almost. It was welcoming – exactly the type of place one could imagine setting up a little shop and living quietly. If only one had a husband with which to do it.

There was, however, little point in musing, not when action was needed. The countess it would have to be. By now Amy had walked from the canal, where she had come first thing in the morning, to the town square, off of which the arriving party had been lodged. The chorus of voices grew louder, and the fresh sea air gave way to the sting of vinegar from an ale vendor, who was on bony knees scrubbing out his flasks. She stepped around him, knuckling sweat from her forehead.

She entered the narrow lodging by a side door, which lay halfway down a cool alley, and went upstairs to the countess's suite of rooms. Before she reached them, she could hear Cottam's querulous voice rising, and another, lower one responding.

'… launch upon her rescue. In Lancashire they are thwarted.' This was the deeper voice.

'It will be bloody,' said Cottam.

'The cutting of a tumour is always bloody. Impress upon the lady the necessity.'

'I shall, I shall. She will want a list of names of men who can be trusted in this land.'

'Lower your voice, sir. She is resting now. She will have it. And a horoscope shall tell us when she might move. I shall have one drawn up, if you have payment.'

'Er … my lady has neither a penny nor halfpenny. Coming away in such a hurry, she had not time to bring her jewels, her things.'

'Alas, this is not what my friends would wish to hear.'

'Yet she shall – once it is known who she is and why she comes, the whole of the faithful in Europe will give aid. The Holy Father, the Spanish king, French –'

'I have warned her of France,' growled the other man. 'That fellow Walsingham is there. Cecil's dog. In Paris. They are in fine fettle now that they have captured Storey, but the stars shall not align for them. It shall not rain in England until John Storey goes free. The dogs will lick the heretic queen's blood and her body shall rot before she dies.' As he spoke, the timbre of his voice rose. 'Only then shall the Scottish queen rise to take England.'

'You've told my lady of this?'

'I have. She has promised me payment on receipt of further news. Further prophecies. I will away and draw the horoscope when the time is most fitting.'

'Very good, Dr Prestall.'

Amy flattened herself against the smudged plaster wall as the speaker swept into view, and she drew in her breath at the sight of him. Tall, with a shaved head and an enormous trailing beard, the man was smirking. The sly smile disappeared as he saw her. 'Out of my way, girl,' he hissed, pushing past her, the robe he wore trailing and jingling under the weight of the amulets and charms hanging from it. His stubbly scalp was only a whisper away from brushing the ceiling. Amy watched him go.

Prestall, she thought. Not a name she had heard before, but one she would be sure to remember. A sorcerer of some kind, a conjuror, promising the downfall of Queen Elizabeth and the rise of Queen Mary. What was the other name? Storey – John Storey. She would have to remember that too. And Walsingham was in France. It could not be more than a few days' journey to Paris – and this Prestall had just given her information to pass on.

The English secretary's face rose into view in her mind, serious and solid. Walsingham had friends at the heart of government, and through them he could do anything, if only he could be persuaded. She was just beginning to wish for a pen and a sheet of paper to write down the words as she had heard them when Cottam's voice stabbed her from behind.

'You should be gone. We want none of your eyes and ears here. Gone off to find your husband, I should have thought. Unless you do not care what has become of him. Unless you already know.'

'I wish to see Lady Northumberland.' Without waiting for the sarcastic response, she moved past him and into the antechamber where he had been speaking with Prestall. Caught off guard, he tried to move around and ahead of her, but she reached the narrow door and pushed it open, stepping inside.

The countess's rooms were shuttered, and it took Amy's eyes a moment to adjust. When they did, she saw that the maid, Kat, was asleep on a cot, the baby at her belly. The sleeping pair seemed oblivious to the countess, who was on her knees at a prie-dieu, chanting prayers in a low, steady voice. She did not respond to the intrusion. Amy stopped, and Cottam was able to grasp her arm and try to force her violently from the room. Their struggle was a silent one, enacted only to the sonorous Latin. Neither gave way, and eventually the countess stopped praying.

'Why do you disturb my prayers, Amy Cole?'

'She is come again to disturb us all,' snapped Cottam. 'A busy, listening creature, she is – she has no place here.'

'I'm not the one listens at doors,' snapped Amy, 'no, sir, that's you!'

'Shrew! Madam, a thankless shrew!'

'Help me to rise.' Cottam stopped ranting to do so. 'Bless you. Now leave us.'

'My lady?'

'Leave us, Will.'

'But –' She cut him off with a warning look. 'My lady.' He bowed his head and backed from the room, looking up only to glare at Amy. In return, she smiled as triumphantly as she could manage.

When Cottam was gone, her smile faded. The countess had crossed the bed and she took the sleeping girl in her arms, nudging Kat awake with an elbow. 'Go and seek out Lord Seton,' she said. 'Discover if his men have found us anything to eat'. Rubbing her eyes, the maid did as she was bid, following Cottam from the room, yawning as she closed the door behind her. 'She is a fair child, is she not?' The countess held the baby up.

'A beautiful lass, my lady.'

'You have no children?'

'No, madam.' Unconsciously, Amy's arms crossed over her flat stomach.

'I have four. Four girls. And only one to tend.' Amy knew this

54

already. She lowered her gaze. 'And a husband. The earl of Northumberland – the finest man you could care to meet. Handsome as a girl could hope for. And yet lacking wit and without courage.' At this, Amy looked up in surprise, and found the woman smiling at her. 'Yes, girl, it is true. Many men are not born with the wit God gave a goose. Your husband, is he so witless that you must harken to his side, wherever that is?'

'Madam, I …'

'Do not expect sympathy from me, girl. You have lost your husband as I have lost my family, all save this child. Tell me, is it Cecil who has taken him? Is it Cecil who had you come to my side and your husband to the den of the Scotch heretics?'

'Sir Henry Norris, my lady, he –'

'Sir Henry Norris is a nothing,' said the countess, rolling her eyes. 'It is William Cecil who rules England. He and Elizabeth, like a monstrous chimera. She the lion's face and he the old goat behind it. Grasping thieves, both. A supposed queen. My mother had the measure of her mother, to be sure. And for revenge she would have me undone, till I straight am nothing, closely mewed up.' Amy coughed, her fist a demure little ball at her mouth. The countess echoed it before speaking again. 'I have heard Norris is to be relieved of his post in Paris. He might be already in England. So you see, my dear, you are quite masterless, with neither husband or patron to protect you.' Her voice had grown harsh, and she seemed to soften it as she saw Amy crumple. 'You would rush mad to England, would you? A foolish caper. You must learn to bear your burdens. Anything can be borne if you trust in God that it is not forever. Anything.'

'But … but I have to find him, my lady. He'll be punished for what we done.'

'Perhaps. Yet I cannot but notice that you were left to me.'

'Just a woman, my lady,' Amy shrugged, diverting her eyes to the floor. Then she hardened her features. 'Cecil will have him. And that other one, Walsingham.'

'You have met these creatures?'

'I … yes. Last year.'

'Then I am sorry for you. It might interest you that it is Mr Walsingham who is said to be in Paris now, relieving Norris.'

'He is? Then he can't have Jack yet – there wouldn't be time, would there?'

The countess smiled, years falling from her face. She really was quite beautiful, thought Amy; she could see what Seton and the rest of the Scottish Catholics who had been her saviours saw in her. After replacing the child in its makeshift cradle, the older woman sat. 'You have a very strong desire to protect that young man of yours, do you not?' Amy did not respond, falling to her knees instead and clasping her hands before her. She had no desire to parade her love, in whatever form it took, before this grand lady. There were some things you didn't let masters or mistresses have. Little displays of entreaty usually satisfied them. 'No, girl, do not kneel. You have a mind. A mind, and a husband you wish to protect. Alas, I fear you do not have the wit to hide it. You will learn. Never reveal what you calculate. Then they know you've a mind of your own.' Amy nodded her head, only half-listening. Though her pose was all supplication, her eyes had slid down and to the side. So Walsingham really was in Paris. A messenger with the benefit of post-horses could surely make it in a day or two.

'Who was that man?' she asked abruptly.

'I beg your pardon?'

'I'm sorry, my lady. A man left just now. He frightened me. A tall man with a beard.'

'An apothecary. A friend. Or he would be.' The countess's tone had hardened again. 'At any rate, you can do nothing more foolish than chase your husband. He saw you last in my train. If he comes to find you, it shall be me he seeks, for it is I who am known. You will only get yourself lost otherwise. If you truly do have a shred of wit, you will not roam far. Good day, Mrs Cole.' Amy had worked for enough titled women to recognise a dismissal. Besides, she wanted to be gone. Bowing her head, she backed from the room and closed the door.

Thankfully, the unpleasant Cottam was nowhere to be seen. His things, though, were; paper and inks and sand, all laid out on the top of a coffer. She had wit enough, she thought, chancing looks behind and ahead of her. Hastily, she scribbled a message on a piece of paper:

Mr Walsynghamm

Wee tryed to stay the c'ess but ytt was safer to get her out of Scottlonde where in Bruges shee is visyted by a man called Prestall, the sayd Prestall calling himself friend and speaking of Mary of Scottlonde. My husbonde ys at no faulte for the whyche I woolde you showlde protect him and I wyll wryte more.

Your servant,

Amy Cole

Her heart in her throat, she sanded the page and folded it into her bosom. There, she thought – you really are a filthy traitor now. She noticed that her hand was shaking and her legs unsteady as she fled the building and wandered the market place, searching for a merchant who would be travelling to Paris. Using the few coins she had to her name, she found a wine-seller who claimed he would be leaving the next day to replenish his stock and urged and goaded him to get moving until his wife chased her away.

Regret and panic descended. The countess had invited her to stay, though not, Amy suspected, out of trust. Rather, she supposed the woman intended to watch over her. Still, the thought of returning to a house in which she had just betrayed the mistress was distasteful. She was still debating what to do, sweat tricking down her back, when she heard the screams.

A crowd had gathered at the entrance to the alley down which lay the countess's lodgings. Pushing her way through, Amy found the ale-seller she had spotted earlier lying just outside the door, bent double. Loudly she asked, first in English and then in French, 'what is this? What's happened?'

The unfortunate old wine-seller groaned, jabbing a finger at her. He croaked something out in a language she did not have, and she turned an uncomprehending face to a man in the crowd. In French, he replied, 'says he was ordered to bring ale directly to this house. Give it to the lady as a gift, on account of the heat.'

'Who? By who?'

Her interpreter looked at her almost apologetically. 'Diamond?' he shrugged. Amy looked again at the aged seller, rolling around now in a puddle of his own wares. No one was helping him; instead, people stood back in fear. They drew back further as he vomited – a thick, bloody foam. Cries went up for the local burgesses as he convulsed and stilled, only his legs twitching. The door opened and Cottam stepped out. 'What is this noise, my lady is rest–' He took in the sight, his eyes roving the crowd who were pressed against the walls of the alley. They landed on Amy and his mouth fell open. 'You!' he gasped. 'What have you done?'

***

The poisoning of the ale-seller – and poisoning it was roundly declared to be, as preferable to plague – roused the countess and her people. A greater number had gathered around her in the days that followed, seemingly coming from all corners of Europe. Many had fat purses and promised to carry messages to the duke of Alba, the Spanish king, the Pope. Plans were made for the countess's safety; as soon as enough money could be raised, she would be moved to a house under the Spanish king's protection. Of the mysterious diamond leaguer who had poisoned the vendor's ale and bid him bring the tainted batch to the countess's house, nothing could be found. Cottam, she was certain, had been encouraging the countess to believe she had done it – that she was somehow still in the employ of Queen Elizabeth and plotting the murder of her Catholic enemies. Thankfully, few paid him heed, instead speculating on the number of these so-called diamond men. It was, Amy thought, lucky that it had been a day hot enough that the fellow would drink of his own wares before he could do as he was bid. That meant it was a sudden rather than a planned attempt. She kept these thoughts to herself, as she kept the treachery of her writing to Walsingham to herself.

It was the second week after her arrival in Bruges when the merchant returned and she found cause to visit him and ascertain that her letter had got to Paris, albeit not directly into Elizabeth's man's hands. There had been nothing in return, and certainly Jack had not found her. Early one morning, she judged that her new mistress would be up but not yet disturbed by her many suitors, knocked on the chamber door and stepped into the reek of unemptied chamber pots and baby vomit.

'Begging your pardon, my lady, but I would speak with you.'

'Then speak, girl.' The countess was standing in a patch of light as Kat fixed sleeves to her dress. In the preceding days, the influx of cash had got her out of her worn clothes and back into fashion.

'I ...' her nerve threatened to flee her, and she nipped at her forearm. 'I can no longer stay in your service.'

'Is that so? That is fine, girl, leave me,' she added to Kat, waving her sleeved arm.

'It's just ... I think that if my husband looks for me, he'll go to Paris. Where we lived awhile.'

'You do love Paris, bless you.' She knew, thought Amy. She knew, and she knew Amy knew too. 'Well, I am not your gaoler. But tell me, do you think to travel alone, to live alone there?' Amy said nothing. 'Did you know that Mr Walsingham is likely to become Elizabeth's man in Paris? No, you do not hear all the news that men carry to me. Yes, indeed – some time in the new year, perhaps. It may be that he has news of your husband.'

'My lady, I–'

'Hopes to make a name for himself, does Walsingham. Ambition, the curse of all who hang on Elizabeth's petticoats. And greed.' She let silence fall between them as Kat fixed a pearl necklace on her. 'I shall be honest with you, Mrs Cole. I would not take you to ... to where I go next. Not,' she added, falsity colouring her words, 'when I know you have such pressing troubles on your shoulders. Yet I have a proposition.' Amy waited, her head bowed. 'You recall these fellows who attempted to poison me?'

'The diamond men?'

'Yes. I heard in Scotland that they had a man about the French queen. And one in England. Hot Protestants, is my guess. Puritanical. Yet I have as yet had no means to make good acquaintance with the French.'

Amy kept her head down, but her mind worked. It was true. Men had visited from Spain and Italy, but none from France. She should know; she had been watching out for them especially. 'No, my lady.'

'And now I find you wish to go to France. You know the place well enough by your own account.'

'Yes, but –'

'More, you spent time with Queen Mary. Last year, you told me. The French shall wish to know of her conditions, her imprisonment. How she is kept.' At this, Amy looked up. 'Queen Mary might be a captive, but she was once that country's queen. In dishonouring her, England dishonours France as well as Scotland and the world. So, you see, you have much intelligence in your head. That has value. The kind of value that will keep your husband alive more than news of who comes and goes to this house.'

'Alive?' gasped Amy, grasping at the word. 'You know what's happened to him?'

'No. Yet I have a mind. It is clear to me that England has taken him. Why they left you … well, that is not difficult to understand. So I cannot have you near me, not when I find I have guests coming and going who should like their names kept hidden from prying eyes. And yet you know a great deal, as I say. My proposition.' She clapped her hands together. 'You will go to Paris as my emissary and kinswoman.' Her head tilted to one side. 'A distant kinswoman. Very distant. My companion. There you shall carry news that a Puritan works evil in the French court, and you might share your knowledge of the Scottish queen's captivity.'

Amy's mouth fell open. 'I can't go to a court! My lady …'

'You have lived in service to great men and women. A great queen, no less. You have observed, I've no doubt, how to speak. It only takes some dresses, and those I now have.'

'But I … my French is not so good.'

'Good. The French think all English girls are ill-educated. You will confirm their prejudice. Make them more likely to believe you are what you say you are if you do. I assume you can ride well?'

'Yes, madam.'

'Hunt?'

'No.'

'Then you shall learn before you go. Do you have any knowledge of music? Dancing?'

'Only to hear it and see it.'

'Then that too I shall instruct you in.'

'But madam, I can't be a lady – I'm … don't wish to.'

'What you wish to do is of no consequence, I'm afraid.'

Amy put a hand to her forehead. The thought of playing the part of one of the overblown creatures she had seen in great houses irked her beyond measure - the posing, preening types who would put their hands to their foreheads and say 'oh fie upon' everything. Her own hand dropped as the thought occurred. Besides, she had always had some vague idea that apeing one's betters was ungodly, though she knew of no religious arguments as to why.

The countess was still talking. 'We have some weeks, I think, before I have money enough to move from here. And I have some other matters to attend to beforehand. None of which concern you. A few weeks, then, and you shall be a passable distant kinswoman to a lady. Kat shall go with you – you shall need a serving woman.' Kat, who was fussing over the sleeping baby, looked up in alarm, but said nothing. 'Do not distress yourself, girl. Think on it – you shan't have to risk tasting my food any longer.' Amy and Kat both gaped. 'Don't give me such a look. I fear no poison. I have lived through too much already to let some desperate men get the better of me.' Was that brave, wondered Amy, or merely foolish? The countess continued. 'King Charles is to be married soon. You will take my letters of introduction to the queen dowager. Queen Catherine. She is the most powerful woman in Europe as long as her son remains … young. Attach yourself to her. I regret I cannot go myself, but … well, it might bring blushes to the cheeks of the French to have an enemy of the English queen turn up on their doorstep. A minor kinswoman, however, seeking peace...'

'But–'

'But me no more buts, Mrs Cole.'

'But why,' pressed Amy, 'are you doing this for me?'

'I am getting rid of you, bless you. If you fail, I shall deny you. Now, I suggest you set to work. And work it shall be, I warn you. I have seen you eat, girl – with all the manners of a slavering idiot attacking a bowl of pottage. If you are to pass as a young English lady, you must learn to stop walking like an ape in a periwig.'

3

Autumn had painted the courtyard of the house called The Papey orange and gold, and left it carpeted in brown sludge. When the horses arrived, laden with goods and people, their hooves threw up the strangely fresh scent of musky woodland. Jack had been resident for over a month, sleeping above the stables and having little to do. No one spoke to him, even when he joined the other small band of resident servants to eat meals out of doors. If he was not a prisoner, word had clearly gotten around that he was far from a friend of the absent master.

Living under Walsingham's pretty, tiled roof, the same dream had come to him each night. He was in a cell, a trencher of food before him, staring up into the secretary's face. 'What are their names?' the man asked, as he had asked it when Jack had last been his guest. 'What are their names?' It had gone on and on, and so it went on in the dream. Never violent, never overtly threatening – but somehow terrible in its measured, almost mindless regularity. When he had finally spoken, beaten down with time and repetition, Walsingham's eyes had changed. Small and dark, they had glimmered like polished marbles. In the dream, the man had the look of a thin cat. Soft at first, inviting you to stroke its belly. And then, when it had you where it wanted you, the eyes sharpened. It sprang.

The dream did little to settle his nerves as the days passed and the black cat crept closer.

When Walsingham returned, Polmear was riding behind him, dressed in grey and now sporting a finely-trimmed beard. The harassed-looking secretary shot down a sour look before turning to Polmear and murmuring something. When Jack moved forward to help him dismount, he grasped his hand and winced his way down, but did not acknowledge him.

'No more stay of execution?' Jack asked as he helped Polmear. They both turned to Walsingham's departing back, swathed in black fur.

'He wants to speak with you,' was all the other man offered.

'Soon as he's settled.' Then, absurdly, Polmear clapped him on the back. 'He might even have news to please you.'

When the horses were stabled, Jack waited for his summons. When Polmear arrived with it, his jocularity had gone. 'He wants you now.' Jack nodded, and followed him out of the stables, and through a doorway in the corner of the yard. It led to a winding staircase, which Polmear took three at a time, pausing at the door at the top. 'Wait here.'

Jack waited. It was a day he had been expecting for weeks now, and yet he was curiously unmoved by it. In truth, he had had no clear idea of what to expect, and so had opted instead to expect nothing. Had he been in for punishment, he would have been clapped in jail – Newgate or the Fleet, perhaps. Had he been in for reward, there would have been no need to steal him away from his wife. 'Enter,' rumbled from within. It was Walsingham's voice, and before he touched the door handle, Jack remembered it, low and lugubrious. It was richer than it had sounded in his nightmares.

The room was an office. Shelves lined the walls, forming dockets, reminding Jack of a room he had once seen in the late earl of Moray's house. It was strange, how things seemed to remind you of other things: as Polmear had said, life was like an unpleasant wheel. The shutters had been thrown open, allowing indifferent October sunshine to filter in. Somewhere outside church bells rang out the hour, and immediately the sound of a crowd singing their way down the street joined them. Walsingham sat back in a chair behind a denuded desk. Polmear stood against one wall, his hands behind his back and his head bowed as though in prayer.

'Jack Cole,' said the secretary at length. He leant forward and steepled his fingers. 'Turned traitor, I hear?' Jack did not respond, which seemed to unease the older man. 'Do not stand there grinning like an idiot at me, boy. Have you nothing to say?'

'I thank you for your kind treatment, sir. It's better than I deserve, far better.' The show of humility seemed to please and then unsettle his patron. 'I let the countess flee Scotland. I couldn't do otherwise. Morton's men … they were rough.'

'They are friends to England and her Majesty. And to our faith. Or is it our faith?' asked Walsingham. 'If I recall, you were too friendly with the papists.'

'You know my faith, sir.' Jack hoped dignity coloured his words. He suspected that Walsingham's faith in the English style of religion was deep, deeper than Jack's drunken father's had ever been; but the secretary's desire to succeed and impress his betters was as strong or stronger. Faith and ambition seemed to be the twin rowers on the black-sailed galley that was Mr Francis Walsingham.

Again, Walsingham leant back. 'We do. Which is why you were supposed to be useful to us. And yet you let that treacherous woman take ship to her filthy rabble. Where she plans, as I understand, to build a centre of Catholic intrigue and spiery. To spread their poison across Europe, into every royal court.' Silence fell out again. For the first time, Jack noticed that the bare desk had one piece of ornament – a single sheet of paper. Walsingham began pushing it around with his finger. It slid easily, the surface of the desk polished to such a sheen that Jack could see himself reflected in it.

'What is that, sir?'

'Do not ask me questions, Cole.' He sighed. 'It is a letter from your wife. From Bruges. Brought me by a cut-throat in Paris.'

'Amy? She is well? You're not harming her?' At this, Walsingham turned to Polmear, a quizzical look on his lined face.

'Mr Cole thinks it is we who are cut-throats! No, Mr Cole, your wife is quite well. And has more sense in her head than you.'

'Do as you will with me,' said Jack, looking up and flicking his fringe from his eyes. 'As long as she is left alone.'

'What do you imagine I wish to do with you? The Tower, Mr Polmear says.' Something like a smirk passed his dark features and was gone. 'No, Mr Cole. Nor the Newgate either. I do not wish the faces and names of men I have use for known.' A little hope entered Jack's breast. 'So, you obeyed the orders Norris gave you in Paris and joined the Scotch Protestants?'

'I did, sir.'

'Did you find them true friends to England?'

Jack swallowed. 'To themselves, sir.' Then a memory stirred. 'And I heard there was talk of a group of plotters. Called the diamond league. Lady North– the lady asked about them. Said they were hot Protestants who'd made entreaties to the Scotch.' Walsingham turned to Polmear, his eyebrows raised in question.

'Never heard of them.'

'Did you speak with these men when you rode with Morton's men?'

'No, sir. But the lady and … Lord Seton, sir, who went with her – they said that these folks had men about the queen of France and one in England.'

'Polmear, find out if any of your friends have knowledge of them. If they are Protestant intriguers, we would know about it. No sense in being as split amongst ourselves as the papists.' Then something seemed to dawn on his face, and he lowered his voice. 'Discover if these men exist – if they had any hand in that business with the papist priests in the north. If they have plans that harm her Majesty, you know what to do.' Walsingham returned his attention to Jack and raised his voice. 'Seton. I understand the lady went also with a clerk called Cottam. We know of him. A filthy Catholic raised in Calais. I must say, Mr Cole, you seem unashamed to stand before me having let this treacherous countess seek fresh pastures.' Jack bowed his head. 'You let her go,' he added, squeezing every last bitter drop from the words. 'Good. Exactly as we knew you would.'

Jack looked up, unsure if he had heard correctly. Walsingham was staring into his eyes. 'Oh yes, exactly as we had hoped.'

'I … I don't understand, sir.'

'Do you take us for fools?'

'Who, sir?'

'Silence. We had Sir Henry send you precisely because we knew you would let the woman go. We wish her at liberty in Europe. From there we shall know all of her doings. She shall reveal to us every last plot, every cursed den of plotters she can court. You did just as we hoped you would. Regard.'

Walsingham tapped the paper on his desk with a bony finger. 'Word from your wife that the traitor entertains a false conjuror lately expelled from England. He has had traffic with another creature called Storey, who lately has encouraged the Spanish duke of Alba to invade. He will now go to the gallows. Yet this Prestall creature we now know plans to procure the liberty of the Scotch queen, whether Storey dies or not. We see all that passes in that foolish woman's house. Her very heart is open to us. So, you see, you did the right thing. Though I mislike and distrust of your reasons.'

Jack squinted down, unable to contain the dismay on his face. Oh no, he thought – what have they made you do, Amy? The thought of her entangling herself with men like Walsingham and Polmear was crushing, especially if she thought to help him by doing it. The older man drew back in his chair and nodded to his colleague, still stationed against the wall.

'You cannot win against Mr Walsingham, Cole. He knows a man's actions before he's done them.' Walsingham tilted his head back against the carved headrest of his chair, satisfied.

'And we have further use for you. Your wife too.'

'Threats against Amy–'

'I do not make threats, Cole. Mr Polmear?'

'Mr Walsingham would have you return to the north. There you will gain the trust of the papists. They flock there. Seminary priests out of Douai, Rome, wherever else exiles and would-be martyrs breed. So drunk from the well of Rome they forget they are Englishmen born. They meet in York – England's festering, papist-infected boil. Thereafter they spread throughout the country. Just lately they've had a good Protestant minister killed. Brutally killed. Worked up the locals to murder, best as we can fathom. You will find them. Gain their trust. Give us their names. And then they will die.'

'If I can't? If I won't?'

'Then you will die. And your wife will be left to starve. It'll go hard for her, fighter or not. There it is, Jack.' Polmear held up his hands. 'Blood or secrets. You can't help but spill one or the other.'

'Why can't you do it?' spat Jack. 'You're well trusted, aren't you?'

'Mind your tongue, boy.'

'I'm sorry, sir.'

'Good. Mr Polmear is known in much of the north,' said Walsingham, his voice quite calm. 'And our work requires that he moves and watches about these islands. You will appreciate, Mr Cole, that we have extended you every courtesy. My own home has been open to you and you have proven you will not run.'

'And I thank you for the honour of your house, sir.'

'If you work for your country,' said Walsingham, dismissing the flattery with an eye-roll, 'as you have done thus far, you might reasonably expect to live a long and fair life. As will your wife. We will see to it that you meet again. Do you understand?'

'Yes, sir.'

'Mr Polmear, you will run through the instructions.'

Polmear cleared his throat. He put forward his chest, adopting a military bearing, staring straight ahead, and began speaking. 'In Mr Walsingham's service you'll observe the following strictures. You will avoid buying and selling property. You will avoid engaging in legal disputes with neighbours or any other common folk. You will avoid anything that results in writing your name on documents.' Walsingham nodded approvingly, his eyes on Jack. 'Avoid fighting you are not trained to,' went on Polmear, 'remembering that others might be and that you might again trouble the law and have your name put to it. If you are known, you … you are weakened.' What was that, wondered Jack – a slight hint of regret? Of embarrassment? Again, Polmear coughed. 'You will observe always the following general rules: you are what you wear, and you are what you say. You will let your words fashion you. However, you will impersonate no man greater than yourself. You will remain always aware of the days of the week and month, noting when you observe what you observe. If you find you must take extreme measures with any man, avoid using any weapon that can be traced back to you.' The cadence of recitation dropped. 'Plainly speaking, I reckon if a man needs a gun or a fancy blade to set to work, he'd better not set to it at all. If you can't kill a man with your own two hands, you've no business doing so.'

Walsingham sucked in his cheeks at the change in tone and frowned at the word 'kill'. 'We need none of your opinions. It is better any man in my employ should run from common brawling. As you ran, Mr Polmear. In that, you did do right.' A lull fell, tension filling it. Jack sensed he had no part in it. Walsingham banged a fist on the desk. 'Pray continue – with what you have learnt at my table.'

'Begging your pardon, sir. Ah, where was I?' He coughed. 'You ... you ...'

'My name,' prompted Walsingham.

'Yes, sir. You will use Mr Walsingham's name never. You will mention him only to trusted men of authority. Even then, only in the gravest of situations. I mean, when your life can't be saved by any other means. And know that even then it might not save you.'

'I see our friend understands,' said Walsingham. He sat back and clasped his hands over his stomach, the image of a man satisfied with his own genius. 'Each item approved by Sir William Cecil as meet for the training of men of intelligence. Though of my own devising.'

'Er – just one more, sir?'

'Oh?'

'My own rule, sir: sleep well and sleep often.'

'Very good, Mr Polmear. Very full of wit,' snapped Walsingham. He turned to Jack, who had stood listening to the oration with his jaw clenched. 'You understand all that you have heard, boy?'

'Yes.'

'Yes, what?'

'Yes, sir.'

'Good. Then there is one thing only that remains. Remember always that you are to watch. To gather intelligence and report what you see. No more. Make no constructions on your observations. Do not think you are to employ such wits as you have in discovering men's motives. It is for we men of state alone to think on such matters. In matters of intelligence, you are a watcher, not a thinker. Now go out, would you?'

Jack slumped and left the room. As he closed the door, he heard some mumbling about diamonds and priests. He rubbed at his temple and began inching down the steps. 'We' repeated in his head. Walsingham had been very careful to say it often. 'We' meant the whole state – queen, Cecil, Polmear, every rotten agent under every rock in England, himself now included. As he reached the bottom, he began to wonder at the necessity of such a deliberate display of strength. Surely, he thought, only men who were weak felt the need to continually show off how strong they were, how much they knew. Did Walsingham really know he would betray his orders and help the countess to Europe, or was he merely making the best of a bad situation? Was Polmear present in Aberdeen to see that it all went off, or to act as insurance if the plan to hand her over to the Scottish Protestants failed? As he stepped out into the courtyard, he realised one thing: whatever Walsingham knew or not, he would never be privy to it. And he could not beat what he did not know.

By the time he had crossed the yard, suspicion had matured to certainty. Walsingham had masters of his own – the queen and Cecil. He did not seem a man to admit he was wrong, but he did seem one to try and cover up his miscalculations and make them work to his advantage. Jack looked around the quadrangle, suddenly thrumming with life. York, he thought. It was hardly seeing the world – and yet it meant that he was alive. It was an odd sort of punishment, but, he supposed, it was bad enough that he should be punished at all for making what he felt was the right choice.

4

Mr Acre turned the card over in his hands. A knave of diamonds. Written on the back was the word 'YORK'. It had been left at the tenement in which he was staying, presumably by one of the temporary messengers. The diamond league had only four leaders, each named for one of the face cards. The suit was chosen deliberately – diamonds signified strength. Diamonds were unbreakable, it was said, and steadfast. Though the four faces formed the mind of the operation, nine messengers were scattered across Britain and Northern Europe. Those men, however, were simply hired mercenaries, none knowing the next, none knowing the true plan, and none even knowing that they were part of the great card game.

Acre folded the card into its pocket. The code was clear enough. The man called the knave of the suit was coming to York and would no doubt wish to meet with him. There they could discuss the progress of events. It would not be a particularly edifying conversation.

The truth was that the deaths that had mounted up thus far had not had any discernible effect. The problem, he suspected, was that the priests were simply viewed as disposable sodomites, and Lansing, the reverend, had served only to infuriate the Protestant civic authorities – and what they thought did not matter. They already hated everything and everyone that did not suckle at the teat of their church. He closed his eyes and tilted his head back. His best thinking was done in the dark.

Yes, he had to admit it: he had enjoyed slaughtering Lansing. That was a grievous fault. It was not just that it was supposedly wrong to enjoy killing – that had long since ceased to concern him – but that enjoying it meant he was likely to make mistakes. Enjoyment brought sloppiness. Groping in the dark, he removed his jerkin and shirt. He could not see his arms, but he could feel the welts and scars that criss-crossed the foreparts. For years now he had disciplined himself with thin cuts. They focussed his mind. If he found that he was losing clarity, that he was drifting into the dark days of unclear and ill-directed wildness, the sharp pain would set things right. The bleeding never lasted long; he was careful about that. The faces of the diamond league – his family – knew that he did it, but they accepted it as part of him. They accepted everything about him. It was they, after all, who had set him to work, knowing that he had the nerve and the skill to ensure their great design was carried out in England.

When he slid out the thin blade he kept at his hip, he grimaced, knowing what was to come. His mind he trained on what would likely be the task ahead: something bigger, gaudier, something that would truly provoke outrage rather than being met with sniggers, closed ears, heretical head shaking, or delight.

He clenched his teeth as the blade bit into his flesh.

It was a foolish and sloppy plan, he thought, as pain gripped him. He did not even believe in their God, however much he loved them.

Again, he cut. He could feel the wetness of the blood trickle. If he had to cut down to the bone he would cease the prattling thoughts that, in the dark, told him that the whole thing was directionless – that those above him, from king to knave, were making it up as they went along. He did not even allow himself to think about the angel who had saved him, and for whom he would lay down his life. It was his place to deliver up the bodies of those that his elders demanded, not to question their decisions. As the blood flowed, he let his doubts and his weakness wash away with it.

Part Three: Double Dealing

1

Jack sipped at a wooden mug of ale at the far end of a long table. The tavern was nameless, squatting over an alley off the Colliergate. He had been in York for weeks, laying his head in common lodging houses and earning a few coins here and there tethering and brushing horses. Each night he had taken to haunting taverns, looking out for groups of men who seemed out of place, brooding, or who simply kept their conversations quiet and sober. Polmear had escorted him to York, leaving him with a fat purse which he laughingly told him not to spend in one whorehouse or piss against a wall, before departing for God-knew-where. Jack opted to save the money in case of trouble, dipping into it only when he could not earn enough for food or a bed. It would not do to be taken up by the law as a wandering and idle vagabond.

Astoundingly, Jack found he missed the bawdy man, though he would never have admitted that to him. It was the company he missed. A familiar face, even a knavish one, was a beacon in an unfamiliar place. If he could not listen to Amy telling her stories of those who had annoyed her over the course of her day, it was necessary at the least to have a companion to whom he might listen. Other people were around him constantly, but they were strangers, speaking only of practicalities – the price he was charging, the oncoming winter, strange deaths in the county. Living amongst strangers in France had been fine as long as he had had Amy passing judgement on all around him, forming a shield around the pair of them. Without her, he found himself wondering what kind of cutting remarks she would make if she were there. It was both comfort and curse.

He set down his mug. A little way along the table, a trio of men were conversing in low tones, their voices a mellifluous hum. They had been visiting the same tavern for several nights now, never arriving or leaving together. Promising, Jack thought. They always paid their bill and they never got themselves involved in any of the numerous arguments, good-natured or otherwise, that punctuated the evenings. He burped as theatrically and loudly as he could. Though he despised heavy drinking, he had seen enough of it in childhood to know the behaviour. He fumbled for a coin, dropped it, and hissed, 'shit upon the queen,' loudly enough for the men to hear. Others heard too, and that was alright. It was rather freeing knowing that you could say what you liked, break any laws of speech, and if some interfering goodman reported you, you could frighten them with the name of one of the queen's own secretaries. Not, of course, that he had been encouraged to do that: cause too great of an affray and he would be left to hang as an example. 'Stay out of the eyes of the law,' Polmear had instructed him: 'operate under it. Townsfolk are the worse for causing scandals and scandals break intelligencers'.

Good advice. But then, the half-formed idea had come to him that being a poor spy might be the best means of escaping a life of intelligence-gathering all the sooner.

As he stumbled from the table, he saw movement from the corner of his eye. One of the three men had risen, and another put a hand on his arm. 'You have been loose with your tongue. You might be hanged for it,' said the first, his eyes mild as he shook off his restraint and slid down the bench towards Jack, his blonde curls bouncing.

'Good. What's there to live for when chaos reigns? I would die a martyr.' Jack turned to the man who now sat by him, challenge painted on his face. 'You think you'll be reporting me? A man's speech is his own. I said hang the heretic queen and I meant it.'

'Talk you of dying? Peace, son,' he said. 'We are not heretics. But you should guard your tongue, lest any of that colour mean to prick it.'

'Not heretics?' Jack repeated, blinking stupidly.

'No. We're true in the old ways.'

'Adam!' hissed the baby-faced man who had tried to stop him. 'Mind your tongue.'

'Are we not here to salve true souls?' said the blonde man, Adam, quietly. 'It is meet we should encourage as many as have the strength to speak up, is it not, Red Robin?' Jack guessed that the nickname came from the youngest man's flame-red hair.

'What do you say, father?' asked Robin to the man who had continued to sit. Jack squinted at him. Older than the others, bald as an egg, perhaps twenty-five. Certainly not old enough to be father to either of the others. He sat with his arms folded, studying Jack right back.

'I say we leave this place. We are causing a scene.' Jack looked around the room and saw that they had attracted some attention. Even in the half-light, it was clear that heads had turned to the long table, and the chuntering conversation had dimmed. 'Now.'

'As you say,' said Adam, tossing his blonde locks. 'What's your name, friend?'

'Jack. Only Jack. Son of a gentleman, fallen on hard times since the southerners took our land when the north fought back.' It was an invention, of course, but one he felt had the ring of truth. A great many old families of the north had had their lands and goods confiscated and their patriarchs hanged for rebelling against Elizabeth the previous year.

'Very good, Jack. We shall speak further, if you like.' He leaned in and breathed into his ear, 'the cellar of the old Carmelite Friary. You know it?'

'Aye.'

'In a half hour.'

'Mebbe,' Jack burped. He slumped down again and stared morosely into the brown pool of ale as the three men took turns leaving. It had not been hard at all – it was exactly as Polmear said. The fellows had even betrayed themselves, using 'father' and calling him 'son' when two of them were only about his own age. After a while, he pulled himself up from the bench, handed over a few coins to the tapster, and slipped into the evening.

Winter had come early to York. Though it was still only touching November, frost sparkled on the ground, forming white veins over puddles and fallen leaves. The streets were silent and empty. Something had shifted across the north of England following the failed rebellion. Beyond just the hundreds of men who had gone to their grave – or to hang, crumbling, from trees – there seemed to linger a morose, suspicious stillness. He had noticed, on his nights moving from tavern to tavern, that those abroad on the streets went about their business silently, as though afraid of who might be watching from the shadows. More than once he had shivered, not out of fear, but because he knew that he had become what they feared. He was the narrowed eyes. He was the pricked ears. He was one of those who had brought about their men's deaths and would, if he could, soon bring more to the gallows. The only way to live with it was not to think about it. If he did, if he leapt into the life Walsingham had prepared and enjoyed it, as Polmear seemed to, he would lose a part of himself. He would slide down the hierarchy from man to the animals, scrabbling about the ground, picking at carcasses.

He did not creep. To do so would only mark him out. Instead he strode the mostly empty streets, hard by the frozen sewer channel, and made his way to the old tenement building on Stonebow Lane, which he knew to have formerly been the home of the Carmelites. It was a tall building, partially decayed. To whom it belonged now he did not know – someone wealthy, probably, who rented the rooms above ground out for crippling prices. That had been the purpose of England's reformation, as everyone in Europe knew. It was not to reform or root out problems in the old church, but to grab its wealth and share it amongst those loyal to the crown. No windows were lighted above, and so he slipped around the side of the building, going slowly until he felt the ground sink to a low opening. He inhaled the cold night air, breathed out, and knocked. A small door opened immediately, and he crouched his way in.

He shielded his eyes from the sudden burst of light as Adam closed the door behind him. The other two men, little Red Robin and the older one, were affixing torches to the walls. The cellar was low and vaulted, so that none of them could stand to their full height, and the floor alternated flagstones and dirt. It was a grubby, shameful place for the faith which even now commanded great cathedrals across the continent. 'You are priests?' asked Jack, willing hope and awe into his voice. Shoots of fear helped it tremble.

'Speak you of priests?' asked the older man, who attempted to cross his arms. The effect was almost comical in the tiny room.

'I'm a true Catholic,' said Jack. 'Why did you bring me here if you're not priests?' The fellow shrugged, turning to Adam.

'You were speaking immoderately. Could have got yourself killed, my friend. It is up to us to protect the liberty of men's tongues and hearts, if they be true.' He sighed. 'We are lately arrived from Douai. Sworn to protect those who oppose the heretical faith in this realm.' Jack felt his heart leap and then sink. They were exactly what he had sought, and yet had feared finding. 'Did you speak true? You are of the old gentry of the north?' Jack only mumbled noncommittally in response. 'My elder friend here is Father Thomas. Born in Newcastle. Moved abroad to take orders years since. He does not trust strangers.' The bald man shot him a dark look, his lip protruding. In response, Adam thrust a fist into his palm. 'But it is boldness we need if we are to reclaim England.'

'Can we trust you?' asked Robin, moving to Jack's side and taking his hand. Instinctively, Jack pulled it away. Physical contact with men he might have to betray was too much. It did not seem to bother Robin, whose open, ingenuous face, sprayed with freckles, remained smiling. In the torchlight his hair glinted like beaten copper.

'Why did you bring me here?' he repeated.

'If you are as you said,' Thomas said, looking down his nose, 'you must know the names of those who stand with Rome.' Jack paled. He had not thought far enough ahead, so intent had he been on finding hidden priests. An idea occurred.

'How do I know this is no trap? That you're not men of Queen Elizabeth?'

'There is no Queen Elizabeth,' spat Adam. Jack turned, surprised. He had expected the vitriol to spill from the older man. 'A filthy, degenerate southern whore who must be destroyed.'

'Peace, Adam,' said Thomas. 'You set your two young friends a poor example with talk so bloody. What is your name? Jack what?'

'Wylmott,' said Jack, on the backfoot, using Amy's maiden name. 'I can share with you the names of the true faithful. When we trust each other more.'

'Tsst,' hissed Thomas. 'The boy has nothing. Knows nothing. A troublemaker in a tavern is all. A fast talker.'

'No, wait – I … I have heard things. In taverns.' He thrust his mind into action, knowing he would have to offer them something to keep them in his orbit. 'I heard tell there's plans in the north. Heretic plans. Men calling themselves the diamond league.'

The atmosphere shifted, Jack's voice echoing around the vaulted chamber before fading entirely. 'Who are you?' said Adam.

'A man of chance,' answered Thomas, again folding his arms, this time in triumph. 'Diamond league – I've never heard of any such thing. It is the names of the faithful we need, not heretical conspiracies.'

'I say only what I've heard.' Jack held up the palms of his hands.

'From whom, Jack?' asked Adam.

'Men who attack the faith?' Robin put in.

'I can't say. Only saying what I've heard.' Eager for something else to say, he almost asked them what their plans were. He bit his tongue; nothing could be calculated to arouse their suspicion more. Instead he said, 'I can only offer you my word. I swear to you, fathers, I'm a true Catholic. I will pledge myself to help you, if you need means of escape or places to go. I'll find them for you.' As the words poured out, he found himself believing them.

'I trust you, my son,' smiled Robin, pulling a crucifix out from under his doublet and kissing it. 'God has led you to us and us to you.' Thomas tutted, but nodded. Adam only stared at him. 'Will you hear Mass with us?'

'Yes. Yes, please.'

'Shall we meet again, then?' asked Jack, after their devotions.

'If we are not torn from our beds in the night and slaughtered by officers of the stolen crown,' said Thomas, 'then … then yes. We shall meet again. Leave us now, Mr Wylmott, if you please.

We must discuss what our plans are. We cannot stay in any single place long.'

'And yet we have nowhere yet to go. Not in safety,' said Robin. 'Two good men who came before us … they died. Killed, as we understand, but the manner of it …'

'Is a thing not to be spoken of,' snapped Thomas. 'I knew them as you did at Douai. Fine Jesuits. Not what is said of them. Good evening to you, Mr Wylmott. I pray we can trust you, though I confess it is against my judgement.'

Bowing to them, Jack left the cellar and took the empty streets back to his lodging house. Dark thoughts threatened him as he walked, and he pushed them away, focusing on putting one foot before the other. The worst thing about being alone, about not having Amy, was having his own thoughts as company.

Soon he came to his lodging. It was the one he had lain in the longest, and the reason why soon made itself apparent. 'Good e'en to you, duck.' Doll, the heavy, middle-aged widow who kept the house greeted him with pat on the arm. When he had first enquired about a bed he had made the mistake of showing her warm gratitude – a rarity, apparently, from travellers – and he had since become her pet.

'Good e'en, Doll,' he said, the mimicry unconscious.

'Anythin' to eat?'

'No, thank you very much, ma'am.' She patted him again.

'Oh, "ma'am", you've mickle good manners. It's a good-fortuned wench as takes you to husband.' Jack essayed what he hoped was an impish smile. There was something motherly about her – she could kindle something childish and needy in him that usually only Amy managed when she was in one of what folk had always called her 'mammish' moods. He passed out of the taproom part of the building and went into the back room, where he had a small blanket in the corner.

When he was tucked up, unable to focus on the walk, he could not resist the siren call of his conscience. The three men whose trust he had just, he hoped, earned, might soon be dead. When he pulled the cover over him that night, he again considered the enormity of what he was doing. He knew names – first names only, but names – and faces. He had no idea how to contact

Polmear or any of Walsingham's men, and had been told to gather as much information about priests' movements as possible, encouraging them, even. But could he do that? Could he send three men to the gallows, whose only crime was their faith? They were so foolish and inexperienced, as young as himself, that they were willing to trust the first coney-catcher in a tavern who had made the right curses and oaths. They were honest men, stupidly honest. He must betray them in the hopes of keeping Amy safe, or find some way of saving both them and her. How that might be achieved he did not know, but he did know that if he secured their executions, his soul would suffer for it.

He knew how Walsingham and Polmear would excuse it, of course. It was for the greater good. It was for England. These men were traitors, sowing sedition, inciting hatred and violence, putting the queen's life in danger. Jack did not care. If the country was so divided that a cluster of men in a cellar could endanger it, then it was not worth saving. The taproom, already chilly, felt suddenly colder.

2

The ambassador's house on the Faubourg Saint-Germain was laid out along stately lines, and stood proudly, as though it knew it was to serve as the dwelling place of foreign princes' proxies. To Amy's fury, it was locked up. She remained on her horse, decked out in a cream-coloured dress and fur-trimmed travelling cloak. As she had witnessed on the road from Bruges, anyone might take her for a lady. Rather than a dreary cap, she even had a small chiffon headdress, her hair daringly curled and visible. It was remarkable that looking the part somehow made one feel the part, she thought. Unlike Jack, she knew she was not capable of mimicry. Yet she had learnt, instead, that the real trick to fooling people into believing you belonged was to appear completely at ease with yourself in their company. She looked up again at the shuttered house as she waited. Eventually, Kat came trudging back towards her own tethered mule. 'Lad up there says there's nae ambassador now.'

'None? No man?'

'No.'

Amy glanced around the street, where servants were carrying baskets and buckets to and from the doors of the other mansions. 'And you used the French I gave you? Said the words right proper?'

'Aye, madam.'

'Well. Shit.' The first thing she had done on arriving in Paris was not, as the countess had instructed, to inflict herself on the royal family, but instead to seek out Sir Henry Norris. Apparently, though, Lady Northumberland had been right in that he had been relieved of his post. If a new ambassador, Walsingham or anyone, had come to take his place, he had not arrived yet. There was no one from whom she could seek news of Jack's whereabouts. Silently, she cursed to herself again. If Jack was dead somewhere, she would dig his bones out of the grave and kill him again for the nonsense into which he had gotten them thrust.

'What do we do?'

'What do we do, my lady?' grinned Amy. She had enjoyed wheedling the girl throughout their journey. Much of the pleasure had gone out of it, though, when it had become apparent that Kat did not greatly care who she served, lady or false lady. She sighed. 'We try the palace.' She patted her bosom for the hundredth time, although she had felt the crinkle of the countess's letters with every beat of the horse's hooves.

They stopped to buy food from a street stall, picking up the latest gossip – the queen-mother is ruling over the pretty new queen, the Austrian Elisabeth; the queen-mother has been meeting with a man of the Holy Father; the queen-mother is ruling France whilst the king has gone hunting, or to ride his mistress; and what a terrible shame it was that the wedding had had to take place in some distant provincial dump – the queen-mother would not have liked that at all. Their bellies full, they then wound their way through the streets to the Pont Saint-Michel and across it to the Pont aux Meuniers. The Louvre and the new semi-built palace of the dowager Queen Catherine lay to their left.

'Do you not mind being so far from home?' asked Amy, when there was room for them to ride side by side.

'No' really, madam. No. If I can pick up French, I can get work anywhere. For anyone. I have my letters too.'

'You've picked up English fair enough.' The girl smiled. 'And who do you seek to work for? Not some servant done up as an English dame?' Kat seemed to consider this before speaking, giving them time to skirt some people on the Boulevard Saint-Germain. As they approached the range of palaces, the smell of people mingled with the fishy stench of the river and the churned muck from hundreds of tramping feet and hooves. Paris was bustling, despite the cold.

'I'd like to work for a queen.'

'You aim high.'

'No queen in Scotland. Not anymore. And the king still in skirts. He won't be marrying awhile yet.'

'You'd like to be a servant forever?'

'It's a good life,' Kat said, shrugging her shoulders and setting her mule stumbling forward. 'Don't starve. Don't have to marry.' The word sent Amy into contemplative silence. It could not last.

'Nothing wrong with being married. But it's good you wish to get on. I did too. You'll find your queen. My mam always said the Scots get everywhere.' She did not add her mother's final assessment on that: they got everywhere like rats and fleas and were harder to shift.

'That too – I like to be out in the world, seeing it. Travelling.'

'Ha,' said Amy. 'You sound just like … my husband. You sound like Jack. He loves to travel.' Sadness threatened. She had never understood his desire to be out seeing the world. Life was the same everywhere – tiring and unfair. Personally, she would be more than happy to sit in a home she could call her own and just listen to the tales of some other poor soul who had worn out his boots and who could tell her of the world's sights. She cast the thought aside. 'Here we are. This is the palace, anyway.'

Amy craned her neck towards the gatehouse, which loomed up, its roof light blue against the grey sky. Her heart sank. She had spent weeks and weeks training to walk, to speak softly in the French with which she had struggled since the start of the year; she had even tried dancing, playing a lute, terribly, and shooting a bow. At best she could say she was competent in speaking. In that she had been strict on herself. If she found herself stumbling, even thinking in English when she should not be, she pinched her upper arm. Even now it ached. Yet the desire to turn around and ride away came gusting down from the palace bell-towers as they rang out the afternoon hour. Another of her mother's sayings came back to her: if in doubt, do nowt. It did not help very much.

'Let's go, my lady,' said Kat, nudging forwards, the mule dragging the tiny little cart on which their belongings were stowed. Her boldness shook away the fear, exciting her urge to go first.

'You follow my lead, Kat. And mind what I told you. Treat me like as though–'

'Like you were the countess, aye. I ken.'

'And keep your mouth shut,' said Amy pressing ahead, her chin tilted. She had grown to like the girl, but she did not want a smart little Scotch mouth getting her into trouble.

A steady stream of men and women, some on horseback but most walking, were making their way into the palace precinct. Others were leaving. Amy opted to follow the crowd, having no clear idea of where to go. The majority of the people, she noticed, were in aprons and the garb of masons, gardeners, and craftsmen. It felt rather like a great building project was underway, but she supposed that it was just another ordinary day at the French court. As they made their slow progress, a man on a black horse came towards them in the opposite direction. Walkers and riders cleared a path for him and a few of them cheered. He waved in return. The horse was caparisoned in hangings, the words, 'Dederit'ne viam casus've Deus've' emblazoned in gold thread.

'Shall chance or God provide the path?' said Kat. Amy turned in wonderment but had no time to question her unexpected knowledge. The rider turned an exceptionally handsome, swarthy face in her direction, looked past her, and then returned his gaze. 'My lady,' he said in French, moving forward and taking off his hat.

'My lord,' she said, hoping her accent gave the language some semblance of culture. 'You might help us – we seek an audience with the queen – uh, the old queen. I am kinswoman to her Majesty's friend, the countess of Northumberland. I come bearing her greetings.'

'An English lady. How very charming. And such a beautiful one.' Amy did not blush. She knew what noblemen were like and had heard rumours enough in England about the French ones. 'I do not know this … ah, but yes. The lady lately come out of England. You are her kinswoman, you say? And she brings greetings to the king's mother, then, and the new queen? The court is not yet arrived from Mézières. The king is hunting. Marriage has given him vigour.'

'Yes,' said Amy. It would be better, she guessed, to say as little as possible. The more she elaborated, and the more unwieldy she made her lies, the harder they might fall. 'Their

Majesties are not here?'

'The king's mother is here. At her own house, beyond the gardens.' He gestured behind himself, where, above sculpted hedges and trees rose a huge, lone building with scaffolding on one side. 'To see that all is in readiness for the entry of the king and his new queen.' He rubbed his forefinger and thumb together and winked, before waving a hand encased in a shimmering black glove at the sky. 'This rain across France, the sky weeps with joy. Yet it is too much for a young queen and her court to travel in. The roads.' He shook his head. Amy frowned. The weather had been poor and the rain strong, but if the old queen, this man, and she herself could have travelled, she did not see why the king and new queen could not, unless they were carrying half the treasury and goods of France with them. She rolled her eyes without thinking; probably they were. 'It is a miracle you made it here, my dear lady. I am the duke of Guise,' the man said, his black eyes boring into hers. 'A dog lately made friends again with the king's mother. At present her Majesty is making ready to take the air.'

'Your Grace,' said Amy. The forest of correct forms of address came suddenly to mind. The French were very particular about those. She had heard of Guise. Amongst the Protestants he was a holy terror – a monster who devoured heretical babies and washed them down with their mothers' blood. To the Catholics he was a hero, valiantly defending the honour of the true faith and protecting it from Satan-worshipping Antichrists. Looking at him, Amy saw a pompous, arrogant creature – the kind who was acutely aware of how attractive and important he was.

'You were not to know, my dear lady.' He snapped his fingers and there appeared three men at the side of his horse, each dropping to bended knee. 'See that his lady is taken to meet with her Majesty. See to her horses. See that her girl is given warmth and good cheer. Now, dogs. Madam, I must away. I have business to which I must attend. These men will see that you are well cared for. You will, I think, wish to refresh yourself before you attend her most Christian Majesty?'

'I should like to see the king's mother as soon as I may,' said

Amy. 'If it please your Grace.' God, but she despised the fiddly titles such people used – they were nothing but a tongue-twisting bother. The good thing about being a lowly servant was that wealthy men in England seldom spoke to you and were instead quite content to let you take out their filthy laundry in silence.

'Oh, you English. So famous for your direct natures. But of course. I bid you good morrow.'

Before Amy knew what was happening, she was being helped down with much bowing, hand-kissing, cap-doffing, being led along a gravel path which bordered the gardens and passed from officer to officer. She had been at the English court once, at Windsor Castle, but the French was something altogether different. The Tuileries itself looked statelier and less old-fashioned, and its staff somehow more powdered, polished, and efficient. She expected that she was being led to some inner sanctum of the palace and was surprised, after taking a detour off the main path, to find herself winding her way into a frosty sculpted garden. The latest officer to escort her spoke to someone else, and eventually she was bowed to and the man's white-gloved hand invited her to step forward. She did, into one of several concentric squares of grass and bush. The sound of women's conversation tinkled from somewhere ahead, and a deeper voice said, 'come forth.'

Amy dropped low. 'Rise,' rumbled towards her. She did, and found herself staring into the flat, expressionless face of a middle-aged woman bundled in furs. 'From England?' She spoke French, but the accent was something else – Italian, she supposed. She realised that the woman was the king's mother, Catherine de Medici. The ladies' chatter was coming from somewhere else in the garden, where the dowager's attendants must have been strolling.

'Yes, your Majesty. I come from the countess of Northumberland, who lately left England.'

'I know. The countess sent me a letter speaking of your coming. I had it at Mézières. Walk with me. These are my privy gardens. A poorer sight in wet weather.' Catherine began to walk as she spoke. In addition to the accent, her voice had a flat, emotionless quality. It fit her statue-like face which, though not ugly, was rather bland.

'I … my lady, she said …'

'Your lady? Your kinswoman?'

'She is …'

'She is not your kinswoman.' This had the cadence of a question, but Amy suspected it was more statement, and she felt her legs wobble. 'You or she have lied to me. Or both have. Why?' Amy said nothing. Humiliatingly, she felt tears prick, though more of anger at how rapidly things were going wrong than anything else. Why had the countess not told her that she had written ahead? She might then have prepared something else to say. 'You do not deny it? This letter, it said that you have news for me. Of the dowager queen. Mary of Scotland.'

Amy resumed walking the raked gravel path, keeping pace with Catherine, who seemed more interested in the building work going on around the edges of the garden. 'I have been with her, your Majesty. In England.'

'You were her companion?'

'Yes.' That was stretching the truth, but she was past caring.

'Scotland is truly lost?'

'I … Queen Mary is a prisoner in England.' Catherine waved a dismissive hand, looking almost irritated.

'The child has lost Scotland to us. It is in the hands of the heretics now. I warned her. Warned her against those melancholy humours. It was having a son destroyed her, as it will weaken us all in time. The heretics would never let her raise a Catholic prince. She should have broken them sooner. Broken all of them. Instead she gave them power enough to undo her before she could undo them. Strike before struck, I said, and said, and said again.' She tutted. 'Yet she was once our queen. I would that she was well kept.'

'She is. The earl and countess of Shrewsbury keep her. They are fine people.'

'Fine, fine. She is Elizabeth's now.' Amy lowered her head. Mary Queen of Scots had been Catherine's daughter-in-law, as all the world knew. Yet the woman spoke as though she was simply a lost piece of property, snatched away by someone else

– regrettable, but nothing to weep over. Amy had not particularly liked the woman – she distrusted most women who appeared overly friendly and sweet – but she had felt sorry for her. 'Is that all you come to tell me? That the Scottish queen is a prisoner. That which I know already?' They had come to the edge of the garden, and Catherine turned and began moving towards a stone wall with an iron gate set farther down it. Strange chirps and hoots came from behind it.

'The palace here is finer than Windsor,' offered Amy.

'You have been a guest of the English queen? You have seen her?'

'Yes, your Majesty. Once.' For the first time, some animation came into Catherine's doughy face.

'What does she look like? Her face – is it handsome? Does she walk straight? I have only the word of ambassadors who serve her. You, I think, are with her enemy, this Northumberland lady who writes me. A spy for this countess, are you not? The truth of that queen will lie somewhere between what you say and they say.'

'Queen Elizabeth, she is …' Amy thought back to her brief glimpse of the English queen, and could picture only a long face, black eyes, and red hair. It was hard to know how much her mind might have distorted it in the past year. 'A handsome woman.'

'A beauty?'

'No, your Majesty. I don't say beauty. Yet she has a queenly air.' Catherine nodded, as though savouring something.

'Does she look old? Too old for children?' The older woman mimed a distended belly with one arm.

'I can't say. She … looks strong enough to bear them.' Again, the nod.

'I understand she is not well liked by your countess and her people of the north. And yet very well loved by the most part in the south. Is this the truth?'

'Queen Elizabeth is … she makes herself loved when she can, I think. Where she can. Tries to.' Amy did not feel she could say that the majority of people she knew did not spend their time either loving or hating their queen.

'Elizabeth has sat on the English throne for ten years and might sit for ten years more,' boomed Catherine, as though beginning a sermon. 'Each year makes her more acceptable to the people. Each year brings her closer to a husband. I confess, it is hard not to admire your sovereign lady. Yet she cannot fight time. Time always wins. It presses her to make a child.' She gave her first smile – a brief knife-slash. 'And what other news comes from your English countess? I own I see little reward in taking her hand over her queen's.' The laughter of the other ladies somewhere in the maze-like garden was growing louder, and Catherine's voice fell in volume as she reached her last few words.

'That … there is some Protestant plot. The diamond plot. The men say they have someone about the queen of France. This was months ago – when the only French queen was your … uh … most Christian Majesty. They've tried to poison my lady.' Catherine stopped walking and turned cold eyes on Amy.

'Poison?'

'Yes. An old man's ale was poisoned. He was told to bring it to my lady's house. He drank of it first and died in the street.' Catherine digested this, looking towards the sound of the chattering ladies and then up at the palace walls.

'I think this grand palace shall never be finished, the expense of weddings and entries and peace.' She coughed. 'My son is newly married to a good and faithful Catholic. A girl I love beyond all others – a true daughter to me. Worthy of protection, as is my son. France is at peace. We have the finest physicians and apothecaries in the realm in our service. All food is tested, and clothing, and cushions. A unicorn horn. Pure emeralds with a special magic about them. What know you of this plot, of these Protestants? A Huguenot who has lingered about me for months? Who are you girl, truly? I know the difference between a great lady and … and a shop-keeper's daughter. Quickly. Out with out.'

'I …' Amy blurted out everything, from her time in service, to her husband, to Walsingham and Cecil, the trip to Scotland, and her journey back to Paris. It came out so quickly she doubted it made sense. Just as she was finishing, a pair of well-dressed women rounded a hedge and stopped respectfully, their servants following behind. On seeing Catherine, all fell to their knees, but the women at the front could not resist looking up coyly to study the new arrival. Amy felt herself bristle.

'My ladies. Bianca Gondi and Vittoria de Brieux. Too old and too ugly to join the new queen's household. My eyes in Paris when I am from home.' The expressionless tone had returned to Catherine's voice, which she did not trouble to lower. 'They will remain in this city to make its great places ready for France's new queen. Once I have raised … once there is wealth enough out of Paris, I shall bring her Majesty and the king here in all triumph. Your name, girl?'

'Amy, your Majesty.'

'You will remain at this place also. With these ladies. You will be treated with all honour, as your fallen mistress of Northumberland begs. You claim you have served the Scottish queen, yes? So you know something of fine taste. I doubt that that lady will have lost her fine fancies even in an English prison. You will not try to leave. I will have you named a dame of my own household, but you stay here until I escort my son and daughter to Paris. I shall wish to hear more of your story and make study of the truth of it. I shall discuss with the king the names of those who have come into my service this past year. Which, if any, might favour the Huguenots. If there is truly some person about me or my family, you will discover the name and bring it to me. If they call themselves a diamond … we have emerald, coral, amethyst – all enemies to foul poison. And if I find you have lied about anything – anything else – or if this is some stratagem, a plot to get the lady of Northumberland's eyes in my house … I shall have you thrown to the dogs.'

Amy let Catherine trundle onwards, her carriage slow and deliberate. She waved away the two ladies, gesticulating sharply back in Amy's direction and mumbling something. They came towards her, the women she had not allowed herself to imagine living beside. To her own disgust, she felt butterflies stir. On the road she had imagined a flock of delicately feathered birds with sharp talons and beaks, mocking and judging and despising her. Despite her best efforts, her mind had weaved her fears and insecurities into a tapestry that would be hard to unpick. It was always better, she thought, to expect dislike and be relieved than to expect love and kindness and be disappointed.

The younger of the women, dripping in jewels and furs, took her by the arm. 'My lady,' she said in a high, brittle voice, 'what a charming dress.' The other, far older, gazed at her with milky eyes, before grumbling something under her breath. 'Ah, pay no heed to my friend. She distrusts the English. Yet we shall be friends, we two young things.' Amy looked the woman in the eyes and smiled. She was almost certainly some distance past thirty, the thick layer of white makeup emphasising what it was intended to hide.

'Yes,' said Amy. 'I'd like that.'

'Come, let me show you where you shall take your rest.'

Amy allowed herself to be led, but her attention had returned to the broad back of Catherine de Medici. The old woman had, she realised, set her a nigh-on impossible task: discover the plotter said to be in her household, whilst remaining only with a small part of it in Paris. It might be weeks before the king and queen took up residence in their capital, and thus weeks before Catherine's entire household was together. The whole thing was a ruse to keep her confined. She had been seen through as a spy of the countess's and was being retained, to be watched. Probably the dowager queen thought the entire tale of the diamond league a fable. Amy would just have to prove her wrong.

3

Acre strolled the streets known as the Shambles on the first Thursday after Christmas. He had bought several apples and crunched on one of them conspicuously, his cap pulled low. The smell of blood in the air was invigorating; it gave him appetite. Chunks of meet hung on hooks outside butchers' shops, and offal was being swept into the channel running between the cobbles.

The fellow he was to meet was in York and would know him by sight. He circled around two florid women who were kissing each other on the cheek and exchanging loud greetings, raising their voices against the nearest merchants' cries. Neither seemed to care that the hems of their dresses were being splashed bloody.

'Our ace of diamonds,' whispered a voice at his ear. He did not jump, though he had not seen the man coming. The street grew alternately wider and narrower as the thatches overhead crookedly conferred, making it an ideal place for surprise.

'Our knave,' Acre said, chewing the last of the apple and throwing the core into the sewer. It bounced off some frozen blood and then stuck in nearby sludge melted by the pressing of boots. 'Where shall we talk?'

They joined the street that led to the old Bootham Bar, running past York Minster on its way. The cathedral's outer walls offered no shade on a cold, grey day, but they did offer an escape from the press of people thronging the Shambles. They did not speak until they were walking alongside them, damp and chill reflecting in icy blasts. 'What are you calling yourself now?'

'Acre.'

'Acre. Ace. Very good,' smiled the other.

'All is well?'

'It is. The Jesuits are here. Stupider even than the last.'

'Pfft. Their deaths brought no great fury.'

'No. No, nor did the killing of the heretic.'

'He was well hated.'

'Yes. We must think of something else.'

'Our king? Our queen? What do they say?'

'They are plagued, brother. And if they are plagued, as are we all.'

'By whom? How plagued?'

'A pair of bustling interferers. A husband and wife. They took ship with that ridiculous countess and her people from Scotland. The wife has departed for Paris, where she can be well watched and well dispatched. The husband is here in York. He disappeared at sea, probably intending to be thought lost so that he might work his tricks here. A spy for the English queen – though he claims he is a Catholic. Calling himself Jack Wylmott about the town, but the name is Jack Cole. A nothing. Yet he speaks of us. We were too loose in Scotland, too eager to enlist those filthy Calvinist savages. Now he is in York.'

'In York,' echoed Acre. They had come to a gate in the wall, where more people were huddled, and they turned back. 'Show him to me. I will get rid of him.'

'Very good.'

'What about the wife?'

'Ah … our attempts to rid ourselves of her failed. It was poorly done, and thereafter she was careful. The countess was too. Any attempt after a failed one is a risk.'

'Where is she?'

'She has taken up residence with the old witch-queen of France.'

'What?'

'Yes. We do not know how they know what they know. When they aided the countess's flight out of Scotland, it is possible they worked in the Scotch camp. Heard of our overtures to those stupid heretical savages. They know that we have someone at Catherine's door.'

'But … I cannot be in France – I have much to do here.'

'Nor need you be, brother. Becalm yourself. Our own queen of diamonds, she will deal with the little English wench.' Acre relaxed, but not entirely. He would prefer to have completed both jobs himself. 'You, young pup – you will have other work, as you say.'

'Beyond the husband?'

'Yes. Our plans thus far … they have not progressed as we would wish. Some priests and a corrupt old man. None have been stirred to anger over them. Forgotten.' He cut the air with a bone-white hand. 'If we wish to provoke the greatest outrage, to have the people railing in confusion and anger, to wash away the sins of corruption with blood–' He stopped himself when Acre gave him a warning look; his voice had been rising dangerously. 'You have doubts?'

'No. Never. Now you are here, though, are two of us needed in the north? I could go south. Raise the southerners' heat.'

'I think not. Not yet. When we have instructions, I shall journey south.'

'Mmph,' said Acre, knowing how sullen he was beginning to sound, how very like a child caught doing something that made his mother scream. 'Only … would it not be better to have some dark day of reckoning.' To Acre's mind, a plot was not a plot unless some day were secured on which all hell would break loose. Thus far their actions had the complexion of scattered acts, however much he prepared each one individually. The other man stopped walking.

'A day planned is a day to be discovered,' he said. 'Great days of attack exist in the minds of intelligencers only. Gives them something to believe in and search for.' Acre felt the rebuke. He had known it all his life, the gentle sense that he was wrong, but that he would be set right. His partner jabbed a hand in the direction of the Minster walls. Above them, the two western towers stood sentinel against the lowering sky. 'You see that? What we seek to do is like bringing it down. Flat, to the ground. So that we can rebuild. Yet there are many who would stop us. How could we do it? Yes, we could plan a great act – hire soldiers, hire a great gun, organise all so that on a certain day – Christmas Day, perhaps – BOOM. It would fall about its archbishop's ears. You like that? A pleasing image, I admit. Yet think. Could we trust the soldiers? The cannon-maker? I said there are many who would stop us – they would be listening for such a plan, bribing soldiers to find out the day of the enterprise.

'Then there is another way. Each day we could pass by the place in all innocence. Removing bricks under the nose of its keepers. Gradually. Steadily. It would take some time, but none would know what we were about. We might not know the day the thing falls but fall it will. This is our way. And as each brick is torn out, we judge the mood of the people. When they have had enough rot and corruption and evil from the men they believe to have the care of their souls … then we might release the cannon.' Acre nodded, drawing his eyes away from the Minster. He still did not like what they were doing; it was still too unfocussed. Too slow. 'We must destroy one who is beloved by all. Remember, it is not the English queen's heretics we must raise to anger. That was our error. Those fools are angry at everything already. The Catholics of this country must be turned against themselves, against Rome's men. If we are to spark total war, we must heat the blood of all. You recall what it has been in France. So will it be here.'

'France,' repeated Acre, softly.

'Yes. The English will not succeed in bloody revolution but by degrees. You know them as well as I do. In France, perhaps, we shall bring about something grander. Something that will rouse the English from their slumber. Put fire in their bellies. But first we must warm them up. Through fear and hatred. We have greater funds coming to us than ever before. Rich men are at our back now. The Pope too.' Acre did a double take and the other laughed. 'Not that any of them know it.'

'Whom do you have in mind?'

Rather than answering immediately, the other man looped his arm through Acre's and the two began strolling back into the Shambles.

***

'You say you're a Catholic? You know I'm not of that faith. Not for a long space.' Mrs Oldroyd smiled, the deep wrinkles crinkling her eyes. 'What brings you?'

Acre had been shown the woman as she handed out coins in the market. Over seventy years old, apparently, and had been trained as a nun until the monasteries fell. Though she was a religious turncoat, she had lived out her life in the north, continuing charitable works and becoming known as a friend to any who struggled with faith, trouble with the law, or food to eat. She lived alone, thankfully, and employed no woman to cook or clean in her little shack near the River Floss.

'I heard tell in't market that you were right good to folks that are in want.'

'You don't look in want,' she said, still smiling. 'Though a good meal never hurt no one. Please, eat.'

Acre picked up a piece of the bread she had set before him and essayed taking a nibble. He despised the formidably pious. Each one he had ever known or watched had been a hypocrite of some kind. From observing the old woman for a few days, it was not clear what she was – too old for whoring and too generous for hoarding. Perhaps her having turned her back on one faith and accepting the one that infected her native land sufficiently warranted what was about to befall her. The important thing was, as his friend and brother had pointed out, there were none in York who called her an enemy.

'You don't believe in confession, in the here- in the reformed faith, do you?' he asked. If she was surprised by the suddenness of the question, she did not show it.

'No. No, we need no priests to ask God for our salvation.'

'Nor any charity. But I've saw you give it.'

'I share what I have from humanity. Not faith.' She looked around the one-room house from her position on a stool and smiled. The place was mostly empty, though a good fire was going in the grate with a pot bubbling over it. 'Not that I've much to give, eh?' She laughed, showing that she still had most of her teeth. 'Are you seeking to turn to the new faith? Sometimes it happens. Fellows go to the services or not, don't understand them, but are too afeard to speak even to the deacons. In case they're accused of being papists, or having been them, or … well, you know how it is, sonny. It's a sad time, people afraid. Is that why you've come? You wish to accept the queen's faith? I can help you. I have books.'

'Books?'

'Aye. In English. Books of faith. Would you like to see them?'

'Yes,' he said, smiling. The foolish old goat thought she had captured one like herself – a convert. He could almost sense the fire kindling in her at the prospect. She had already pulled herself up from the stool and crossed to a corner of the room, where an old wooden coffer sat. She opened it and leant in, sorting through papers, chattering as she did so. 'Pages from the Book of Martyrs. Some of the people mentioned, I was alive when they were murdered.'

Acre slid from his seat. 'Murdered?'

'Aye. Many've fallen on the path to salvation. When the queen's sister reigned ...'

'She burnt, didn't she? When I was a child.'

'It would be around then, to be sure. Not so very long ago. Cast a right long shadow.'

'Then we've something in common.'

'What's that?' She was still bent over the coffer, digging away.

'I burnt my parents. Burnt their house to the ground, the false creatures.' He had crept up behind her, and he stood with his legs apart.

He was not prepared for what happened next.

The old woman, astonishingly spry, wheeled around. Rather than retrieving books from her little chest, gripped in her hand instead was a small, sharp dagger. She swung it at his face and sent him stumbling backwards. His legs hit the stool and he went over it. His heart, which had not sped up as he advanced towards her, started to race. 'You old bitch!'

'Who are you? You killer! Who sent you into my house? Papist assassin!' She held her arm in the air, the dagger pointing downwards. She lunged. He rolled. He heard her blade splitting the floorboard where his head had been less than a second before. The attack seemed to have winded her, and he sprang up, twisted around, and fell on her back. She let out a low moan.

'You'll die for that!' he hissed. He lay for a moment, crushing her, and then felt her weak movements as her arms stirred. She was trying again for the knife. 'Traitor! Foul old carcass!' He grasped her arms and twisted them behind her back. An internal snap told him that one of them had broken under the sudden pressure. The fight departed her. For a moment he panicked, expecting her to scream, to draw attention from someone on the street outside, despite the hour and cold. Instead, she moaned again.

Acre grappled her to her feet. She weighed very little. Her head lolled forward as he pushed her ahead of him. 'Mhmm,' she said. Then, with more strength in her voice, 'who are you?'

'I'm of the true faith, heretic. You know what we do in the true faith?' Her back stiffened, but she lacked the strength to fight.

'Oh God,' he heard her whisper. 'Oh God.'

'God hates you,' he spat. 'He hates you. He hates me. He hates the false new faiths and the corruption of the old.'

'Mmph,' she mumbled. And then, with surprising strength in her voice, she said, 'boy … you must be an unhappy boy to do what you do to me. God forgive you.'

Still gripping her arms, he pushed her towards the fire and thrust her, head-first, into it. Her screams were brief. She tried at first to rear back, but he knelt down on the back of her legs, leaning back himself to avoid the flames. The pot of stew which had been bubbling away fell in with her.

It took the blessed and much-beloved Mrs Oldroyd longer to die than he would have imagined. As the flames consumed her upper body, still her legs remained stiff. When he judged her to be gone, he got up and pulled her out, using the skirts of her dress to put her out completely. From the waist up, she had become thoroughly blackened. Heavy smoke had wafted back into the room, and the stench of burning meat clawed at the inside of his throat. He left her body lying in the centre of the room and then went to her coffer. The books were there – the dagger must have been hidden beneath them, as an old woman's last line of defence. He removed them and began shredding them, casting the pages about her corpse.

Before he left, he scrawled on the wall, 'SO BURN ALL HERETICS'. He doubted Mary Tudor could have done better herself. Mrs Oldroyd had, so he was told, been a fixture of York life, respected both by the heretical and pious Protestants, whom she worshipped with, and the so-called Catholics who pretended their faith and would have the rule of Rome restored, with all its fornicating priests and greedy, grasping bishops. Both camps would be outraged at the discovery. This would be a scene that would stir the blood. Death was always fanned into tragedy when those who suffered it were very old, or very young, or very beautiful. The Catholic north, famed throughout Europe as having tried to resist the heretical English queen, would now draw hatred and scrutiny to the Jesuits. Whatever the knave said, a day of reckoning would come which would see Catholicism washed clean of its venality and corruption, and fit therefore to wipe away the foolish and false sects which had been set up in vain to replace it.

Acre straightened himself up. His little diamond pin had worked its way loose during his labours. He pulled it out and held it to his lips before forcing it back through the loose thread in his doublet and concealing it under his coat.

4

Jack nibbled on a pie crust, careful lest the gravy spill out. It was a communal pie and he did not wish to appear greedy. 'You tuck in, duck,' said Doll, watching him as he ate. 'You eat like a duck, too – there's nowt to you, like a half-starved whippet.' The truth was the pie was vile. Jack had heard from other customers in the main taproom that their hostess had once had a success with a homemade stew, and it had gone to her head; now she boasted her taproom as the only one in York that prepared and served its own meals. Grinning his way through another couple of bites, he thanked her, passed the pie on, and retreated to the back room. It was early, but the night was dark. January always seemed to have the dreariest and most miserable of days, and he had grown used to contemplating things in isolated silence; his fellow sleepers had departed for warmer houses with finer fare. He strode into the chamber and threw the door closed without turning.

'You shouldn't enter a room without looking around it first.' Jack jumped. Beside the door stood Polmear, a grin on his face. His beard had grown thicker. 'Another lesson for you, and for free.'

'What do you seek?' It came out more abrupt than Jack had hoped – it betrayed his surprise too much.

'I've come to see what you have for me,' Polmear said easily, bounding across the room and hopping up on a low table. He drew his legs up and sat, child-like, on top of it. 'Well? Have you ferreted out the papist scum?'

Jack swallowed before speaking. 'How did you get in here? Doll – the tavern mistress warned me of no guests.'

'I'd no traffic with her.' He tapped the side of his nose. 'You've got to learn how to enter places unobserved, unremarked. You've already been schooled in how to change subjects. Not well, though. What've you found here? Or who?'

'You're just like Walsingham. Just as bad. Just without the same power.'

'Pfft. I've the same authority as our master. The same authority as the queen too. It's just I don't have as many folk who believe it.' He winked. 'Now, come on. What have you found? I'll be put off no more.'

Jack swallowed before speaking. 'I've met some men. Might be papists. Hard to know until I win their trust. Where have you been, anyroad?'

'You've missed me, my friend?' Jack rolled his eyes. 'Lancashire, if you must know. Lot of trouble in Lancashire these past months. I swear before God, no sooner have these Jesuits been rounded up, or buggered each other to death, than more sneak in through the ports. Devil of a business. How many?'

'How many what?'

'How many are "some" men?'

'Oh,' said Jack, making a sham of getting comfortable on his pile of blankets. His old false smile twitched at his cheeks and he resisted it. 'Three, I think.'

'You think?'

'Three.'

Polmear swung his legs off the table. When he spoke, his voice had lost some of its cheerfulness. 'Jack, you can't be playing at this. Our people want papists found, their plots discovered.'

'Speaking of plots,' said Jack, eager to change the subject, 'I've cast around for news of this diamond plot. Have you heard anything?'

'Nothing. Nothing that suggests that men of our faith are doing anything. There … well, there was some business in a village not too far from here, mind.'

'The vicar? I heard tell of that.'

'Lansing. Rotten fellow by all accounts. Looks like he was done in by papists, only … well …'

'What?'

'Not really their style, is it? Unless they've been given orders from the Pope to start butchering Protestants in their homes. Hard to see how that would win them the love of a country turned away already. More likely to do the opposite, to my mind. Keep us turned away. Disgust us.'

'The diamond league are meant to be all Protestants,' yawned Jack. 'Leastways, the countess and Lord Seton heard in Scotland that they were trying to win the Scotch lot over to them. Protestants wouldn't be killing their own.'

'Our own,' said Polmear, folding his arms. 'Don't forget who you work for, Jack. Or who you work with' His voice turned sunny again. His hand went to his belt. Jack's eyes narrowed.

'What's in that coin purse?'

'Remarkably,' said Polmear, 'some coins. Come, let's go and have a mug of ale somewhere.'

'I'm tired.'

'Wine then. If we can find any. That wakens the blood. Don't like it myself. Rotten stuff. For women and rich bastards. But I've a lesson for you.' Jack groaned in response. 'No, a good one this. Listen up.' He tugged on his own earlobe. 'A man should drink.'

'I don't like it.'

'Life's full of things we don't like. A man should drink, and he should drink every kind of drink that men can brew. Ah, there's curiosity writ on your face now. A fellow ought to learn exactly what his humours can stand. How much of any drink can sit on his gut before his lips loosen and he starts telling strangers things that might get him killed. Or make him piss himself. Whichever of these things comes first. Come on, let's have a cupful.'

'You go, if you like.'

'It wasn't a request.' He skipped over and yanked Jack up from his bed. 'I've a thirst on me. And I'm in a talking sort of mood. Here, you know who's an arsehole?'

'What?'

'Do you *know* … who *is* … an *arsehole*?' Polmear repeated, slowly. 'No jest.'

'Who?'

'The old dame who runs this place – what did you say her name was there – Dolly?'

'Doll.'

'Doll, then. Arsehole.'

Jack laughed, surprised at the randomness. 'Why?'

'Too easy to get by. I can read folk.'

'Well,' said Jack. He closed his mouth and grinned, diffidence stifling speech.

'Well what?'

'Well … I reckon her food comes out of one, anyway.'

'Ha!' Polmear slung an arm around him and ruffled his hair. 'So you can play Sir Jester when you wish. Good lad. Come on, let's have that drink and a talk and be merry.'

One reluctantly, the other eagerly, they left the lodging house. Out in the street, a crowd was moving. Excited chatter bubbled from it, growing with each step as people were drawn from doorways to join. 'What's this?' asked Jack. Polmear shrugged.

'What news,' he shouted, grabbing at a man who was pulling on a coat and stepping out onto the road. 'What's happening?'

'A murder,' said the man, pulling away. 'So they're sayin'.' Jack and Polmear looked at one another as the fellow launched himself into the crowd. They followed, winding their way along the streets until everyone reached an old, single-room house. The crowd fanned out before it. City officials were holding back those at the front.

'What's happened,' asked Jack, his voice barely above a whisper. Polmear repeated the question more loudly to a woman at the back of the group of onlookers. Jack turned to see that it was Doll.

'Old Mrs Oldroyd,' she said. 'Been murdered.' She saw then that Jack was standing with Polmear. 'Oh, it's you, duckie. No night for a good lad like you to be out. You'll catch your death.'

'He's a big, strong boy,' said Polmear, giving him a slap on the back that sent him stumbling forward. 'A mountain one day, not a maypole. You say a woman's been murdered?'

Doll looked between the two men, curiosity on her face. She seemed to be weighing whether to ask her young friend who his companion was, and evidently thought better of it. Instead she nodded. 'Set aflame. Sayin' it's Jesuit priests what've done it.' She shook her head. 'Old Mrs Oldroyd. She was a good soul. A poor old woman. Be hell to pay for this. Bloody Jesuits. Haven't they caused enough trouble in't north?'

'Did you know her?' asked Jack. Polmear shook his head. He had turned his attention to Doll, who had in any case dissolved into tears, and was surveying the crowd. 'Should we say to the justices who we are? Find out the truth here?'

'No. No speaking to the men of the city. They have their work and we have ours.'

'What are you looking for?'

'Strangers. Strangeness. Sometimes the men who do their crimes lurk amongst the crowd.'

'Why? Don't they run?'

'I don't know – madmen do mad things. Just the usual looky-loos here. News-seekers. Nothing. The devil among us is too clever for foolish mistakes, by my truth.' He took Jack by the shoulder and steered him away from the crowd, looking around as he did so. 'Another good Protestant killed. Could your new friends have done this?'

'No,' said Jack.

'You sound right sure, for a lad who says he don't yet have their trust.'

'They wouldn't harm an old woman.' He shook his head to emphasise the point. 'This, and the others … this diamond league. It can't all be chance. Something strange is happening, Polmear. I don't reckon it's Protestants or Catholics. I … something strange is going on.'

'I think you're right, laddie.' Polmear looked again at the crowd, and then back at the direction from which they had come. 'We'll have to have that ale some other time.'

'Where are you going?'

'To get word out. Never mind. I'll be seeing you.' Light on his feet again, he disappeared into the thick of the crowd and then into the darkness of the night. Jack stood awhile, looking towards the house. A gasp and then a chorus of cries went up as a covered stretcher was taken out. The news then rippled through that the woman's books had been destroyed and a message from the Jesuits left on the wall. When it became clear that there would be no more from anyone official, the people began to disperse. Jack noticed that they were arguing furiously amongst themselves. He turned his back and began to make his way home.

Something stopped him.

Father Thomas, the eldest of the trio of priests he had befriended, and with whom he had recently shared the names of places known for Catholic sympathies, was standing by the porch of a building. He seemed oblivious to the thinning crowd, and simply stood, whistling. Jack paused, watching him. The priest cast a look to his left and right and then tossed an apple in the air, catching it, the model of nonchalance. Too casual, thought Jack. Thankfully, Thomas did not appear to have seen him. He stowed his apple inside his coat and began strolling, his hands behind his back. At a distance, Jack followed.

The priest was up to something, of that Jack had no doubt. His manner, his gait, were odd. He would take a few steps, look from side to side – causing Jack to bob down behind some goodwives – and then continue on his way. About halfway along the street, he disappeared altogether. Jack frowned and moved to where the man had been only moments before – just beyond an alley which ran between two houses. Nothing but the women, still pressing forwards.

Somewhere down the alley, the snap of a twig.

Jack turned and slipped between the houses. Their heavy thatched roofs shrouded the place in darkness, and he could barely see the ground. Yet Thomas could only have gone this way. He crept his way along the right-hand house, his hand to its wall.

On the other side of the alley, from a servants' doorway cut into the side of the other house, came another sharp crack. He half-turned, expecting to see a dog or a cat, when a black figure loomed out of the darkness and grasped his arms.

Before he could scream, he was being drawn deeper into the space between the houses, was pivoted, and a hand was clamped over his mouth. A voice whispered in his ear – a voice he recognised as belonging to Father Thomas. Something ran through his head about hunters and hunted, and he cursed himself for a fool. 'Thank you for following me, son. A good pair of eyes you have. You've been playing us false, Jack Wylmott. If that's your name. You've much to explain.' Jack

106

whimpered, gnawing on the hand over his mouth. First the Protestant lot stifling him, and now the Catholics. Thomas took it away.

'I do. And I will. Jesus, let us go somewhere safe.'

Within fifteen minutes, he and the three priests were assembled in the cellar of the old Friary, where the other two had apparently been saying Masses all evening for visiting Catholics. Thomas had bundled him in as though he were parading a thief freshly caught in the act and threw him down. The other two had looked up in surprise as the door was locked. Jack remained half-sprawled against one wall, the Jesuits with their backs to the one opposite. Thomas seemed ecstatic. 'I told you, didn't I? I said this lad was playing us false.'

'Peace,' said Adam. 'What do you know?'

'I followed him. Watched him, as he's been watching us. He left his rooms in company with one of the English queen's men, or Cecil's – the one spoken of by our true friends. Some old woman has died out in the town this night. The pair of them followed the crowd, thick as thieves. Old friends, or so it appeared, him and this fellow.'

'Who? How do you know?'

'Polmear. The gypsy-looking fellow. Watches the ports – boats coming to the north and going out. We were warned to be wary of him even in Douai.'

'Is this true?' asked Robin. Jack looked at him and then looked away. Robin seemed younger than ever, not a trace of hair even on his trembling upper lip. Somehow that made losing his trust all the harder.

'They have my wife,' he said. 'The queen's secretary, Walsingham, and … and that man. But I've told them nothing. I swear. It's true that I'm Catholic – what I said was true. Please, fathers … let me confess.'

'Liar!' spat Thomas. 'Traitor!'

'Let him speak,' said Adam. 'Who are you?'

Sighing, Jack told them his story, his head bowed, beginning with his instruction to deliver the countess of Northumberland to her enemies and ending with him being deposited in the north, his wife a hostage for his pursuing and betraying Catholic priests. Throughout, he maintained that he intended no harm, and had been all along trying to think of ways of protecting both them and Amy.

'I believe him,' said Robin.

'Of course you do,' spat Thomas, turning away. 'Though he admits to consorting with our enemies.'

'Yet we are still alive,' said Adam. He moved to stand under a torch. 'You haven't delivered us to this Polmear. Why?'

'I ... In truth I said I have met three men who might be of the old faith. But no more. We were interrupted by the news of this woman's death. They were all saying Jesuits done it. Killed her. Destroyed her books.'

'Heretical books,' Adam said. Robin looked at him, his mouth falling open, but Thomas nodded.

'But ... it can't be true. The Holy Father has not turned you into killers. You didn't do this?' Jack realised he sounded more like he was pleading than questioning.

'Of course we didn't bloody do it,' said Adam. 'We're here to save souls, not burn old women.'

'Then it was the diamond league. I told you of them when I first met you, remember? Polmear – he thinks – I think too – that they're neither Catholic nor Protestant. They're something else. If we can just–'

'Enough about this fantasy,' snapped Thomas. 'Let him and his friend chase after these ghosts. If they are destroying heretics, so be it.'

'Father!' Robin cried.

'Not just them,' said Jack. 'The priests who came here out of Douai before you, the ones ... the ones there were all those dirty tales about. It might be they were killed by this league too. A conspiracy.'

'Then you and your priest-hunter can spend your time sniffing it out,' Thomas said, folding his arms. He dropped one and slapped the palm of his other hand into his forehead. 'They warned us about the wildness of England. At home – at Douai – they told us. But the things that go on here! This whole blasted country is waxing dangerous. Every man, even the faithful ones, are but two pots of ale away from doing whatever mad thing runs in their mind. You, boy, might be the worst of them. It's clear we cannot trust you.' Finality tinged his words.

'Yet,' said Adam, putting a hand on the older priest's arm, 'he might be of use. If we keep him by us.'

'How so?' asked Robin. Jack detected enthusiasm, faint but definitely there. Young Father Robin would be his ally. Adam shrugged.

'A man who is loyal to neither side, who works for both … tell me, Jack, in the grace of God and in all truth, do you bear love for our faith?'

'I do,' said Jack.

'And yet none for Walsingham, or this creature of his?'

'No. No, I am their prisoner, really. They have my wife.'

'Across the sea?'

'Yes, but they've given me no word of her safety. They will be using her too.'

'Well, then, I think we must have faith,' Adam concluded. Robin smiled, but Thomas threw his hands in the air.

'A man who is loyal to neither side might get us all killed. Taken to London and torn apart.'

'Then he will suffer for it,' said Robin, his eyes shining in the torchlight. 'And we go to God as martyrs.'

'Let us pray it doesn't come to that. Thomas, Father Robin and I are agreed. We shall continue to trust this man – to some small degree – rather than cut him from our side.' Thomas said nothing but glared stonily at Jack. 'If we flee from him, we lose any chance of knowledge of what the heretics do.'

'You trust him as you list. On your head be it.'

Robin crossed the room and held out a hand. Jack reached up and took it, allowing the fellow to help him to his feet. 'I promise,' he said, with all the dignity he could muster, 'that I will do all I can to protect you. I will warn you of any danger. As long as I can be sure my wife is safe, you will be too.' He hoped that he could prove the truth of his words, and yet had a nagging doubt that he could not.

5

Amy rolled over on her cot, the double blanket doing little to keep out the chill that crept into the room despite the low fire. It was normal for her mind to work her into a fury when she slept alone – her thoughts were like fire themselves, and she could not extinguish them. For weeks the thought of Jack had kept her up. When she did sleep, it seemed to be only for minutes at a time; some nightmare would intrude, in which he was drowning and she desperately reaching over the side of a boat trying to save him. She would fail. He would sink deep, leaving her staring at her own reflection in the glassy surface.

She would stir from the recurring image not with fear, but with renewed determination. If he was dead, she would know it; she would have felt it happening somewhere inside herself, as she had known the night her ailing mother finally slipped away. There would be some crack in the heavens, a sign of some kind. He might well be on the moon, for all she knew, but he was alive somewhere and trying to get back to her. The thought sustained her like strong meat and drink.

Weeks had passed. Christmas had come and gone. Gradually, Amy had accustomed herself to the life of a dame, which, she swiftly realised, was simply glorified service. She had had no time alone with the rather frightening Queen Catherine, who had made only sporadic visits to the capital to gather money for her son's and daughter-in-law's state entries and deposit more lower servants to aid in making the royal palaces ready for their new mistress. The king and queen were apparently making a slow and stately progress across the country, partly because of heavy rains washing away the roads from the Austrian border, and partly because young Queen Elisabeth was a sickly girl.

Amy's days had thus been a stultifying round of Masses, walks, choosing and arranging furnishing, rubbing her hands on cushions and doorframes to check for poison, and, rather enjoyably, watching as a doddering old physician waved a magnificent spiralled unicorn horn, its tip sharpened to a needlepoint and coated in solid gold, about each chamber to ward off poisonous airs. She was no longer carrying armfuls of laundry, to be sure, but now she was folding and perfuming clean clothes, refreshing ewers, and waving jewelled rings around doorframes. Everything was regimented, beyond anything she had ever known in service – from the order they processed to Mass to who got to sit first, the most senior amongst the ladies down to herself. They had even to bow and curtsy before the closed door to the empty royal bedchamber and innumerable empty chairs of estate. Why so many poor girls dreamed of the life of a court lady she had no idea. Even dressing was a hideous chore – fine for one evening, but a trial when each morning brought several rounds of lacing and pinning. And the silence! Vittoria de Brieux's claims of friendship had been hollow – hollow, Amy supposed, like most of what came out of the mouths of noble ladies. Kat was useless, always off somewhere doing the kind of work Amy used to do herself.

Her investigation into the dowager queen's household had not progressed far, as she had known it could not, despite the royal apartments filling up with those who wished to claim sleeping places ahead of the royal arrival. Yet there was one thing that did bother her. Each night, during the course of her tossing and turning, she had become aware of nocturnal comings and goings from the antechamber off the queen-mother's bedroom in the unfinished Tuileries Palace.

She had no idea of the time beyond that it was still some hours until dawn. She lay with her eyes half-closed, and, sure enough, the sound of bedclothes moving and footsteps skipping lightly from the room came to her. There followed the soft opening and closing of a door. Her eyes shot open and she carefully turned on to her side. The fire gave off very little light, making only a semicircle around itself. Heavy velvet curtains cut out the moonlight. In the room with her slept her two earliest, unfriendly companions – the wizened Bianca Gondi, whose stertorous breathing still rumbled, and the younger Vittoria de Brieux, of the doll-like face paint. In addition, their servants, Kat included, slept on scattered rugs in various corners. This room had been their exclusive domain as the first ladies left by Catherine to sweeten the building. It was one of them who was slipping out at night.

Amy sprang up, dragging her feet silently towards where she knew the door was, careful not to step on anyone or anything that might make a noise. She slipped open the door and crept into the next chamber, where more snoring greeted her. The whole palace, or what there was of it, was built in a series of interconnecting rooms, with a service corridor running parallel. She guessed that the departing woman would not have opted to stroll the darkened chambers, and so she felt along the wall for the door to the corridor, stepping out into light and blinking away the shock of it.

Once her eyes had accustomed themselves, she set off, not sure exactly where she was going. There was something strange about palaces at night – something unnerving. Small houses and even large manors all slept when the sun went down, but palaces seemed to hum with life at night, as guards patrolled, servants made ready to get to market before dawn, and cooks rose early. There were few guards about with the royal family officially still in residence outside the city, but even so the place was eerily quiet. Amy wandered the corridor, which was still clean and sterile thanks to its relative newness, and came to a set of stairs. She stood at the top, looking down, debating whether to continue what was probably a fruitless mission. At length she descended. A doorway led outside. She opened it, peering out into the mizzling rain. Narrowing her eyes, she looked down at the gravel. There was one set of disturbances, something like footprints, to trouble the gardeners in the morning. Whether it led to or from the building, she could not say, and she could gain nothing by stumbling about the gardens, where only occasional beacons cast festive light.

Amy sighed, closed the door, and began trudging back upstairs. She could simply stay awake until the missing woman returned, but she would be none the wiser as to why she kept disappearing at night. As she made her way back along the service corridor, though, a new sound came to her and she froze. At first, it seemed like someone was being attacked, and she made to cry out. Before she could, however, she balled a fist and put it in her mouth.

Though it had been a while – months, in fact, since she had seen Jack – she knew the sound.

Although she stifled her laughter, she could not stifle the giggling voice in her head. You might scarcely remember what it feels like, it said, but you certainly recall what it sounds like.

She hurried past the door of the closet from which the sounds of the copulating couple emanated and opened the door back to the royal apartments. As she was about to step inside, she heard the closet door open behind her and she ducked in, popping her head out just enough to see a man in black leave, buttoning up his breeches as he did. Her brow furrowed. There were few men in the makeshift household: Catherine's knights and gentlemen of honour, her maîtres d'hôtel, her cupbearers, esquires, and carvers, were all with her. Yet she knew him. The door clicked again. She started. The woman, whoever she was, would be coming her way. Amy jerked inside and hurried back to the ladies' bedchamber. She was back under her covers, both pulled up to her neck, when the adventurous woman came back. Still she could not see who it had been. Instead she let the glimpse of the man return to her mind. Over and over, she scanned her memory, visualising his profile as she had seen it before he turned his back to her and left.

She had it.

He was one of the men whom the duke of Guise had commanded to help her get to Queen Catherine the day she had arrived. Satisfaction hers, she drifted into a fitful sleep, in which opening and closing doors might have been real or imagined.

The steady pulsing of her heartbeat in her ear woke her. Amy could almost feel the dark smudges sagging under her eyes. The light, which was unforgiving in the white-, cream-, and gold-painted room, did nothing to mask them. She sighed, wrinkling her nose. Whether in the newest French palace's bedchamber or a squalid hovel, dawn rode in on a pungent tide of urine and sweat. The only difference was that here the morning's piss-bucket reek mingled with herbs and perfumes. Something irritated her and blurred her vision and she shook her head to clear away loose strands of hair. No good. It took a few seconds for her to realise that it was the grit of sleep stuck to her eyelash, and she rubbed it away.

It was fitting, she supposed, that she had joined Catherine's band of women too old to serve the new queen. The others were already up, Gondi preparing for Mass by worrying beads in corner, her lips moving silently over toothless gums, and Brieux having her face repainted whilst holding a small mirror. She caught Amy looking in the reflection and deigned to speak. 'You sleep late, my lady. You had a restless night?'

'I slept poorly.' The words came out on a gust of sour morning breath and she put a hand over her mouth. She watched, entranced, as the woman's maid pasted the decoction onto Brieux's skin. It formed a thick sheen, like the glaze one would see on a pie crust. The wrinkles and pock marks disappeared under it. The goal was to make time melt away, but instead it made her look artificial, like the frightening images painted in French chapels.

'Forgive me, but you might do well to put something on your face. Do you not have such things in England?'

'We do, my lady,' said Amy, puffing out her chest. Amongst the small number of bodices, sleeves, and kirtles that the countess had sent her off with had been a small box of vials – a gift from someone that Lady Northumberland had claimed to find insulting.

'Well, use them. I was beginning to think the only thing your kinswoman provided were those … uh … charming dresses. Her Majesty never did tell us – what are you to the countess exactly? Her needlewoman?' She delivered this with as much of a smirk as she could manage under her makeup, and then returned her eyes to the mirror. She nodded sharply. Amy bit her tongue as Brieux's maid finished painting her dark skin white and began affixing the plethora of jewels she habitually wore. From Kat's gossip with the other servants, she had divined that Vittoria de Brieux was a wealthy widow, who had bought her way into Catherine's household, and thereafter done everything she could to seduce the young king, apparently without success. As her mother would have put it, the lady was a jade on the make, and a fading one at that.

Instinctively, Amy put her hands over the old nightdress she had been given – a plain thing, but of good quality. Then anger rose. She would not let a painted old French whore mock her – a woman pushing forty with thin hair and a face plastered in milk, eggs, and piss. She would not allow herself to be a figure of laughter, she who has always sworn and cursed at the opinions of others.

'Kat,' she whispered, crossing the room and taking the girl by the arm. She spoke rapidly, low and in English. 'You remember the men who looked after us when we got here? Someone in this room is swiving one of them.' Kat's mouth fell open in scandalised delight. 'Listen to the servants' gossip. I know how they do. If you hear anything, tell me.' A curt nod, almost military style. Amy switched back to French. 'I'll dress now.' She selected the gown which required the least amount of lacing and the fewest pins, pining for Kat's own plain smock. Having endured the pain of being dressed, she breezily said, 'bring out the little box. I'll use the stuff in it today.' She took the stool Brieux had been using when the older woman was helped up and looked on with trepidation as Kat began pulling out tiny bottle and silver boxes.

'You may use my glass, if you wish,' said the older woman with amusement. She held out the jewel-encrusted hand mirror. Amy accepted it without thanks as Brieux sashayed away. A desire came over her to crack the woman on the back of the head with it, and to the devil with bad luck.

'I don't know what these are,' said Kat in her broken French, holding up a bottle and looking at it as though it were a strange little glass creature.

'Me neither,' Amy said out the side of her mouth. 'Just do what the other girl did. Rub it all on.'

The first thing opened was a circular jar full of what appeared to be red jelly. She recoiled from the smell, bitter as almonds, which leeched out into the room. 'Your lips, madam?' Amy shrugged.

'Do it.' She tilted back her head and pouted. Out of the corner of her eye, she could see Brieux watching her, giggles fighting their way out of her unmoving face as her girl brushed down the front of her dress. Bitch, Amy thought. Kat stuck her fingers into the red stuff and began smearing it. Amy held up the mirror, watching her lips redden. It looked rather good, actually – like life was being brought into a dead and colourless face. When it began to feel heavy, she mumbled, 'that'll do,' trying to not to part her lips too much. 'It's heavy. It's …. Kat, stop!' Her mouth fell open. The paste, which had felt cool at first, had started tingling. The tingling had begun to burn. Invisible needles were stabbing at her. The mirror fell from her hand, landing on the rug with a dull thud. Kat did nothing, and Amy turned to her.

'My fingers,' the girl screamed, not bothering with French. 'Mistress – my lady – it burns!' Sure enough, Kat was staring down at an index and middle finger which were turning livid. Amy reached for a cloth on the table, still dirty from Brieux's toilette, and put it to her lips. As soon as it touched them, the burning intensified. She screamed, leaping from the stool and letting it fall. Brieux and her maid had ceased what they were doing, the former holding a hand over her face, her mouth a silent scream. 'Poison,' screeched Gondi, her beads falling to the floor. She crossed herself, and began chanting, over and over, 'guards! Poison! Guards! Poison!'

Amy fell to the ground, tangling herself in her gown, in blankets, coiling and uncoiling her body in an effort to get the sudden, searing pain out of lips which had turned to fire.

***

Amy woke in a small closet room, whence she had been carried immediately the poison was discovered. Physicians had been sent for, and had smeared her face with oil, milk, garlic, and honey – an admixture they called theriac. They had had her kiss healing rings. Nothing lessened the burning, and her gratitude at being helped had swiftly soured into anger as the two men began arguing over her about the merits and demerits of fetching the unicorn horn. At this, her pathetic pleas for help had lessened. Instead, she realised two things: that the physicians thought her much more important than she really was, and that they would prove useless. The important thing was that she had not died and had in fact managed to rub off most of the foul red jelly without it getting into her mouth. On realising this, she had felt safe to vent her frustration at the men, telling them to leave her alone, to go and gaze at piss, for that was all they were good for. Abashed, they had left her to rest in the tiny, dark, airless cubby.

On waking, she put a hand to her lips and pulled it away. The skin was raised and tender, swollen but not yet scabbed or flaking – and thankfully they were only sore when she touched them. She cried out for water and, receiving no answer, felt around the floor next to her. Sure enough, there was a tray with a jug and some bread on it. She jerked away from it, suddenly afraid. Someone had poisoned her. They might do so again. Her stomach growled in sullen resignation.

She had no idea how long she had been lying in her new bedchamber – surely it had been a day and a night. As she swung her legs over the low cot, intent on finding out where she was, the door opened and light framed a solid figure in the doorway. Amy hopped down and fell to her knees. It was Queen Catherine, the two physicians at her back. The old woman said nothing, but stared down at her, a pomander held up to her face. 'Your Majesty, please. I am hungry … afraid to eat … I …'

'Becalm yourself,' hissed the queen-mother. 'You have cheated death.'

'But .. I …'

'The water is honeyed. The bread good. I had it prepared myself. Tested with most care. These gentlemen have eaten of it. Your room guarded since it was brought.' Her voice carried no sympathy.

'Someone tried to kill me.'

Silence greeted this. Amy had noticed that the queen-mother had a curious habit of pausing before responding, so that one could never tell if she were slightly hard of hearing or just measuring her words. 'Yes,' breathed Catherine eventually. 'A foul act. But rather here than where my son and daughter are.' Amy said nothing but looked up at the face shrouded in shadow. 'This potion – could it not have come from your countess

117

already with some taint to it? You said there was an attempt on your mistress's life in Bruges.'

'No, your Majesty. I saw that coffer given to the countess. It was locked tight. She only opened it to look before she gave it to me. To take with me.' She could remember the countess unsealing and looking through the contents, offence growing at the audacity of one of her European friends to suggest that she needed artificial beauty aids.

Catherine sighed. 'You told me there was a plotter in my household. I did not believe you. For that … I am sorry.' The apology seemed to come with difficulty. 'Yet you have done good work. You have had this creature reveal its presence. Tell me, who might have touched your coffer?' Amy thought, lifting a hand to her throat. The glands felt swollen and tender.

'Anyone. It was in the bedchamber. Anyone.' A thought occurred. 'Has your Majesty found anyone come newly to your household? In the last …' she counted, 'six months or a year?'

'We have indeed made searches. You, girl, are the only one who has come into my household in that time. And Madame Gondi. But she is of an old Italian family. Cousin to my dearest friend, Marie-Catherine.' Something like emotion twinkled. Briefly. 'Even the servants of my ladies are of long standing.'

'But the Italians are –' began Amy, before biting down hard. She had almost said that Italians were notorious poisoners. 'But the diamond plotters – the countess said they had a woman about the French queen in August last,' she said instead.

'Ah yes, the diamond plot. From your countess's lips. And again I remind you that you said there was an attempt to poison the lady in Bruges.' Amy nodded once, hard. 'And so there is poison there, and now there is poison here. It seems to me that this plot was begun with your countess and continues with her woman.' Amy hung her head, unsure what to say. 'It seems to me that this entire plot might have been invented by your mistress. To win the love of the great people of Europe she might invent and then save us from a plot of her own imagining.'

'It's not true,' said Amy, looking directly to where she knew Catherine's eyes were. 'I tell you, your Majesty, there is something evil here. Here, and in Bruges, and in England, too.'

'In England? Then I shall speak with our new ambassador from that realm. Mr Walsingham.' Amy's mouth flopped open and her hand flew to it.

'Sore,' she offered lamely.

'It will be, for some days. The new queen is a delicate child. Neither my son's entry into Paris nor hers can take place until she is well rested, and the best dates predicated. These gentlemen are needed at her side. As am I. You do not have long to find proof of your plot, girl. If you cannot, then our arrangement will be at an end. You will leave this place. I do not wish you near the queen, a child of your … quality.'

'Wait! Uh, please, your Majesty.'

Catherine, who had half turned away, inclined her head. 'What?'

'Before I was attacked – the night before – I found a woman of the bedchamber not in her place.'

'Which woman?'

'It was dark, I couldn't see.' Catherine tutted, making to leave again. 'But I followed! I found that she had went to … to make love with a man.' Again, the dowager tutted. 'A man I knew to belong to the duke of Guise.' At this, Catherine paused. She said something rapidly to the two physicians, who reluctantly moved away.

'You are sure of this?'

Amy thought, but could not be sure, that there was little surprise in Catherine's voice. If anything, perhaps there was a purr of triumph. 'I am. The man helped me when I first came here. The duke ordered him.'

'The duke … the duke is a friend to our family. This is a time of peace.' She seemed to consider. 'Yet he is a young man of great passions. He would have us at war again with the heretics. He would have blood on the streets of Paris if he could. That is not my way. Nor the king's.'

'But someone in your household is having traffic with him. A lady or one of her people.'

'Hmph. I will discover what this is about. It is none of your concern.'

'But if it is connected to this diamond league plot –'

'Then you shall be absolved, girl. And so you had better recover your wits and your health and set to work. It is clear that someone wishes you not to do so – unless you were behind your own poisoning. As I said, you have only until the king and queen take up residence in this city. The royal entries are arranged. They will take place at a date to be divined in March. I suggest that you rouse yourself. Go to, girl. And do not wear these cosmetics. They thin the skin and sour the mind. Oh. Your girl, your maid. She is unhurt. She will be grateful for your concern.'

Amy blushed. She had forgotten about Kat. She really was becoming just like them.

Catherine stomped from the room, closing the door behind her, leaving Amy in the dark. She got up from her knees and sat down on the bed, staring into nothingness. She had no idea what to do. What she needed was an ally, and it was clear that the old queen neither liked nor trusted her, despite what had happened. If anything, the attempt on her life had only brought more distrust. Yet something the old woman had said shone with hope. The new ambassador, Mr Walsingham, was back in the city. She disliked the man intensely, but he was English, he understood plots, and he knew her. More than that, he probably knew where Jack was. It might even be that he would relieve her of all her cares, get her safely out of Paris, and let her forget all talk of diamond plots, royal entries, and exiled countesses. That was unlikely, the rational part of her mind said – he would want a great deal in return, he owed her nothing, and she and Jack were almost certainly still under a cloud. Still, the image of his serious, lined face loomed large in her mind, offering sense and order in a world of glittering, jewelled madness.

6

Jack allowed Robin to embrace him. The boy had tears in his eyes and his travelling cloak was tightly knotted about his shoulders. He might have been off to his first day at university. 'Father Thomas said not to tell you where I'm going,' he said, blinking away tears. 'But if not for you I wouldn't know to go there. Newcastle,' he winked.

'You'll be safe in Newcastle. Good Catholic men there. They'll be glad to protect you.' Robin beamed, and then strode off in the weak, wintry sunshine. Of the three Jesuits, only Adam remained in York. Thomas had gone the previous day, refusing to say goodbye to Jack or to tell him in which county he had received assurances of protection. He preferred it that way. It meant that even if Polmear turned on him, sent him somewhere to be starved and tortured, he could not betray his conscience and reveal knowledge of where the men of his religion were going. He had not the heart to say that to Robin.

As the red-haired priest disappeared from view, he felt a tug at his elbow. It was Adam, smiling. 'Do you go soon too?'

'Perhaps. In time. Though I will be sad to leave the true faithful in this city without comfort.'

'More will come, though, won't they?'

'Oh yes, with God's grace. No matter what becomes of us, the seminary will always have men willing to risk their lives and come here.'

'What brought you to the church?' asked Jack. He realised that he had not pried into the lives of the three Jesuits at all. Knowledge, again, was something to be avoided – but he was interested. 'Are you from England? You sound it.'

'Yes, I was raised in an English town. It's still Catholic in its devotions.'

'Most are. Outside the rich ones in the south.' Adam nodded.

'Yet even the northern ones will turn their heads against us if these … these desecrations continue. Fewer folk each day come to the Friary to hear Mass.'

A chill ran through Jack. It was true. In the taverns and alehouses, even the men he had once heard speak openly about their hatred of southern Protestants were now decrying the savage acts of foreign Jesuits. The murder of the old woman had turned them fickle. Talk was now of rotten foreign men coming over with rotten instructions from rotten foreign masters, murdering decent English folk. The violence seemed to have sparked something in northern hearts – hatred of foreigners and their black acts was replacing hatred of southerners and their made-up religion. It reminded him of the kind of angry, hateful talk that he had heard daily in Paris. Blood for blood. A religious war to end them all. 'Will you be coming to Mass tonight, my friend?' asked Adam.

'Tomorrow morning, if that's good?' Jack felt a blush creep into his cheek. Earlier, Doll had passed him a hastily scribbled note dropped by an unknown messenger indicating Polmear's return that evening. How he would explain the departure of two of his quarry for destinations unknown he had not yet figured out.

'Of course. God bless you.' Adam stalked off, his hands clasped behind his back. Silently, Jack prayed that he would go too – find some rich benefactor who would hide him away in his household. Otherwise, there might be no choice but to deliver him to Polmear. Jack shivered again.

Who, he thought, do you work for, Jack Cole?

His life seemed to have taken a dark turn since he had lost Amy. It seemed to have become a confusing maze, in which different voices were calling out to him from different directions.

He waited for a horse and its rider to pass and then crossed the street, heading in the direction of his room. The street was not crowded, but there were people enough to cause him to step around sewage, skirts, and hand carts. Few people, he noticed, were speaking with one another. Since coming into York, he had found the town suspicious, its people quiet; but it had lately fallen under an even more unpleasant cloud. People seemed not just afraid of the queen's informers but of one another. Neighbours glared at one another sullenly. Goodwives crossed the street to avoid each other. It was like living in one of the Italian romances Amy liked to read, albeit it was scented with peat and ice rather than citrus and sun. Jack kept his head down as he walked, and it was still down when a burly man bumped his shoulder. 'Sorry,' he mumbled. The man grumbled an oath under his breath and Jack turned to give him an angry look. As he did, he caught sight of someone ducking into an alley.

He watched for a few seconds to see if the person emerged – perhaps, he thought, it was simply someone pissing. After a few moments, he began moving again, and this time he himself slipped behind a carter's stall. 'Away wi' ye,' hissed the carter. 'Unless yer buyin'.' Jack shook his head and stepped out. Sure enough, the fellow in black, a cheap cap pulled low, was steadily walking towards him. Panic gripped. He looked around to see where he was. On the street near the Mercers' Hall. If he did not want his pursuer knowing where he slept – and still slept alone – then he would have to shake him off. He began crossing back and forth across the street, hopping the sewer, each time moving a little farther in the direction of the River Ouse. The man, however, never seemed to slacken his pace or waver in his direction. With a start, Jack realised that he was not being followed. He was being herded. He turned and began jogging, towards and over the bridge. Buildings began passing in a blur as his chest tightened, strain squeezing his heart. The grey started to thin, replaced by open greenery as he hung a hard right. He knew that over the bridge and along the river there lay a ruined Dominican Friary, tangled now in woodland. Without looking back, he headed in that direction. When he reached it, he threw himself amongst the trees and fallen stones, only peeping his head out and over a tangle of brush to see if his pursuer was still abroad. His heart sank. The man had kept pace with him. Worse, he was coming towards him, twisting what looked like a dagger in his fist.

Jack turned and looked deeper into the little wood. He began crawling, thankful that the ground was wet, when he heard a low, tuneless whistle.

He froze.

A voice growled, 'there is nowhere for you to run, Jack Cole.

You have come where I've bid you.'

His head low, Jack continued to crawl, pressing himself into the spongy ground. Suddenly, it opened up before him, and the smell of wet, turned earth rose to greet him. A rectangle of ground had been dug. An open grave, freshly prepared. Abandoning silence, he sprung up and away from it as the dark figure barrelled towards him. Jack kicked backwards, catching his attacker in the forearms, which seemed to startle him. His cap flew into the air and Jack's breath caught in his throat on seeing his face.

But rage had overtaken fear. He wanted to punch and stab at the man who was attacking him. He fought the desire. Escape – find people, his mind cried. Escape! As the assassin launched himself to his feet, wasting time scrabbling for his cap, Jack began running, bouncing and flying over the undergrowth. He leapt over the wall which bordered the old Friary and into the half-empty street. Away from the centre of town, there were always fewer people. Crashing and cursing in the woods behind him sent him moving, back in the direction of the bridge. He did not stop to see if he was still being followed.

Over the bridge, there were plenty more people, and Jack did stop, putting a hand against a plaster-fronted house and straining to catch his breath. He looked up.

The man in black was moving towards him, not quite running but moving quickly enough.

Jack hissed to himself. Then, with regret, he reached down to his belt and yanked free the purse of coins he did not trust to the lodging house. Fingering open the knot, he loosened the string and cried out, 'largesse! Largesse!' Heads turned in confusion as he launched the contents into the air, and a shower of silvery coins rained down on them. A mad scramble ensued, men and women throwing themselves into the street, stretching out greedy hands. Jack was nudged, jostled, and pushed in the scramble. So too was the man who had followed him. The jumble of people came between them. Before he slipped away, Jack locked eyes with the furious creature which loomed over the bent, screeching bodies. It was a face he recognised, but not entirely – he could not place it. He took a circuitous route back home, entreating strangers to crowd the direction from which he'd come, where a madman had lined the streets with gold.

'Duck!' Doll cried when he burst into the taproom. 'What's happened to you?' She pushed through a crowd of drinkers and barrelled towards him. 'You've been through a hedge backwards.' Her broad hands reached out to him and he pushed them away. He could not get words out, and instead gave her what he knew to be a ghastly smile. She recoiled from it and he threw himself through the door to the backroom.

Polmear was waiting for him, picking dirt from his nails with a pin. He looked up with his usual expression of sardonic amusement. On seeing him, his face lost its smile. 'What happened?'

'Attacked,' Jack wheezed. 'Fucking attacked.' He let the anger rage, kicking the blankets, kicking the wall. Spidery cracks traced their way out from where his boot made contact. 'Bastard chased me into the woods. Grave already dug. Ready for me.'

'How did you escape?' Polmear took him by the shoulders. Jack's eruption of anger vanished.

'Ran. I threw money. All of it. People got in the way. Blocked him.'

Polmear grinned, and the grin became laughter. In spite of himself, Jack began laughing too, and the pair dissolved in it for some time. Only after they had calmed down did the older man say, 'well, you'll be demanding more in your expenses from Mr Walsingham, eh? Tight-fisted old shit, is the queen's man, God love him. Looks like I'll be buying the ale. Don't think of arguing, laddie – you'll take a cup or three with me this night.'

'I recognised him,' said Jack, when his nervous laughter had subsided. 'I don't know how, but there was something familiar in his face.'

'Describe him.'

'I dunno,' Jack shrugged. 'Young. Dark. Thin. Beardless.'

'Sounds like me,' smiled Polmear. He had been shaved since he had last visited, and he ran the back of his hand over his neck. 'The young part especially.'

'Younger than you. More like my age. Maybe a bit younger

125

even. Eighteen?'

'And you've seen him before?'

'No. I don't think so. I can't place him … but he looks like someone I've seen before.' His mind worked. It was useless. Recognition danced on the periphery of his mind like a coy mistress, refusing to come closer. The man might have been stalking him for some time. He might be a fruit-seller, or a baker's boy he had seen but not really looked at. 'He saw me looking. He knew.'

'Aye, well, if he's been sent to kill you and failed in it – and you've seen his face … an assassin whose face is known is worse than dangerous. He's useless.' Jack lapsed into silence for a while. 'You say a grave was ready dug?'

'Yes. I saw it. Out in the old Dominican Friary.'

'Well, it was certainly a bit of work planned, then. No lad you know from the town who spied your purse and decided to turn cut-throat. No crime of chance. No, I'd say that it was definitely our local madman at play.'

'What do you know of the French wars? The religious wars?'

'What, are you turning Sir Schoolmaster? "The second Punic War was fought between Carthage and the Republic between …"' He ceased the whining impression. 'You're serious?' Jack nodded. 'I know that the papists and the Protestants have drunk of each other's blood for years. Damn near brought down the country, brought both churches into the people's hatred. Found a kind of peace now, though, so Mr Walsingham says. Fragile kind of peace.'

'Would anyone like the wars to start again? Spread, even, out of France?'

'I can't …' Polmear scratched the side of his nose. 'There'll always be jackasses want to bring wars on.'

'Why?'

'Who can say? For profit. Glory. Revenge. Anger. Madness. War is just martyrdom for whole countries. There are as many reasons for wanting it as there are wars. You think that's what's been happening here? Someone's trying to bring the French religious wars here? Neighbour against neighbour, that kind of thing?'

'Is it possible?'

'It's possible – of course it's possible.'

'It would explain why different folk have been killed. Catholics, Protestants … to raise a great tumult. Have each side blaming the other. You know when men argue they reach for their weapons. And you've seen it out there – people all in anger and fear of each other.'

'I'll have to take it to someone.' Jack thought Polmear's voice sounded a little reluctant, and embarrassment flooded him. 'Perhaps. Best not to lay out plots and fancies before we know the truth of them. And with Mr Walsingham abroad–'

'Where is he? Is he in Bruges? Has he word of my wife?'

'Peace. No, he's not.' Reluctance paused him. 'Paris. He's in Paris. I'll write and ask him. I promise. Soon.'

Jack bit his knuckle. That, he supposed, would have to be good enough. 'There's something else, though. Something that's … uh … disturbed my mind.'

'Can it wait till we're at table?'

'No. I need you do so something for me. It might be nothing. Might be wrong. But I don't think so.'

'My God, boy, you do like to be mysterious.'

Jack said nothing. If he was right, he would shortly have answers to at least some of what had been going on. If he was wrong, he would be sending an innocent man south to have his guts torn from him at Tyburn.

***

Acre, his arms heavily bandaged, stood with his head bowed. Cold anger simmered. 'How can it be that you failed us?'

'He is one of Walsingham's men, you said. They are … they must be trained to avoid detection. He's no foolish young priest, no old man or old woman.'

'Yes, yes. And no poor little dog nor cat either, asking to be buried alive. He cannot be allowed to live long. Not if he knows your face. He must be made to disappear.' Acre looked up, aggrieved. His role throughout had been to dispatch those he had been called upon to dispatch. It had become a source of pride. His willingness to take lives had been his strength. The stupid brat had robbed him of it – made him weak.

'I promise you, brother – he will. You know his lodging – I will risk taking him from there.'

'No. I will be rid of him.'

'But –'

'But nothing. You know his movements. He will go to that damned Friary in the morning to hear Mass. He lives by routine. I shall get him at that place, make an end of him there. After it is done, then I will call on you to get rid of his body. Can you do that, or will you allow his corpse to run from you?'

Acre kept his mouth closed. He gripped at his forearm, letting the blood ooze under the bandages. The pain was a tonic. 'I will.'

'Good. He knows and says too much. The man is a blundering fool with a headful of knowledge. A danger admixture, is it not? A conscience too, more dangerous than that. Ach, but I am not sore angry at you. These things happen. He is nothing. He dances with both the Jesuits and the heretics. Neither side will miss him.'

'I … I do not like that you should have to bloody your hands. This is my work. Always has been.'

'It is all our work. I … we … never intended that your days as our dagger should last forever. We share our labour. And God knows, there will be daggers enough drawn soon. I mean to say, you cannot go to France and get the wife, can you?'

'Is there news from there?'

'None. But let us hope that his woman is more accepting of death.' He shrugged, his face in shadow. 'It might be that she is dispatched from this earth already.' With a hand under the chin, he raised Acre from his kneeling position. 'Do not let it trouble you, brother. Remember why we chose our name. Diamonds are steadfast.' He gave him a long, indulgent look. 'There,' he said, brushing Acre's belt. 'Is that the blade you took from the old heretic witch?'

'It is.'

'May I?'

Acre slipped the dagger out and handed it over. The other man held it up close to his face. 'You stabbed her? I thought your burned her?'

'I did not stab her.'

'But there is …' His voice trailed off, as his eyes fell upon the minute flakes of blood that still stood around the hilt. Acre looked at the ground. 'I see. I will put this to use, do not fear. And do not punish yourself. It is a sinful thing, self-flagellation – one of the fripperies our faith should do away with. Your grave will be put to good use on the morrow. Go now. I will come to you when it is done. We will then both have shed blood in the name of cleansing the true faith.'

As Acre left to seek his own nameless lodgings, he let his hatred of the boy who had escaped take charge. He would put him in his grave, to be sure, but not before he tore his body limb from limb, taking the head off and making it watch. Shedding blood for the true faith was a fable, but he was happy to let the rest believe it. For him, their plot had always been about humiliation and revenge. Since the day he had discovered the truth of his birth from his ugly, greedy mother, and destroyed both her and his father, he had been intent upon lancing the corruption that had brought him to them. He could remember the day clearly, the salon bathed in sunlight. He had only been a child, and already his mother and father despaired of him. Wanted rid of him. Told him he was sick and corrupt. And then they told him why, and in the night he had watched them burn.

7

Amy looked up at the house in Saint-Marceau, south of the old city walls on the left bank. It was, though, nothing to look at. The district was crowded, the houses shabby and overhanging the street, and the tannery smell of industry seeped out from innumerable workshops. It could not have been more different from the grand mansion from which Sir Henry Norris had conducted his ambassadorial duties, and in which he had lived like a prince, supposedly projecting the might and glory of England's queen. If the house Mr Walsingham had chosen was any indication, England was a small, ugly nation and its queen a toothless labourer. Yet, whatever the face of it, inside lived the new ambassador, and he might have news of Jack. In fact, on the walk to the district, she had convinced herself that he would. She took a breath, went up to the peeling wooden door, and rapped.

A maid answered, looked her up and down, curtsied, and then called into hall, 'A lady come to call on you, sir.' She spoke in English. Before Amy could object, she was ushered into a small sitting room where Walsingham was prodding a fire, absently reading a paper held in his other hand. He turned to look at her and his face registered no recognition.

'Mr Walsingham,' he said. 'It's me, sir. Amy Cole. What news of my husband?' He paled and his eyebrows lifted.

'You,' he said. 'But you … why are you dressed … who the devil gave you permission to come here? You are to …' He seemed to recall where he was. 'I will not speak in my parlour. Follow me.' She did, almost tripping over a small wooden horse. 'Mind yourself, girl. That … that is a gift … my daughter, not yet come to Paris.' He cleared his throat and then mumbled, 'she will play with toys, fond things. Come. My office.' He coughed again and went up the stairs. Amy wondered if his abruptness was surprise, awkwardness around women, dislike, or some combination of all three.

'I cannot seem to be rid of you Coles,' he said. He made to

close the door, seemed to think better of it, and eventually shut it. 'By my truth, you have a pert manner about you.'

'Thank you, sir.'

'It was not a … do not bandy wits with me, girl. I counsel you to weigh your words with care.' And then, more gently, 'sit.' She did. He took a seat opposite her, behind a mirror-like polished desk, the edge of which he gripped with both hands, as though he were at sea and it likely to roll away. It was a utilitarian room. On the desk, carefully placed, were a stack of papers, held in place with an onyx paperweight. The only sour note was struck by a jumble of brightly coloured materials – gloves and doublets, by the look of them – stuffed in a corner like a shameful secret. 'Gifts,' said Walsingham with distaste, following her gaze. 'Fripperies of welcome from the peacocks of this city. The stuff of vanity.'

Amy wondered if the introduction of Walsingham's wife and child would make a difference to the house. Even if it did, she suspected this room would always be dry and cold. It was the brain, not the heart. 'You are in Bruges. You are supposed to be. I have heard no word of the countess of Northumberland leaving that place.'

'My lady commanded me to Paris, sir. I tried to tell Sir Henry Norris. He was gone.'

'Gone, yes. He's gone home. And I forced to this dreadful city again. Why did the wench order you here? And in such array?' He gestured at Amy's fine, rose-coloured dress.

'Happen she wanted rid of me. She said as much.'

'A fine pair of eyes you are to me if she distrusts you,' said Walsingham. 'Had she some reason for sending you hither?'

'To give her regards to the dowager queen. The French royals. She thought that someone involved in a plot was about the old queen. Thought her Majesty might welcome the news of it. But all the women here talk about is trifles, sir – the supposed bastards of dead noblemen and who'll be picked to hold a napkin before the new queen's face when she spits.'

'What happened to your mouth?' Amy sucked in her cheeks, and Walsingham's colour again faded. 'I mean … forgive me, my lad- Mrs Cole … I … your lips.'

131

Amy knew that her lips had grown scabby and duck-like as the effects of the poison faded. Her hand rose to cover them. 'I was poisoned, sir.'

'What? By whom?'

'By one in Queen Catherine's house. They poisoned the face washes my lady gave me. It's one of the plotters, sir, I'm sure of it. There is a league of men calling themselves the diamonds, that's what the countess heard. They seemed to be Protestants, courting the Scots.'

'This name again, this diamond league.'

'You've heard of it? It's real?'

'Only from your husband.'

'Jack?! You've seen him – where is he? Is he here?'

'No – he is not. Cease your prating. First, tell me what you have discovered, girl.' In response, Amy let her swollen lips protrude in a ghastly pout. She thought, but did not say, that Walsingham's little girl was not the only one in the family who liked to play with her toys. When she did speak, the pain had gone, leaving a strange numbness that made her voice sound odd to her.

'Nothing. Until you tell me what has become of my husband. I said I would tell you of the Lady Northumberland's doings in Bruges, and I did – I wrote you of the man Prestall.'

'Prestall is a known troublemaker – a fool and a gambler, out only for money. If the lady is trusting such men as he, Queen Elizabeth can sleep soundly at night.'

'Well … that's as may be – but I sent you information and I hoped for some in return. You know, don't you? You know who took Jack and where he is.'

'Moderate your tongue, girl. It is ever women's tongues that breed their cares. And their sorrows.' His eyes roved over her gown. 'And their vanities.'

'Please, sir.' She licked her lips. 'I'm not a proud woman. I'm begging you. Please tell me.'

Walsingham rolled his eyes and released the desk, sitting back. Amy felt her heart begin to skip erratically, fear and hope buffeting it. 'You are a remarkably single-minded creature. Your husband is well, I assure you.' She exhaled and closed her eyes. 'He is kept well in the north of England. He does his country good service in return for your safety. I confess, I had thought that ignoring you and your silence from Bruges was fair recompense for his service. I did not know you would turn up on my doorstep. In truth, I dislike the using of women in grave and weighty matters.' Acid fizzled in his tone. 'Your husband, I recall, observes with right humility the humble station to which he was born. He does not beautify himself in false feathers.'

'You promise he is well? Unhurt, despite what we did? It was me who made him do it,' she lied. 'I was to blame.'

'Enough. You have my word that he has come to no harm. I daresay he is at unaccustomed peace without such a wife.' Amy started to rise. 'Forgive me, girl. That was rude of me. Beneath me. These past weeks have been a trial. Coming here, my own wife and daughter apart from me.' She reclaimed her seat, fixing her dress over her lap.

'I came to you for aid, sir, beyond all else.' He stared blankly, but she thought she caught a flicker of interest. 'Do you recall I begged your aid once before?'

'I do. And I did not listen to you. That was an error.'

'And me and my husband, we saved the queen's life. Two queens.'

'You were given recompense. Forgiven your part in the affair, sent into exile. And have since repaid us with this business of the Northumberland woman.' Then he added, a little too emphatically, 'as we knew you would. That is why you are both quite well. Now pray come to your point, girl. I have to make this place habitable for my family. Lay out what you know and let us see if we can make sense of it.'

'First thing,' said Amy, leaning forward. 'The countess heard that some men calling themselves part of the diamond league were pressing the Scotch Protestants. Saying they had fellows in the north of England, France, and across the seas.'

'Yet no such thing has been proven.'

'Please, sir. Now, if we suppose these men exist, then they are hot Protestants. They hate the Catholics and want to work against them. That's why they tried to kill me. And they tried to kill the countess, sir – a man was poisoned by accident when he was tricked into delivering it to her house. I didn't get the chance to tell you. So we have a league of hot Protestants trying murder.'

'I must say, my dear girl, you paint the blackest face of our faith.' Walsingham's voice had dried out. 'Yet here is where your calumnies fall. Your husband is at work in the north of England. And I hear from all voices out of that country that it is good Protestant folk who are being butchered in their homes. It is the Catholics who have never been more hated there. It is those of the true faith who have had grisly deaths and cruel, taunting words written about their walls.' Amy sat back, feeling deflated. 'So you see, if any men of this diamond league are behind it, they are not of the true faith, but papist scum. Yet …' He drummed a finger on the desk.

'Yet?'

'It is nothing. Probably it is nothing.' He hesitated. 'Some months ago, there were two men found. Both dead. The baubles of the Romish religion were found and our men in the north discovered that they had been seminary priests, smuggled into England. It looked … it appeared that one had killed the other, before taking his own life. I shall not give you the details.' Amy tutted, disappointed. 'It did not look right to me. The manner of it. I was glad to see the creatures gone, it is true … but the manner of their going disturbed me.' He sighed, and she sensed a note of regret. 'It made the papists look bad it is true – I let it lie. But …'

'But diamond plotters might have done it.'

'Why should any plotters kill people of both faiths? If they are papists, they attack Protestants. If they are Protestants, they attack papists.'

'Who is coming out of these attacks looking worse?' asked Amy.

'The papists. The news from our good capital of the north is that the Jesuits have turned wicked. Too wicked even for those who share their faith.'

'Have you ever been a servant, sir?'

'What?' Amy repeated the question. 'We all serve someone,

girl,' he replied.

'But you've never carried someone piss-stained sheets, nor emptied what they leave in a bucket in the night?' Walsingham made a face. 'No, I didn't think so.'

'What does this peculiar line of questioning have to do with anything?'

'It's just … this talk about bringing things into hatred. If you had a master, what would make you hate him?' Walsingham shrugged.

'Cruelty?' he offered.

'Yes, sir. If I hated my master, or my mistress, and some new servant arrived, I'd want them to be on my side. To hate them too. And so I'd make sure that this new girl saw them as a monster.'

'I do not understand.'

'Well, think. Think about it. This diamond league must look to be Catholic – must seem to be, I mean. That's how come they can settle into the north of England, and especially about the French queen-mother. Maybe they even are Catholic. But they must hate their church, as if it was a bad master. And if it isn't, they'll make it look like one.'

'So …' Walsingham placed his elbows on the desk and began rubbing his temples. 'Your belief is that these men exist. They are scattered about these places, and their mission is to bring their own church into hatred?' Something dawned on his face. Moving quickly, more quickly than she had yet seen him move, he got up and went to a chest, opening it and retrieving a book. He flew back to the desk and sat, flicking rapidly, absorbed. 'Listen, girl,' he said. 'The word of God … what does it tell us has led us to chafe against the chains that bind us in the past? When those holding the chains are cruel, when they are monstrous and evil. We fear them, yes, but we gather strength and resist them.' He began quoting in a deep drone. 'Overthrow the wicked … And the house of the righteous standeth.' He flicked more pages. 'This is what the Lord says …. Don't kill innocent people here. If you carefully obey these commands, kings who sit on David's throne will come through the gates of this palace with their officers and people, riding in chariots and on horses … But if you do not obey these commands, says the Lord, I swear by my own name that this king's palace will become a ruin.'

He closed the bible in triumph, its gold edging twinkling. 'These men are plotting to bring their own church low. To make it hated. To rebuild it from blood and ashes and ruin. If you desire to make a man hated, you might make him look guilty of some heinous crime – rape or murder. If you desire to make a great body hated, make it look guilty of causing a great and general slaughter.'

'It could be,' shrugged Amy. Her bottom lip jutted. Somehow, Walsingham had taken her idea, wrapped it in bible verses, and made it his own. Something the countess said came back to her and she retracted her lip and lowered her lashes. 'I wouldn't know sir, being only a simple maid.' She chanced a peek up.

Confusion had etched twin lines on Walsingham's brow. 'Whatever wiles you are trying, you foolish girl, cease them.' She dropped the act and put her lip back out.

'Would you prefer they were hot Protestants who killed their own kind?' she asked.

'I would prefer the whole thing to be but fond fantasy.'

'But you said people are being murdered.'

'So they are. And if this thing is true – if there are mad Catholics with a grudge against their Romish church, I should say leave them to it. Let them damn themselves and their false religion. But for … but for the fact that they are killing those of the true faith. I will not let good men die to serve the turn of backbiting papists. How many of these diamonds are we dealing with? It must be more than three, else they could scarcely speak with one another.'

'Do you have a pack of cards, sir?'

'I do not play cards.' Light dawned in his eyes. He called for a servant, who brought a deck. Without Amy asking, he drew out the diamond suit, spreading it on the desk in an uneven semicircle. 'Eleven? Eleven men?'

'Yet with three leaders. A king, a queen, and a knave.' She put her finger on each of the little painted faces in turn and slid them to the side.

'England, France, and Bruges – the murders in England, and poisonings here and at the rebel-countess's house … where else?'

'Across the seas is all I heard. But yes, the Low Countries, for sure. One of them put poison in an ale-seller's wares and sent it to my lady of Northumberland. Killed the poor old soul.'

'All places where men are hot for fighting between the two faiths. I understand the Low Countries are infested with Spanish soldiers fighting honest Dutchmen. Tell me, is the ace card significant in games?'

'Sometimes. Depends on the game.'

'So perhaps four leaders. Involving themselves in a plot against their own church. Some private grievance, perhaps. Yet if they are Catholic plotters, then our queen is in danger, even if their target is just now their own faith. What would help them bring resentment against their church more than murdering the queen?'

Amy bit her lip and then winced. Since the scabbing had started, she could not seem to resist nibbling away the flakes, despite the little pinpricks of blood that sprouted. Walsingham would only be interested in pursuing the matter, she suspected, if there were a threat against Elizabeth. At length, she said, 'possibly.'

'We had better fear that there is, for safety's sake. They must have some date planned. Plotters always have some day of their enterprise. I will write home. I will warn Secretary Cecil to ensure the queen's safety. I thank God her Majesty got through the revels in all safety. Yet there will be the Easter holy days, Lady Day, I–'

'Please, sir,' said Amy, raising a hand. Strangely, years had fallen away from Walsingham's face as he waxed lyrical about the days on which the murder of his queen might be planned. 'Yes, the queen must be kept safe. But remember there is a diamond agent here, in Paris, about the dowager. And she has demanded that I discover this person before the king and queen have their royal entries to the city. First the king's and then the queen's.'

Walsingham sat back, reluctantly, Amy thought. His hands

137

began flexing and unflexing, as though she were keeping him now from an important task. 'I hear Queen Elisabeth is sickly. Not poison? I have not heard rumours of poison – just a chill.'

'I only was thinking … if they wished to do in Paris what they're doing in England – making violence on the streets. Murder. Bringing their church into hatred. Couldn't they do that here?'

'The new queen is a Catholic.'

'Yes, but the two faiths are at peace, aren't they? So at the king's entry, both Catholics and Protestants will be present. Great men and women of each faith. A diamond plotter with a gun of some kind shoots it off and blows away the head of … I don't know … some Protestant leader … then the whole of Paris would fall to fighting. It would be …'

'It would be a nightmare. The Seine would run red.'

'Will you be there? At the entry?'

'I am afraid I must. Our own queen is …' he trailed off, as though realising he was talking to a nobody and a woman, despite her dress. 'She is engaged in delicate discussions with the royal family here. I must do my part if England is to have any hope of heirs.'

'What can I do? I'm living in the Tuileries. Only a few ladies – older ladies and servants – but … the diamond plotter has to be there, sir, not with the royals. That's how come they could poison me.'

'Mrs Cole,' said Walsingham, smiling for the first time. Again, it took years off of him, even though it almost looked painful. 'You are a rare creature. "How come they could poison me" indeed. I see your young man had no need to fear your safety. I would lay money on you over three, or four, or a hundred plotting Catholic madmen.' Amy smiled, and hers was certainly painful.

'Sir, what do you know of the duke of Guise?'

'I have heard things. Why?'

'Someone in the queen's house had traffic with one of his men. I don't know what it means.'

'The duke of Guise,' said Walsingham, his smile gone entirely, 'is a dark creature. Catholic, and the worst of them. A demon in man's form, like all of his foul race. The Guise, they say, will never fall in war, but rise in it. In peace alone the clan has lost its power.'

'I thought he was quite a handsome creature. Charming, I thought.'

'I take back what faint praise I had for you. You have a woman's heart.' Silence fell about the room, the flecks of dust not even bothering to float wildly on the air. 'The duke's father did fall in the wars of religion. Brought down by a shot from a brave Huguenot's pistol. He has nurtured revenge and hatred in his black heart since. If the duke of Guise is in league with one of these diamond plotters, or if he is one of them himself, then all France is doomed. He commands many. If war erupts, he will see the whole country bathed in blood. He hates the peace we have laboured towards. He hates the efforts I made on my last visit to secure the Huguenots the right to practice the true faith in peace'

'What should I do?'

'Go home, Mrs Cole. Back to your fine palace. Keep your eyes and ears open. Watch at night, if you must. Bring me anything.'

Amy got up to leave. Her heart sank. She had felt elated at working out what she felt sure was the goal of the plot and the complexion of the plotters, but it was only at the thought of returning to the palace that she realised nothing had been solved. She found she did not want to leave the relative security of the house. Its owner was English – he was her countryman – and there was something oddly comforting and solid in that. It felt good speaking to someone, even this man, in her native tongue. Yes, her mind reminded, her, Walsingham had given her no more than the news that Jack was well; that was welcome, but she would still be living with a poisoner. Queen Catherine would still be expecting results. 'If I can't find this plotter, sir, can I leave France? Not to go back to the countess, but … but to have my husband back and go?'

Walsingham looked genuinely disarmed. Had she been a man, she was sure he would have laughed at her and sent her on her way. As it was, he said, 'tell me, Mrs Cole, why do you involve yourself in this matter? In the discovery of these plotters?' She looked at him blankly. 'Is it for your queen? Your country? France? To stop the innocent being slain? Or to protect the false faith your husband has forced you to?'

'Jack hasn't forced–'

'Hush. Be plain with me.'

'I … I wish them to be stopped so that Jack might be at liberty. To come back to me. I wish that we could both be out of all bondage.'

'I see. Singularly minded. The right thing for the wrong reasons. You are a well-suited pair.' He sighed. 'Your husband is under the care of a man of mine. If that man is satisfied he has done us good service, then … then yes, girl. You can have your husband and you can both stay out of my sight. Until then, watch the proceedings of this royal entry. If you see anyone behave suspiciously, meet with Guise, anything, then bring it straight to this house. You have protection here.'

Mollified, Amy stood up. 'Thank you,' she said, and meant it. Walsingham was not the stubborn, ambitious mule she had thought him to be when they had last met.

'One moment.' She paused, still smiling, still certain she had got the better of him. 'You asked if I had ever served anyone. I own my ignorance of piss pots and washhouses. Tell me, do you know how often her Majesty's privy council sits, and what items its great men require?' Her smile faltered. 'Do you know by what means summonses are sent for to bring together our parliament? How it is that we have news of the Turk? How our law courts are provisioned with good ink and paper?' Amy bowed her head. 'No, mistress. Think on that, in all your pomp of borrowed raiment wrapped around a prideful servant's heart. Now you may go.'

Amy bowed. He had had the last word, but she was sure to look him in his dark eyes before she left the house in Saint-Marceau. Let him feel that he had won something. The chance to have Jack out of his clutches was more than she had hoped for. All she had to do was wait out Catherine's period, send Kat to the countess, and wash her hands of the whole sorry lot of them. She wandered the city awhile, drawing admiring looks for her clothing and then sudden, awkward looks away as people caught sight of her lips. Probably they thought her a courtesan, riddled with the pox from whoring. One day soon, she might be free entirely of what French peasants thought. French queens and ladies, too.

By the time she returned to the royal apartments, it was quite dark, though the bells rang out the early evening. She was delighted to find the room empty, her peers and the servants having gone to the evening service – in fact, she had dallied deliberately so that she might avoid it. She wandered the room, looking around the scattered bedclothes and cots. When she reached her own, she spotted a note. Lifting it, she read, 'the duke of Guise's man and his whore are in the privy garden together, inside the gate and the left inner garden' scrawled in French. There was no signature. Kat, she thought – she had asked Kat to inform her of any servants' gossip about the duke and his lover.

Yet … what if it was not Kat.

She read it again, and again, and again. It was possible she was being lured into some kind of trap. The clever thing to do would be to rouse the palace guards and take them with her. But to do so would be to advertise what she was and, if the note spoke true, to parade the secrets of the court. Walsingham's voice came into her head: 'I would lay money on you over three, or four, or a hundred plotting Catholic madmen'. She had killed men who had tried to hurt her before, and she would welcome the chance to do it again. With one hand she lifted an empty, gilded wooden candlestick and tested the heft. It would make a good weapon if someone really was trying to trap her. She scrunched the note with one hand and left the room with the candlestick in the other.

Amy followed the course she had taken the night she had found the couple in the closet. She opened it and looked in. Nothing but coffers and wooden eating utensils. The stairs it was. Crunching over the gravel, she let her breath mist out as she passed through the courtyard. Above, stars twinkled behind the frayed edges of clouds.

The ground had been thoroughly churned – a party of men and

141

horses had certainly been stabled. Nodding to herself, she entered the privy gardens, the hedges springing up, maze-like, around her. The pleasant strolling space took on a strange aura in the dark, as though it had another nature altogether. She came to where she had walked with Catherine on their first meeting and spotted the tall wall with the gate standing closed. Passing to it, she found that it was unlocked, the iron bars scraping across the gravel.

Amy had not entered the private garden before. She understood it to be an eastern garden of some sort – a place for strange foreign birds and little trifles from the far east. A place, she more often supposed, for lovers' trysts. That was the French way. She still did not trust the note entirely and was sure to leave the gate open behind her, just in case her poisoner had lured her with thoughts of striking. To her left was another area, this one with a low fence and another gate. She pushed it open quietly and went inside. Sure enough, the sound of laboured panting came to her. Her head cocked, she lifted her skirts and crept forward. Grass and gravel were arranged in squares in the small enclosure, and at the far end, directly opposite her, was a little house, with only a door-less entry. The noises were coming from there. She moved to the left, hugging the outer wall, and crept towards it.

The gate closed behind and she turned, her mouth falling open. All she saw was an arm wrapped in grey or white. She made to move back towards it when the panting sound drew her back to the house. From inside, something lumbered out. A beast, a wolf, a dog – it looked like some monstrous mix of all three. It was dressed, black velvet hanging down over either side, something written in gold picked out. She could not read it, but she did remember the duke of Guise's horse, with its motto, 'shall chance or God provide the path?' emblazoned on either side. A black tongue lolled from its head and it howled, fangs emerging to pierce the night. Amy heard the delicate snick of the lock behind her. As she turned to run, she heard the crunch of the beast's paws on the gravel.

8

He crunched down hard. Warm liquid squirted, splashing to the ground, bloody gobbets flecking it. Vile. Burnt on the outside, bloody and raw on the inside. In disgust, he dropped the meat pie, vowing silently never again to eat of Doll's table. He spat out the few chunks of half-cooked meat that had got into his mouth and looked up. Broken shafts of sunlight pierced the misty morning air. Jack stood before the door to the Carmelite Friary cellar, his breath steaming. It was a dangerous business, coming and going to the place, not because the authorities took an especial interest, but because the faithful Catholics still attending Father Adam's private Masses were liable now to turn violent if they thought they were being watched. Especially by someone whom they might rightfully suspect was a government man, he thought. The door was thin and did not quite meet flush with the walls. He could hear the drone of Latin through it. Returning to the street, he stood conspicuous in its centre and blew into his hands, warming them.

It was a strange thing to start a day knowing that death would follow no matter what fell out.

Within minutes, there was noise at his back. Two voices rose and fell in the alley that ran between the old Friary and the building next door, a man's and a woman's. '… dangerous courses,' said the female, her voice genteel.

'Only way be b'violent means,' said the rougher male. The two appeared, the man spitting at the ground and the woman wrinkling her nose and stepping around it. 'E'en it take blood to rid us o' the heretics, blood it be.' The fellow was short and squat, his face hard. His companion was well-dressed, and together they had the aspect of a mistress and her servant. The woman caught Jack looking first, and her eyes widened in fear. She tugged on the man's arm. 'Come, let us be away.' Thankfully, her friend seemed too preoccupied with his angry excitement to notice her manner, and the pair melted into the

January morning. When they had gone, Jack gave another look around the wide street. Nothing. He blew once more into his hands, turned his back to the brightening city, and re-entered the alley.

The door was locked, and he rapped. It opened. The torches were lit, and Adam stood aside to let him step into the still-freezing cellar. 'Jack,' he said, grinning. He gave a toss of his curls. Jack grinned back and flicked his own tawny fringe out of his eye. 'You were not stopped, nor watched in coming?'

'No, father.'

'I have good news. A gentlewoman just left – says she has a safe place I might be protected.'

'That is good news. Where?'

'Sheffield. To be nearer to the queen of Scots. I can say no more. You understand.'

'Of course, father. When do you leave?'

'Soon. Perhaps. I can't abandon the flock here until more true men come from Douai.'

'I … I shall miss you.'

'You will be taken care of.' He patted Jack's shoulder. 'Please, kneel.'

Jack crossed to the centre of the cellar, where he habitually knelt to take Mass. The damp immediately began to bleed into his knees. 'I will miss all who come here,' said Adam. The young Jesuit had moved over to his strongbox, which had a cloth overlaid and was sporting all the accoutrements of a makeshift altar. The gilt of a crucifix gleamed as torchlight wavered on it. Adam's back obscured it and then he turned back to Jack. 'Bow your head, my son.' Jack did, watching until the priest's lower legs took their position before him. 'In nómine Patris, et Fílii, et Spíritus Sancti. Amen.'

Jack kept his head bowed, but let his eyes swivel upwards. Adam raised his right hand as though to bless him. But too far. The light this time glinted off of something sharp. Jack threw out his left hand, grabbing the man behind the knee. He jerked it, hard. Adam stumbled, his weight shifting to his other leg. His arm swung wildly. Before he could recover, Jack drew free the dagger Polmear had given him. In one swift movement, he gripped the hilt and swung it sideways, into Adam's left leg. It pierced his thigh. He screamed. The blade he had been swinging in the air fell from his hand and he followed it to the ground. Jack sprang up and kicked it away. He then leant over the fallen priest, who was still screeching in pain, and twisted and jerked his dagger free. Retrieving it brought fresh howls of agony and a jet of blood. Red washed over the flagstones, sank into the dirt.

Jack backed away until he hit the wall. He had been proven right, yet he took no joy in it. Instead, he felt a curious detachment. He looked down and was surprised that the hand which held the dagger was shaking. Father Adam was writhing on the floor, trying to staunch the bleeding with the folds of his cassock. Jack turned from him, slowly, and opened the door to the cellar. 'Polmear,' he cried. 'Polmear!'

His shouts echoed down the alley. Rather than Polmear, they hit an elderly couple who had been coming towards the door, already tentatively drawing wooden beads from the linings of their coats. At sight of Jack, they began furiously trying to conceal them and fled. Jack's heart leapt as he saw Polmear step around them and bound towards him. 'You were right?'

'Yes. Yes, I was right.'

The two men stood inside the cellar, the door closed firmly behind them. Polmear put his boot down on Adam's ankle and the man yelped. 'Father Diamond, isn't it?' Adam looked up. Anger managed to crush the pain out of his expression, albeit momentarily.

'Heretic scum,' he said, and then clenched his teeth.

'That's as may be, lad. But I'm not killing old women, sodomising priests, gutting churchmen. Oh, we know all about your plans, don't we Jack? Seems you're no more expert in the art of killing than your mad dog.' Adam managed to spit at him. 'Right proper uncouth too, this one.'

'You've … been … following me,' gasped the Jesuit. His words, when they were out, sounded more like a question.

'I didn't have to,' said Jack. 'You revealed yourself.'

'Aye,' said Polmear, laughing. 'Friend Jack here was mighty secretive last night about what revealed you to him. What was it?'

'He … he knew about the old woman being burned. Even before the other fellow said to him what had happened, he said, "we're here to save souls, not burn old women". But we only just knew she had been killed. Only just brought the news. He knew, though. He's the one wants the religious wars here. I heard people leaving this place – the man was talking of blood. He'd worked him up.'

'Listen to the lad,' Polmear barked, grinning. 'A mind as sharp as the blade he just stuck you with, Father Diamond. What do you think of that?' He squatted down next to the fallen priest and hugged his blonde head as though they were old friends. Adam wriggled and jerked but had no strength to free himself.

'No use,' coughed the priest. 'No use, you fool. I'll … be revenged. The flames … will rise … Paris will burn. Blood … blood will wash away the sinners. Like you. Like … Your wife … will die.'

'What did he say?' asked Jack. He repeated it in a shout. 'What about my wife?'

Polmear's voice turned hard. 'What is this of Paris? Where's your attack dog, priest? The animal you've loosed in the north?' Adam said nothing. 'Who are the other diamonds? What foul act are you plotting? When?' He shook at him. 'Ah, well, there's poor sport.'

'What?'

'You've killed him.'

'What?' gasped Jack.

'A knife in the leg. Sometimes has that effect. Brings too much blood out too fast. Hell's breeches, Jack Cole – you really are bad at making friends.' He dropped Adam's head and it fell to the ground with a sickening crack. 'And if the knife didn't, that did. A damn shame. Our friends in London should've liked to make him sing before the end.'

'What do we do?' Hysteria sang on the edge of Jack's words. He had brought the weapon only on the unlikely chance that Adam somehow smuggled the murderer past Polmear, who was stationed on the main street outside, watching the alley. He had expected simply to draw some confession, some proofs or incriminating words from the priest's mouth, so that he might be arrested. It had all happened too quickly – an accident. 'I won't be protected for this, I'll be hanged! I didn't mean it – not to kill him – I swear – just to bring him down!'

'Becalm yourself, laddie. Not the first time you've killed, as I hear. Can't be helped.'

'But what do we do?'

'Leave the little shit-poll to rot. He's no use dead.' Polmear nudged him again with a foot. 'Filthy mad papist,' he growled. Jack shook his head.

'He said something about Amy – he knows something. He must have friends about her.'

'The other priests?'

'No,' said Jack, shaking his head. 'He was … like a wolf hiding amongst sheep. I'm sure. I'm going to her. I'm going.' Polmear stood and took his arm. He shook it loose, waving the bloody dagger in fury.

'Whoa, laddie. Don't forget that you're a servant of her Majesty. Of Mr Walsingham.'

'Fuck Walsingham,' spat Jack, reddening immediately.

'Not a job I'd fancy. I'll forget that. Listen, boy, Mr Walsingham is on the continent himself, as I said – in Paris.' Polmear bowed his head and rubbed the bridge of his nose. Eventually, he said, 'I'll have to get word to him. Word that this diamond thing is real. That a Jesuit priest was one of them. And an attack dog. If this priest is one of them then are at least two in the north. Well, one now. And that he threatened Paris. It might be that he's found something there himself. Your wife…'

'Amy.'

'Aye, Amy. She's with the countess of Northumberland, isn't she?'

Jack shrugged, a little huffily. 'Wouldn't know. You fellows tell me nothing.'

'Wherever she is, she is Mr Walsingham's. As you are. Both protected, as far as our people can.'

'Paris is near enough to the Low Countries. Closer than the bloody north. I'm going. I'm going to Walsingham and telling him this is all over. And getting news of my wife and getting her and getting out of this and …'

'Easy, lad. You're excited. You need to take a walk, breathe the air. You can't get to Paris in a day. One more night and I promise I'll take you with me in the morning. Might as well, eh? No reason to sit around and wait to be murdered by this,' he nudged the dead priest, 'creature's wild dog.'

'You promise? Your word?'

'I promise,' said Polmear, grinning, and putting a hand over his heart. 'On my honour. Yet … I'll be plain with you – I'm a plain man. I've long since written the secretary that Father Corpse here had two Jesuits with him. Our master will want to know their names and movements, sheep or not. Fair warning to you, lad. You can't protect them.' His features lightened again. 'Come, let's get away from here before more papists come. Let them find him. Christ alone knows what this city will be when the news gets out. Good Protestants murdered, another priest dead. If the folk are twitching for their daggers already, they'll have them out at this. It would be a sore thing if he got his religious wars through spilling his own blood, eh? Mad fool.'

Polmear fished through the dead man's things, finding the key to the cellar door. 'Look here,' he said, holding something else up and whistling. 'I'll be having this.' Light bounced off a little diamond-headed pin.

'You can't rob him. It's not right.'

'Hark at it – it's not right, says the man who stuck a blade in the creature's leg. Go on then, you have it.' He pitched the pin into the air and Jack caught it. He rolled it around in his palm.

'Not so shy about having it yourself, eh?'

'I'll keep it,' said Jack, slipping it inside his coat. 'Maybe … maybe if he gets buried and we know where, I'll leave it on the earth. Some day.'

'You do that. Let's go. Leave him to watch the world burn from Hell.' He took the key, locking the door as they left. It was a flimsy thing, but it might keep the news from spreading until they could be safely away.

The energy had drained from Jack and Polmear guided him like a sleepwalker, first through the market, where he forced food down his throat, and then to bed in the backroom of Doll's tavern before the short, snowy day had even ended. The room was still as bright as it ever got when Jack allowed the blanket to be pulled up around his neck. He stared at the cobwebby ceiling.

'Get some sleep, lad.'

'Can I ask you something?'

'Depends what it is. Something I can answer?'

'Maybe. If you wish to. What did you do? To become known in the north. You said you made errors. That's how come you could train me and watch ports and that, but you couldn't do the quiet, watching sort of stuff yourself.'

For a while, the only sound was that of the drinkers in the next room cackling and swearing. 'A woman,' said Polmear.

'A woman?'

He sighed. 'Gave my heart to a nice northern girl. Alice, by name. Still sore at the name Alice. Pert little thing, yellow-haired and with white teeth. She loved those teeth. Catholic. And I got full of ale and told her what I was about. Bragged, you might say. The next morning, three of her brothers came at me in the street with clubs. Mob of their friends in the town were fitting to join them. Things didn't look too good for young Edward Polmear.'

'In York?'

'No, no – was in Bolton then. When the Scotch queen first came to England. Not long ago, but it seems it. Learnt me a lesson then. Beaten right out of town, so I was. And the news running out ahead of me – "this way comes a southern man, watching for to ruin us all". Clannish lot in the north. Sir William – I worked for him then – he washed his prim little hands of me. I'd have starved had Mr Walsingham not given me another chance. Saw I had a mind, he did. My face was known, my name too, but my mind still worked. I'd sailed a bit – my old dad was a sailor – so he set me to work. Good man, is Mr Walsingham. He'll see me right.'

'So it was a woman that … that put you where you are.'

'No, lad. It was myself. There's a lesson for you – don't blame other folks for your own daft mistakes. When you're a dolt, own your doltishness.'

'Yeah,' Jack yawned. 'I will.' His mind had turned entirely to his departure from York. The next morning could not come soon enough.

***

When the noontime dinner hour came and went without word, Acre began to wonder. Wonder grew into the closest thing he knew to worry. Worry became a cold and angry certainty. Something had gone wrong.

A sudden, heavy snow flurry had forced the people of York indoors, and those who remained on the streets were huddled together around braziers. It looked to him as though those who shared ideals flocked together: the angry, blood-frenzied Catholics fired up by Father Adam were together; elsewhere the Protestants warmed their hands together; at separate fires stood those moderate Catholics, bewildered, frightened, and worried about the perverted and violent turn their church seemed to have taken. Muffled so that his face could not be seen, he ensured that none paid attention to this lonely young man abroad on a dirty day.

The door to the cellar was locked. A bad sign. He had been told that he would be contacted either directly or through one of the hired runners earlier. His fellow diamond, the religious knave, would not have left the boy to rot and gone off elsewhere. He looked up and down the alley. No one. He launched one hard kick at the centre of the door, just by the iron handle. The whole thing fell inward off its hinges. Inside was gloomy, only the faint light from the dull day attacking the dark. The smell of spent torches, acrid and stinging, lay thick in the air. He let his eyes adjust.

Inside, Acre found the body of his fallen brother.

He knelt to the floor, his jaws clenched, and took his hands. Something snapped within him. His eyes glazed over. He saw Adam as he had been at fifteen, two years older than himself. That was when he had found out the truth. His brother had turned to religion, claiming that what the thirteen-year-old Acre had been was not mad, but destined to be an avenging angel. He had believed it, because he had loved him. Love was something he had never believed in – it arose in others as some imbalance of the humours that send them skidding to others who had the same imperfection at the same time. Yet he loved his brother as deeply as he knew how.

And that boy – the boy who had humiliated him the day before – had killed him.

He wondered if Adam had seen his death coming. It was a thing he had often wondered when watching people die – did they know that their fleeting time was at an end? Did they appreciate that every foolish act they had ever done in their lives was about to be wiped away, bootless, of no consequence? Or did their minds continue to work even until oblivion overtook them – did their thoughts stubbornly try and tether themselves to the world of men, unwilling to let it go on without them? Did Adam's?

He felt around under his brother's torn cassock – Jack Cole, who called himself Jack Wylmott – had dug around under it. He felt for the pin that should be there but wasn't. Thief, he thought. Only the religious items remained, and, he noticed, the dagger that had once been the old woman's, Oldyngham's. He slid that into his belt and then sat down, legs splayed, beside the corpse. No tears came, just one low, tortured wail. Acre lay awhile with his dead brother, saying nothing, staring into the abyssal gloom. He thought that perhaps someone came – one of the religious folk – but they ran off when they saw the broken door. After that no one tried.

When darkness had fallen hard, and he judged it to be very late, he lifted Adam's body under one arm and began dragging it out of the cellar. He kept to side streets and alleys, stopping to rest often. The town watch was abroad, but they did a poor job of patrolling the streets – because he, Acre, had done a good job of making them frightening places to be, even for the men charged with keeping the peace. Eventually he half-dragged him over the bridge, looking, perhaps, like a man taking a drunken friend home, and out to the Dominican Friary's overgrown former parklands. There, in the falling snow, he laboured through the night to bury him. The grave that had been meant for Jack Cole was now too good for him. He would lay his brother there, amidst the broken ruins of the religion he had loved for its truth and hated for its corruption.

The snow lay thick on the ground as he made for the lodging house in which the murdering Cole slept. His mind was quite calm. He did not concern himself with footprints. The ground was already a mishmash of them, and it was beginning to turn sleety. It would be dawn soon, and light was starting to shine from around the edges of wooden shutters – the bakers and the servants of fine houses would already be astir. If the tavern wench who kept Cole's house was up, he would go through her. It did not matter.

He trudged through the slush outside the flaking, shabby building and forced the door. Cheap. Useless. Inside was empty, even the ale pots still locked away for the night. There was no lock on the inner door. He slipped inside. It was dark, but ambient light always found a way of helping those who wished to see. A knobbly dark shape signified the sleeping form. Acre took a few seconds to judge head from feet. Both emerged from a blanket on the floor. Just where he judged Cole's neck to be, he plunged the dagger in. It met no resistance. Blood jetted out, soaking the body. There was no scream, only a wet gurgling. It was not satisfying. Again and again, Acre raised and dropped the knife, standing clear of the blood, enjoying every wet thrust of the blade.

He stood away, letting the floor turn red. It had been a mistake to do it so quickly, so easily. It was not nearly satisfying enough. He had acted rashly, out of passion. He would have to punish himself for that; there was no one, now, to counsel him otherwise.

Still, there was the wife.

The diamond league was not dead, even if his brother was. Only he knew of Adam's fate, and he must carry it abroad. It was his duty to ensure the dead man's hopes lived on – his dreams of a world in which terror and fear erupted, bringing those that came through it to a state of purity. If she had not already been dispatched in Paris, he would find Mrs Cole, and her death would be more meticulous. More satisfying. He left the lodging house the way he had come.

9

The wolf-thing advanced with a strange, lopsided gait. Amy had pushed at the gate to no avail. If she wanted out, she would have to climb over it. Set into its centre was a plate with the painted arms of the Valois, and she put a hand up and gripped it, heedless of the chill it sent through her palm. She chanced a look behind her. The thing was watching. Its head hung down low, but the black eyes glinted upwards, reflecting moonlight. It sat back on its hind legs halfway between her and its house and made a strange, throaty laugh. And then it pounced forward.

Amy threw herself upwards, bracing one shoe against the solid silver plate of the arms. The back side of it was unpainted: it dimly reflected her own image. Her foot slipped. 'Shit!' She tried again, not daring to turn. An animal stench washed over her, musky and wild. The candlestick fell from her hand as she scrambled for purchase. She heard it roll away. Her hands tightened on the bars above the arms. She felt herself lift, up, up, up. Both feet were now on the plate, her head only a few inches from the top of the gate.

Craaack!

She tensed, expecting to feel pain flood her. She looked down and saw that the beast had taken the candlestick in its jaws. It had been a thick, ungainly thing. The monster had snapped through it in one bite. It shook its head from side to side, disappointed at the meatless bone. What was it? Her mind raced. A wolf of some kid, but with its spine deformed, making its head curve downwards. The eyes rolled up again to stare at her.

Amy clung to the gate like a fly, her legs up and braced against it, her skirts still trailing to the ground. The beast lurched forward again, jaws snapping. It caught her dress and she closed her eyes. She would fall into its waiting maw, she knew – there was no hope. After a few seconds, she opened her eyes and twisted her head around. Her lips had begun moving in prayer. The thing had bitten clean through the folds of her dress, like scissors through thin paper. With a start, she realised that the strength of its jaws was too great. It could not pull at her gown, could not pull her with it, without slicing through it. Renewed hope got her moving.

Ignoring the pain that was beginning to tear through her hands and arms, she hauled herself up further. It was easier going without the weight of the dress, cut cleanly away below the knees. The animal itself could not leap upwards – it had the weight of its own strange clothing. With more strength that she thought she could muster, she began gracelessly pulling, sliding, and jerking herself upwards. One leg higher than the other, she pulled in her knee and used it, too, gaining a foothold on the plate's upper edge. There she stopped, catching her breath. The animal began its barking laughter again, and this time it raised the chirps and squawks of the parrots that she had thought to be the strangest creatures in the garden. She looked down and saw that it had begun circling its enclosure again, stopping only to stare up at her.

Amy swung one leg over the top of the fence. The sharp rail heads stabbed at it, but the remnants of her gown cushioned them. She positioned her hands between the points and got the other leg over, leaning on her front and letting her corseted bodice guard against impalement. Once she had both legs over the side, she dropped, letting her body fall whilst her hands clung to the top. She could not will them to let go, and so her body jerked, the stress sending fresh waves of pain through her arms. It was the pain that forced her to release her grip and she dropped in a heap to the ground.

For some time, she could not move. Instead, she stared through the bars of the gate at the monster that would have killed her. She had heard of the famous wolves of Paris – creatures which stalked the woods of the country and, when plague came, or bad winters brought starvation, entered the city to devour the poor in the streets. This thing, though, was altogether different. It was no half-starved beast, but a sleek, monstrous devil. At length, Amy used the stout stone wall beside the gate to get to her feet, fearful that the creature would snap at her hands if she touched the iron bars – would bite through them as it had the candlestick. On wobbling legs and with tears born of anger and relief, she stumbled towards the gate out of the garden. Thankfully, this one was unlocked – her tormenter had had no need to seal her in with exotic birds. Only with a monster.

As she trooped back to the palace, she realised that she should say nothing about what had happened until she could speak to Queen Catherine, or even Walsingham again. Yet she could not hold it to herself. Instead, she blurted out, 'I have just been near-eaten by a wolf, for the love of Christ,' to the first guard she found. The man looked mystified, and she laughed at the confusion on his face, knowing how insane she must look. She patted his arm, enjoying even the look of surprise – or was it lust? – that appeared when he saw her half-bared legs. The bewildered boy was of a piece with all the guardsmen she had seen about the Louvre and the Tuileries: young, beautiful, blonde, and arrayed with impressive weapons he had no notion of how to use. There were no scarred and battle-worn soldiers to offend the eye in a French royal palace.

'You, guard! Quickly Murder! Murder!' The shout sounded over both their heads. It came from upstairs – the voice of one of the man's colleagues. 'Don't hang there like a limp prick, man, raise the alarm!' The guard Amy had spoken to leapt into action, running from her, leaving the palace. Her mind worked slowly. But I am not dead, she thought – I escaped the thing's jaws. She kept walking towards the apartments, heedless of the cries, halloos, and women's screams that were erupting around her. Someone has been murdered, she thought, in a detached kind of way. Someone who is not me.

She pushed her way through guards, through servants, towards her bedchamber. As she got near to it, a woman's hysterical sobs greeted her. 'I am sorry, madam, you cannot go in there. There has been an accident,' said a bearded young guard who was blocking the door to the ladies' bedchamber.

'Go and fuck yourself,' she said in English. The guard appeared not to know the words, but he did not misunderstand her tone. Anger flared on his face and then, seeing her dress, torn though it was, he mumbled under his breath and stood aside.

On entering the room, Amy was greeted by a scene to rival the madness of being trapped in a privy garden with a hellhound. Vittoria de Brieux was on her knees, her makeup cracked and flaking, wringing her hands and screeching like a whipped dog. Around the room, the other women – Madame Gondi and her maid, Kat, and a host of new arrivals decked in finery and service weeds – stood with their backs to the wall and hands to their mouths. At the centre of the tableaux, drawing everyone's attention, lay Brieux's maidservant. She was prone on her front. Blood pooled around her. From the centre of her back, like a giant, bony finger, protruded the long, swirling unicorn's horn.

The shock of it was too much. Amy's legs, already unsteady, gave way and she fell to the ground in a dead faint.

***

Amy was on her knees before Catherine, who was seated on a chair in her bedchamber – directly beyond the room in which the unfortunate maidservant had been found dead – beneath a freshly-hung cloth of estate.

'It is not a wolf,' said the queen-mother. 'It is called a hyena. Out of the blackest heart of the Africas.'

'An African wolf then,' said Amy, focussing her glare on the thick carpet into which she had partly sunk.

'A wedding gift from the duke of Guise to my son and his bride. A most expensive beast. A female, very wild and furious, the duke tells me, since being parted from its cubs. It shall give us good sport.'

'The duke,' said Amy, looking up. So it had been his monster.

'He delivered it only yesterday. You stumbled into its presence last night. And then this affair of the girl. The keeper of the gardens pleads his ignorance. He claims his keys were stolen, as my lady Gondi was robbed of the key to the coffer where we keep the great horn. He, though, has not the excuse of age. He will pay with his place. The beast might have escaped and been lost to us.'

'I'm no huntswoman, your Majesty – but give me a bow and

I'll put an arrow between that thing's eyes, I'll put my hands in its blood, I'll–'

'Silence.' Catherine's neat, sharp tone allowed for no argument.

The queen-mother had arrived the morning after Amy's brush with the thing she now learned was an African hyena. The dead girl, it was discovered, had been strangled from behind. The unicorn horn had then been forced into her back, like a gruesome flagpole proclaiming her departure from the world. The horn itself had been an expensive thing, kept in a specially carved, gold-inlaid strongbox in the ladies' bedchamber so that the physicians could purify the air with it before any member of the royal family breathed it. Only the elderly Madame Gondi had a key, and she protested in the querulous timbre of old age that anyone might have taken it from her, hoping to cause her trouble. It was found still in the lock. It would be useless now, thought Amy darkly. Anyone who still thought the unicorn horn had magical, protective properties would have a difficult case. It had certainly given the physicians something to jaw over, as they had been doing non-stop since Catherine returned – pausing only to try and cut Amy after insisting that her shameful fainting had slowed her blood and that it must be forced to flow again.

'This note you say was unsigned – do you have it?'

'I ... I must have dropped it. When I dropped the candlestick. That wolf likely ate it, as it would have eaten me. The duke of Guise–'

'The duke of Guise is a friend to this court. I cannot – I will not ask him questions at such a time. Nor about such a one as you. You have not seen his man about this place at night again?'

'No, your Majesty.'

'Then, as he says, he is a true and faithful friend. You are unhurt. Keep your mouth shut, if you can.'

Amy trembled with barely suppressed rage. 'But this girl ...'

'She had no family. It is to be said that she met with an accident. I will not have scandal touching my house at this time.' Amy could not resist a gasp and Catherine gave her a sharp look. 'We – all who wear crowns, I mean – are looked on by the public. The public are fickle, and in their numbers they are dangerous. One scandal – the murder of a girl under my charge – it might light a fire that will not soon be put out. The heretics will use it as proof of our corruption. The republican creatures will use it likewise.'

'She deserves justice,' said Amy, feeling suddenly bad that she did not even know the girl's name. 'Madame de Brieux wants justice.' It was true – the woman had been hysterical, frightening the other ladies and having to be sedated with hippocras, her face cracked and broken as great chunks of white glaze fell from it onto the dead woman's back.

'That lady wants to remain part of this household more,' said Catherine, a dark smile raising her lips. 'I have already provided her a new maid. The dead girl will be buried. Forgotten.' A chill ran through Amy, making the tiny hairs on her arms rise. It would have been the same had she died and had there been anything left to bury. Gone and forgotten. Would Jack even have been able to find out the truth of what had become of her?

Catherine rested her chin on her hand, staring over Amy's head, and sighed. 'Anyone who lodged under this roof last night might have killed the wretched girl. That is a great many ladies now, and all their servants and attendants. A guard, for that matter, driven mad with evil lusts. They will be discovered.' The queen-mother, Amy thought, seemed strangely uninterested in the girl's death, despite the gruesome manner of it and its proximity to her bedchamber. 'My guards will be ever present from this moment until the new queen takes up residence in the Louvre.' She nodded slightly towards the door, on either side of which two exquisitely groomed, caparisoned men stood sentinel. 'And thereafter.'

'Your Majesty,' said Amy, unable to resist a smug smile. 'It could not be just any of the new ladies. Whoever killed that poor girl – it must've been the same who sent me to the wolf pit. And the same who poisoned me. That was before most of the ladies came here from court. Perhaps this girl knew something – saw too much – and so the person killed her too.'

Catherine shrugged, noncommittal. 'I set you the task of unmasking this creature. And this is what you have? That it was someone?' Amy lowered her head again. 'I shall not return to this palace until the royal entry. My dearest daughter the queen has fallen into illness again, some malady of the throat or chest. It will be some weeks before she recovers fully. I must be by her side again. The beginning of March is said to be the fairest date for the king's entry. His wife's not until after. All say it, the astrologers, the cunning men.' Amy looked up in alarm. That was over a month away. Two attempts had already been made on her life. Increased guards and a greater number of watchful women or not, she would be lodging with a killer. 'You may go,' said Catherine. As Amy rose and began to back away, the old woman said, a glint in her eye, 'Oh, but I understand you were from the palace when the beast was delivered. Before it struck at you. Where?'

'Giving alms, your Majesty.'

'Is that so? And taking nothing with you to give. An English pursuit, perhaps. Odd habits your people have. Well, have a care, my false lady. I shall not see you for some time. I trust you shall not be slain before then.'

10

The woman's screams brought men and women in the street thundering into the house. As they had at the scene of Mrs Oldroyd's murder, a couple of alderman were trying to keep order, to force the increasingly heated crowd back. He heard them before he saw them and tethered the horses at a hitching post around the corner before pushing his way through the crowd. It was thick outside Doll's tavern, despite the early hour, and his heart began racing.

'What news?' he asked.

'Anootheh muh-dah,' said a boy, whose smudged face marked him as a ditch digger, or perhaps one of the wretches who dug in the sewage channel for things that might still be sold.

'That's him!' screeched a voice he recognised. It was Doll. 'See, over there?' She had the grip of an alderman's sleeve. 'Brown hair, down over one eye. That's him!'

On hearing her, the crowd parted around Jack, as though he had an infectious disease. Not knowing what to do, nerves drew a lopsided smile. 'See,' cried Doll, 'smiling like that. An odd duck, I always said it. There's your murderer. Take him up.'

Before Jack knew what was happening, he was being grappled to the ground by the crowd who had been driven to distraction by the pent-up anger and fear of months. He heard daggers being drawn and braced himself, only relaxing when he heard the aldermen and officers punching their way into the crowd to form a barrier around him. One of them, a stringy man, took him by the ear and yanked him to his feet. 'You killed the fellow yonder, lad?'

'What?'

'Don't act the goat with me, boy – your tavern mistress found him, sliced in collops.'

'I … who?'

'He's an idiot,' spat the alderman. 'Anyone know this stranger?' The crowd only jeered.

'I haven't killed anyone,' protested Jack, looking around pleadingly. Unable to sleep, having done so for the majority of the previous day, he had let Polmear take his bed, and went out walking, hoping to find the first ostler to rise that might sell them horses. He had hoped that they might have left York together before the full city had even woken. Suddenly his heart sank. Nausea swept over him.

'Sir, ye'd better come and 'ear this,' said a new voice – that of a heavy-set young man who had just left the tavern part of the building. Jack's captor took his arm none too gently and dragged him along. Together the three went inside, past Doll, who shot Jack a look of disgust and fear mingled. 'Kept him under my roof,' he heard her saying, 'a killer. Fed him too.'

'It's fuckin' Polmear,' said the chubby man, who stopped short of the backroom. 'Papers on 'im fro' t'queen's sec't'ry Walsingham. The one who watches –'

'I know who he is,' snapped the alderman, taking a harder grip of Jack, who could feel the man's fingers sinking into his flesh. 'Jesus Christ and all the Saints. Edward Polmear.'

'We knew 'e came and went. One o' t'south's men in t'north.'

'Aye, came and went. Came and went, not came and met butchery. Christ Jesus, what do we do? We'll have t'blame of this. It'll be another bloody mass slaughter. Polmear, the queen's man. Cut to ribbons.'

Jack began to sink to his knees, and he was pulled up again. 'Help me with this idiot,' spat the alderman to his fellow.

'What do we do with 'im?'

'Buggered if I know,' returned the alderman. 'Doubt even the sheriff'll want involved with this mess. No, not even if he killed poor old Oldyham.'

''E don't look much like a killer.'

'Oh aye? And what does a killer look like?'

'Hard,' said the big man. 'Scarred. Bad.'

'Met many, have you?' A shrug was the answer. And then,

'We'll have to lock 'im up. Question 'im, maybe. Till we get word up from t'south.'

'I know my job, lad. We'll get him to t'castle.' The alderman slapped at Jack's face and he roused a little, staring into the old man's sharp blue eyes. 'You alive, idiot? You're coming with us. To t'castle. You can spend the day in there, until we know t'truth o' this.'

'You think 'e killed the old woman?'

'I don't know. Help me get him shifted.'

Jack allowed himself to be led out by the two men, through the crowd of people. Some spittle hit him in the face, and others began hurling chunks of melting snow and dirt. The missiles kindled him. 'Here,' he said. Then, more loudly, 'here! Let go of me! I haven't killed anyone. I'm one of Mr Walsingham's men. Francis Walsingham. Send word to him.' His words excited the crowd still further. They stopped only when some filth accidentally hit his guards, and the two men began hurling threats of imprisonment back at them.

'There's been a mistake,' said Jack to the younger man, hoping for an ally. 'Is Polmear dead?' It was the old man who answered.

'Aye, lad. And bringing down the wrath of the south on all our heads.'

'He … he was my friend. I lodged with him. Left him sleeping last night. We're Mr Walsingham's men. My name is Cole, Jack Cole. He sent me here, and Polmear, he watches over me.' Then, lamely, 'we're leaving today.'

'You're goin' nowhere, friend,' said the younger man, hooking a thumb into his broad belt. 'Save that way.' He nodded along the Floss Bridge, past the Mercers' Hall. Jack began struggling. In that direction lay the infamous Clifford's Tower, from which the Catholic leader Robert Aske had been hanged in chains by Henry VIII, and the crumbling York Castle itself. Jack continued struggling until his captors twisted his arms behind his back and began carrying him. 'I'm to go to Paris,' he cried. 'Get news to Walsingham! In Paris! You'll all die for this!' He gave full shout to the sudden descent of temper he usually suppressed, but to no avail.

Within half an hour, he had become a curio. Locked in a cell in the tower, the door of which had a barred grate, he endured the taunts and questions of a number of men. Hours passed, the nature and quality of the curious shifting with each; first came the well-dressed, sneering folk, and then the poorer sort, and then only guards. At first he paced, and then he shouted insults back, and then he sat, despondent. He let the news that Polmear was dead sink in. And with that realisation came the enormity of what might happen to him if he were declared guilty. The penalty would be swift. He could only hope that the death of one of Walsingham's known agents would stay the hands of the city officials, forcing them to send him south for investigation. But Walsingham was in Paris. That would delay matters. And all the time the remaining diamond man, Father Adam's attack dog, as Polmear had called him, was on the loose. Had he intended to kill Polmear, or was he himself the quarry? If so, did he realise his mistake? What then?

Jack curled in a ball on the floor. He had supposed he would be on his way to find Amy by now. That is what he should have done at the outset – he should have fled Walsingham's house and taken the first ship he could find to the Low Countries. He might have beaten any searchers or messengers Walsingham sent to harm her. In frustration and anger, he kicked at the wall. A chunk of loose stone fell. Old place, he thought. Old place, with an old door. Hope rose.

Gaining his feet, he crawled along the floor to the cell door and, standing, peeped out of the grate. He was, he knew, on the ground floor of the circular keep. In the great chamber outside, a thick stone pillar stood in the middle, a desk flush against it. Two men were pawing through items laid out there. Their voices boomed around the building, until they reached the high roof. 'Don't envy you. Might 'ave word about that one tomorrow. Well, good e'en to you.' One of the men left, and the other sat on a wooden chair, his back to Jack.

It was getting late. Other prisoners had been grumbling, occasionally shouting for food or water from their own grates. He judged the passage of time by the flattening of their cries and pleas. And by the back of the night guard, who eventually slumped over his desk. Some torches stood in sconces about the central room, but they were weak, letting shadows stretch. It made sense, thought Jack, that there would be only one guard in such a place; the room would allow him to see in all directions if he chose to. What he apparently chose to do, though, was sleep; and why not? Every prisoner was locked in his cell.

Certain that the fellow was in deep slumber, Jack tried sliding an arm between the bars of the grate. It fit easily enough. The lock, however, was set down to the right. His left hand would be useless at such an awkward angle – he had not the skill at using that one for careful work. He retracted it.

Grateful that he had not been searched, he drew the diamond pin out of his coat and gripped it tightly between his left thumb and forefinger. Standing with this right side to the door, he slid his arm out and down. He smiled. He had always been plagued by weak and unnatural joints. It had been one of the things his father had beaten him for as a child – marks of the devil, he had always said: proof that Jack was a tainted beast who had killed his mother on entering the world. For the first time, the strange ability might prove itself useful. He let his wrist unlock and bend backwards. Still gripping the pin, terrified that sweat would release it from his grasp, he felt for the lock with his palm. He found it. And inserted the pin.

Jack had never picked a lock before. However, he had heard his fellow servants in Norfolk's house talking about it – about how easy it was with the right tool; about how any man might rob his master even without a key. Jack had turned away from that kind of talk, despising thievery as he did. Yet now it was useful.

He closed his eyes, trusting that the lack of distractions would be more helpful than trying to twist around now and then to watch the guard. The pin slid into the lock and hit something. He wiggled it around until it slid in farther. He moved it up. Down. Overshot it. Slipped. He removed it entirely and took a deep breath. He tried again, with the same result. Anger and frustration threatened – a desire to snap the thing in a rage. If he gave way to one of his outbursts, he was lost.

Sweat was beginning to burst forth on his forehead. It trickled down the small of his back. Soon it would be running over his arms and hands. In went the pin. He moved it in the other direction this time. Side to side. Again, it slipped in further. This

165

time it seemed to strike home. He had it. He froze.

Having the pin now acting as a key, he was terrified to move it, lest he lose what he had achieved. He stood, immobile, as the seconds ticked past. Snoring from the guard and other prisoners reverberated around the vast chamber. Gingerly, carefully, he twisted the pin between his fingers. He froze again as he heard the dull, muted *snick*. In the stillness of the night it ricocheted to the rafters. He withdrew the pin and pulled his arm back into the cell, pocketing the makeshift key. Then, hardly daring to believe, he massaged his painful right hand, locking it back into normality, and reached out with his left. He had to stand on tiptoes, but he could reach the circular handle. He pulled, and the door slid open easily. He rode it like a child.

He was free.

Crouching, almost crawling, Jack left the cell, fearful not only that the guard would wake, but that some other prisoner would call out to him. It did not happen. He supposed – he hoped – that the others would have no reason to be staring out of their grates in the middle of a cold night.

Jack crept over to the desk where the guard was sleeping, his face down over one arm. On the desk were Polmear's papers and purse. Sadness washed over him. He had hated Polmear at first, and lately hated that he had come to like him. The man was an enemy to his religion, but he was good company. Silently, Jack vowed that he would avenge him if he could. Then he slowly picked up the purse and gripped it tight in his hand so that the coins would not shake. Unable to bear the strain any longer, Jack skipped lightly towards the door of the keep. On a coffer next to it were the guard's cloak and hat. He slipped into both and then opened the tower's main door, the hat pulled down low and the collar pulled up. He did not open the door fully, but slipped out the slightest crack, scared that any swift gust of cold air would waken his sleeping gaoler.

The tower stood on a hill, and Jack strode down the stone path, keeping his head down – just a guard carefully picking his way through the slush as he went about some urgent business. The first trial was a gatehouse, which stood at the bottom of the hill. He passed through without interruption. Thereafter lay an enormous courtyard, the centre of the ancient castle, and he looked around. Ahead, across the courtyard, was the main entrance. He did not have the nerve for it. Instead, he forced himself to walk slowly along a range of stables to his left. Horses whinnied, and he briefly considered stealing one and leaving money. He had not the nerve for that either. Instead, he went to the smaller, northwest gatehouse and passed under the stone.

'Who goes there?' called down a voice. Jack closed his eyes for a moment, his heart thundering, and peeped over his furred collar. A guard was standing on a flight of wooden steps, one hand upraised to the cold stone. He carried no torch, and Jack thanked God for the darkness.

''eadin' out,' he said. ''ad about enough o' t'cold in there. Too cold for t'bloody lice on those dogs.'

'Should try it up 'ere. Colder'n a night in bed wi' t'wife.'

Jack chuckled. 'Good e'en to ye, lad,' he grumbled.

'Good e'en, sir.'

He passed through the gatehouse and began walking faster, and then faster. He began half skidding through the slush, elated. It passed. He realised what he was now: a wanted man. A criminal on the run from the law. The officers of the north would be after him. The queen's men would be after him and might not believe what he told them.

And then, with a start, he realised that none of those things would happen.

Polmear was dead. That was sad, but there was something even sadder. Alive, the man had been important. Dead, he would be forgotten. When and if news reached Walsingham, he would shrug his shoulders, perhaps be irritated, and then find a new and unknown face to spy on the north. Intelligencers, he thought, were something like prostitutes. Worse, in fact. They sold their minds as well as their bodies to the state, to be used and then cast aside.

The justices and aldermen of York would send out no search parties. They would do nothing regarding Polmear's death until they had written instructions from either Walsingham in France or his superiors in London. They would certainly not advertise that they had lost the only man they suspected of being a murderer of a southern intelligencer. The whole network of watchers operated below the level of law and justice. Men true to English liberty would fear to tangle themselves in it.

It might be wishful thinking – it might even be fantastical – but Jack allowed himself to believe it. He was a free man with money in his pocket. As long as he stayed away from the city of York, he would remain so. Paris could only be a few weeks away by land and sea, once he had found his way south, or east, and proven he could work his passage. He would go to Walsingham and tell the man of Polmear's death, and he would then leave his service and find Amy. That was the safest thing to do. He would not risk London, and he would not try and get to the countess without letting the queen's secretary know of all that had passed. For one thing, he did not relish the idea of forcing his wife into a life in the shadows and on the run. For another, he knew that the diamond league was still at large, had threatened Paris, had threatened Amy, and might yet bring about a holy war that would drown Europe in blood.

Part Four: Following Suit

1

The salt wind blew over the new house, which stood over the forgotten ruins of the old. There was nothing left of the old place, no charred foundations or dead grass. Time and the unceasing industry of man had eliminated all, intent on burying the ugliness, the strangeness, the questions which no one cared to ask.

He wondered if the small dogs and cats, some of which he had strangled and some of which he had buried alive, still lay beneath the courtyard in the back.

Acre stood outside the house, blinking in the sunlight. It would be spring soon. The time of new life, supposedly. Already violet flowers were struggling out of the earth. The wind blew again, stronger, still cold but freshening. It was the same tempestuous one he had known in childhood. He closed his eyes fully and let the memories come.

He was thirteen and being dragged by the Scotch woman who had called herself his mother into the hall. She hurled him to the ground as though he were a weightless sack of animal bones. 'Unnatural bairn,' she had cried. Her English husband, glittering in his finery, had known what to do. Without asking the nature of his latest crime, he had drawn out a riding crop, pulled down the young Acre's breeches, and set to him with a vengeance. Still the woman screeched, cried, and sobbed. Acre had not cried – he never cried – and she called out again, 'unnatural!' The only fear that passed through him was that he might be locked again in the cupboard – the punishment to end all punishments – and left screaming, alone in the dark.

'The child is wrong-headed,' her husband agreed. 'A twisted and abominable thing, to do what he does.'

'It's enough I've had,' she shrieked. 'Enough o' these dead creatures. Enough o' this loon.'

'He is ours to care for, as God willed.'

'You say God,' she hissed, her voice low and deadly. 'You're meanin' thon bastard priest. I say we go to England and be quit of him.'

Acre's ears had pricked. 'Priest?'

'You're a foul changeling, boy! Left us by a priest, no creature of my body!'

'Silence, Sybilla! You forget your tongue!'

'Forget nothing. I've had enough o' it. We'll take the children and leave this … this wretch! We should never have stayed here – should have gone with the rest.'

Acre had not bothered listening to the couple's irritating chatter any further. Instead his little mind had begun turning on what they had said. A changeling, left by a priest. Not of the dreadful woman's body. He had carried the news to his siblings, who absorbed it with interest. He told them also that they might soon be carried away by the cold and unloving people who had called themselves mother and father.

That night, he had roused his siblings from their slumber and dragged them out of the house. In the kitchen, the fire had begun spreading from its wide grate and outwards, where it licked at thrown chairs and wooden crockery. The false parents, when the smoke rose to them, would go nowhere. He had barred their door from the outside.

Thereafter, the children, none above sixteen, had roamed wild. Weeks passed, and the neighbours would not help them, would not let them in. The most they could hope was to scavenge the odd crust from the street, or perhaps catch and cook a stray dog. It was hard living. They would not have survived long living thus, had not their saviour come.

Acre had always known there was something wrong about his relationship with the Scotch woman and her English man. It was not just that they were distant and cold, but that he did not look like them. He did not think like them. When they caught him killing things, they looked at him in horror, and tried to beat him out of himself – or to shut him up in the dark, where the really bad things lurked. His siblings, though, protected him when they could. There was kinship there, at least.

And then relief had come, in the form of a shimmering angel, the like of which none of the starving, lost children had ever seen. They were embraced. They were given the entire, horrible truth about the hideous conditions of their parentage. Tears flowed, from the angel at least. And they were promised things. Above all, they were assured of revenge on the cruel people that had separated them, and everything they stood for. Within that revenge, each was promised what most their heart desired: the restitution of a true, clean faith; wealth and comfort; and, of course, the chance to kill and hurt, provided it were done in pursuit of higher goals. The avenging angel did not judge, but gifted them money and their little diamond pins and set them on their way.

Thus, the diamond league had been born.

Acre shook the memories away. The old house was long gone. No one would know him here. Now Adam was gone, his path to true faith still unfulfilled. He would now have to tell the angel. It could only be done in person. Then he could find out where the plot stood. As it was, he had no idea; no messages had come to him since his brother had been murdered. Without instruction he was directionless. The ace, he thought, smiling to himself, could not be played without a hand.

He made to leave the sprawling harbour town. He had made slow progress from the north of England, unconsciously, he supposed, trying to delay the difficult moment. He knew that he lacked delicacy. It would be difficult news to give. Undoubtedly there would be tears. Possibly there would be recriminations. Still, it was his duty.

And, of course, there was the promise of Amy Cole. He had no idea if the woman still lived or if she was even now in the blank void with her husband. He did not allow that for that possibility. In his head, it had become clear and fixed that he would inflict on Jack Cole's wife the most hideous of brutalities. The only disappointment was that he could not force Mr Cole himself to watch each one.

2

As the winter weather turned milder and wetter, and the band of ladies charged with turning the palaces by the Seine into jewelled nests increased, Amy had struck upon a plan. She did not bother attempting to meet with Walsingham to explain or test it. There was little time. The king's own royal entry was to take place the following day. In the streets, artists were at work painting canvases and draping them over elaborately moulded and sculpted wooden frames, and the whole city had begun to throng with people eager for spectacle.

There had been no further attempts on her life – or at least none successful enough even to be apparent. Day after day she had busied herself in needlework, sewing endless white silks to be used as banners and pennants. She had even had the chance to embroider some little samplers, which were to be distributed to souvenir-hunters as gifts, though she suspected that the crowds would much prefer the free bread and wine with which the royal family hoped to win their cheers. At various points – each night, in fact, as she slept with one eye open – she had considered how easy it would be to simply leave after the royal entry. She could hold Walsingham to his word to release her and Jack, and Catherine to her claim that she would be ejected from the palace once the royal court made its entry. Yet, as attractive as it sounded during her sleepless nights, she realised that she would not feel at ease as long the diamond plotters were at large. Even if she regained Jack, they would be more at the mercy of madmen with grudges in the slums or streets of Europe than ever she was in the cloistered, perfumed finery of a French palace. And even in that palace two attempts had been made. Doubtless, if she left after the royal entry, she would get but two steps towards finding Jack before a knife was thrust into the small of her back.

As much as she hated it, she would have to lead her assassin into the light of exposure. The festivities of the following day would be the perfect opportunity for both monster and unmasker.

After eating – which now she did only direct from the palace kitchens, which gave the added fillip of food that was still hot – she began walking purposefully back to the royal apartments. She had grown to hate them, to hate the white and the cream and the gold hangings; to hate the women, ladies and servants. It was they who had made her afraid to eat. Any one of them might be trying to get at her – or perhaps all of them, engaged in some conspiracy. The mind was a maze you could get lost in, and the constant thinking, the overthinking, only led her deeper and deeper into it.

She had even grown to hate the guards, and as she passed two of them stationed in the service corridor, she had to force a smile. As she entered the royal suite, she paused at the half-open door to the ladies' bedchamber. Inside, she could hear the painted Vittoria de Brieux holding court.

'… says the attempt was on her life when it was my dear girl who was murdered.'

'You should not speak of that,' grumbled the cracked voice of Madame Gondi. 'You have been warned not to speak of that affair. Cease prating of the foolish English mare. Damned English.' But a fit of excited, burbling chatter overtook her as the other assembled ladies begged for more.

'I mean,' said Brieux, 'if one wanted that little wench dead in the eyes of French society, one would advise her only to wear one of those ancient, drab gowns.' Laughter. Amy's hands balled into fists. Bitch! Where was Kat, the little traitor, who should be defending her? She was on the point of bursting in, when she remembered her plan. She stood, waiting, until the talk turned again to the next day's events.

'The duke of Guise won't come, will he? He hates this peace.'

'He will come,' said Gondi. 'He has been commanded to come.'

'But to break bread with the heretics! A Guise! What a sight! He would prefer breaking heads. The duke favours violent courses, I hear.'

'And the little maid of Bourbon –'

'They say she's a heretic!'

'She is only twelve!'

'And her father is nothing, a man of no religion.'

Amy had heard enough. She threw the door open. Madame de Brieux turned her glazed face towards her, and Madame Gondi her withered one. Amy could sense some of the other ladies nudging one another and felt the eyes on her dress. It was the same the world over, she thought, from palace to provincial town. People formed vicious little cliques, and she was always an outsider. Well, it was better to be an outsider amongst a coven of society ladies than to feel so amongst one's own people.

'Ah, our friend now of longstanding, ladies,' said Brieux. 'You have quite missed our conversation. Perhaps ladies do not converse so in England.'

'No. Not outside henhouses,' said Amy. A little ripple went through the group. 'Or kennels.' Madame Gondi, appropriately enough, barked laughter. 'The theme of tomorrow's events, you know, is peace. In that spirit, what would you all say to us sitting at rest today and playing a game of cards?' Amy put her hand to her throat and laughed too.

No one was willing to play, and the other ladies left her to sit by herself. She did not mind. She listened again to their chatter which became more muted as the cries of the guards signalled Queen Catherine's arrival. The old woman sailed past them all and into her own room without a glance, speaking all the time in rapid French to the ladies of her bedchamber. In her wake, Kat returned, a bundle of sheets in her arms.

'Where have you been?'

'Washing sheets.' The girl reddened.

'A fine time at it.' Amy was aware that she had taken to the role of mistress a little too well. More gently, she took Kat by the hand and lowered her voice. 'Listen. If I were to tell you something, could you have this palace's servants knowing of it?' When she began to protest, Amy cut her off. 'I know what servants' gossip is, girl. God, but I do know. I tell you and you tell another, who tells another, and soon they all know. And their mistresses will then find out tonight, when the time comes for them to be undressed and put to bed.'

'What is it?' asked Kat, with only a trace of reluctance. Amy smiled, and told her.

***

Jack munched on an end of bread as he surveyed the house on Saint-Marceau. He had missed French bread. He had even missed French crowds, and those filling the city were arrayed in all manner of finery in anticipation of the coming of the king. Huge signs reading 'CONCORDIA' hung across streets. Lodging houses were full, with visitors even ejecting vagabonds from the gutters to claim their spots. On an ordinary day, Paris, with its network of nearly three-hundred streets, was a rabbit warren which dwarfed York and made even London look small. On extraordinary days, it was a seething, pregnant beast.

He spent longer than he had intended watching the house which had been pointed out to him as that belonging to 'Monsieur L'Anglaise'. It seemed a pretty poor place for Walsingham compared to his home in Aldgate. It seemed a poorer place to arrive at after weeks of hard living.

Since fleering York, Jack had taken a circuitous route through England, avoiding major towns and cities on the off chance that there was a hue and cry out for him. He had spent as little as possible, on a horse at first, which he thereafter traded, usually downwards, as he went. Food for himself and his mount had to be worked for: a day of labour here, a day of animal-tending there. He had skirted London and, when he reached Portsmouth, had to work over a week until a ship sailing for Dieppe would give him passage. Then he was free to make his way directly to Paris – a journey of over a hundred miles, without benefit of fresh horses. Yet it had all seemed fine – his only choice. It was moving forward. It was returning to Amy.

Only now did it seem like folly.

Because he had avoided news, he had no idea of what had reached London and gone ahead of him. None on the smooth journey across the Channel had heard of anyone carrying news to Walsingham – or, if they did, he could not get it from them by subtle and indirect means. Yet it was inconceivable that the queen's man did not know of the death of Edward Polmear. And so Jack continued to stand before the man's house, as bustling, singing, cheering people barged past him in all directions, unsure if he was walking into interrogation or accusation.

When the sun was high, he plucked up his courage and knocked on the door. A male servant answered, a little too quickly. The look of surprise told Jack the fellow had been opening the door anyway, and almost immediately a thin man stepped out. It was not Walsingham. 'Black, black, everything black, no colour,' the man grumbled in French. He darted a look at Jack. 'Nothing but black!' he said, and then stomped off.

'The tailor,' sniffed the English steward. 'Can I help you, lad?'

'I'm here to see Mr Francis Walsingham. Was told this is his house.'

'Is he expecting you?'

'No. Probably not. My name is Jack Cole, tell him. Please. I've come from England.'

'Wait here.' The door closed. Jack looked nervously behind him. A reprieve, he thought. A final chance to lose his nerve and flee. 'He is at home to you.' Jack jumped. He had not heard the door open again.

He was shown through the house and upstairs to a small office, dominated by a hand-drawn map of Paris which hung on a wall. Or, at least, that would have dominated it, had not Francis Walsingham been seated at the table, his head low and wolfish, his jaw clenched.

'I saw your tailor, sir,' said Jack, grinning, not knowing what pulse of nervousness drew it from him.

'Jack Cole. Last sent to the north. Now standing before me hundreds of miles from that place.'

'Yes, sir. I beg your pardon, sir. I thought I must make report to you of … Mr Polmear is dead.'

'I heard this. Murdered in his bed.'

'My bed, sir.'

'Do not interrupt me.' Jack bowed his head, twisting his cap in his hands. 'I confess I half-expected you, Cole. I daresay I hoped you might come to me. Yes, you see, when news reached

177

me that Mr Polmear was slain, and nothing of you, rational thought lay before me several possibilities. One: you slew him and ran, having betrayed us to the papists.'

'No, sir, I–'

'What did I just say, boy? Two: you had also been slain and lay dead somewhere. Three: you were on your way with news of what madness has overtaken that country and, I might dare hope, that you have stopped it.'

'Three, sir – it's three. Mostly three.'

'Then I am glad. Not for your sake, nor even Polmear's, but for that I should not like to have to explain either your death or your guilt. What happened up there? As you recall it, boy, I wish to know everything.'

Slowly, methodically, Jack told Walsingham everything, stopping only when the secretary halted him and asked for clarification. When he had finished, Walsingham sat back, looking, strangely, relieved. He wiped a hand across his mouth, making the black moustache crinkle. Then focus returned to his eyes. 'You used your own name in the north?'

'Yes, sir.'

'And mine?'

'Yes.'

'Then you are less than useless there now. Lacking even Polmear's skills of subtlety and force. All you have for me is what little sits between your ears. You say there were two other priests who were with this killer-papist. I have written word from the late Mr Polmear also that three seminary priests were plying their trade in York. Where are the other two?'

'Slain, I believe, sir.' To bury the lie, Jack began to pile on truths. 'He would have killed me too. As I say, he had a man killing for him. Tried to kill me and when he failed, the priest tried. When I … when he died, sir, the one called Adam, the first fellow returned. He killed Mr Polmear – it had to be him. But none would listen.'

'So you fled her Majesty's justice. No, no, I am glad of it. It is bad enough to have lost one man to the north. The expense of finding two fresh ones is beyond me, I regret.' Jack grimaced at the coldness with which he spoke of Polmear, but he was not surprised by it. 'May I see this diamond pin?' Jack produced it and handed it across the desk. Walsingham held it up close to one eye.

'You have noted the marking here?'

'No, sir.'

'It is a hallmark. A mark of the jeweller who made it. French.'

'I used it to open the lock – I might have crushed it a little.'

'It is a mark, you fool. I am not blind. These have been used by the guilds in France and England for hundreds of years. Since the days of the first Edward and Philip the Fair.'

'Does it say who it belongs to? Their name?'

'No. It tells us only which smith or smiths worked the gold. A master jeweller might know – might recall the fellow who bought the thing.'

'You're sure, sir, that it's French?'

'Fairly sure. I need no more. You will go to the guilds on the morrow and discover what you can of it.' Walsingham held the pin out and dropped it into Jack's palm. He returned it to his pocket.

'Tomorrow is the king's return, I heard. It's all that's spoken of out there.'

'Yes,' said Walsingham, his face darkening. 'This wretched royal entry. They say artists are busy at work, turning this whole city into a blasted carnival.' He drummed his fingers on the desk.

'I was hoping, sir … that you might have news out of the Low Countries. Of my wife.' Walsingham shifted in his seat – a little uncomfortably, Jack thought. His heart turned over in fear. 'She's well, isn't she? I mean, nothing's happened to her, has it, nothing bad?'

'Your wife is well. Or was, the last I heard. She … she left the traitor-countess. Not on my orders, I might add, but acting according to her fallen mistress's mad schemes. In truth, Cole, she is here. In Paris.'

'What?' Jack nearly launched himself onto the desk, held back only by Walsingham's hard face. 'Where? There's so many people – I went to where we used to lodge last year first, but there was no room. No Amy. Where, sir, please?'

'Becalm yourself, you foolish boy. Your wife, I believe, is still resident in this new palace hard by the Louvre. The Tuileries. She has been taken in as a lady, no less, by the dowager queen – the king's mother.'

'A lady?'

'Yes. A disgusting ploy. A shameless thing.' He tutted. 'Women's wit and wiles.'

'Can I go there? Can you get me in to her?'

'Indeed I cannot. I am Queen Elizabeth's ambassador in this realm, not a pander to a pair of carnally-minded servants.'

'But ... but I need to see her. It's been ...' Jack began counting on his fingers, and found he was not even sure. 'So long. She'll be worried – must have been worried. Have you seen her? Spoken to her?'

'I have. Be assured, I told her of your continued good health.'

'Why didn't you tell me, you or Polmear?'

'Be careful, Cole.' Walsingham's voice had taken on a silky air of menace. He softened it. 'She is well. Living better than you have been, I should warrant. In fact, it might interest you to know that she has been engaged in discovering the diamond plotter in France. The fellow to your dead priest.' Jack only gaped. 'So you see, both of you have been making use of the knowledge you gained at the traitor-countess's table.'

'But these folk are dangerous, these diamonds.'

'Your wife has proven herself a hard lady. Determined.'

'Has she found anything? The plotter about the French queen?'

'She has not discovered a name, to the best of my knowledge. I did share with her that which I had uncovered.'

'What's that, sir?'

'Only what you have found,' shrugged Walsingham. 'A small group of plotters. Two, I see, were in England. One is now dead. That leaves three. If they travel in pairs, it might be that two are at the French court.'

'Hoping to bring the wars of religion again? As I thought?'

Walsingham's mouth worked, as though he was tasting the idea. 'Perhaps. A grudge against their own faith was my thought. God knows we of the true faith have suffered angry sects enough. It is fair that the papists have their share. Of course, when those of our faith disagree it is by reasoned debate and logic. When these monsters do it, it is by blood and murder.' Almost as an afterthought to his rant, he added, 'Your wife helped me some in discovering the plot.'

'Please, Mr Walsingham – when can I see her?'

Walsingham stood for the first time. It seemed to cause him a little pain. Jack wondered what age he was; he guessed past forty, but by how much it was hard to say. He had the manner of an old man, but his hair remained mostly black, and the lines on his face, though deep, were few. He did not answer directly. Instead, he said, 'where are you living in this city? You said your former house was full.'

'Nowhere, sir. I mean, I thought to sleep under a hedge or in a ditch.'

'Well … you have slept under my roof before. You shall do so again. You are an Englishman in France after all. And I own I should not like you to do anything foolish this night. Lodge here, if you will, and you might accompany me to this blasted royal entry tomorrow. As my serving man, no more. You will keep your mouth shut and your manner civil until and unless I say otherwise. I shall find some means of getting your wife to you. In return, you will do my business. When you are free, you will discover the history of that pin.'

Jack was barely listening. Over Walsingham's last words, he had begun gushing thanks. He was eager only for the day to be over and for the royal entry to be upon him. No feelings of foreboding troubled him.

3

Though not part of Queen Catherine's elaborate ceremonial lever, or waking ceremony, Amy found herself able to sneak into the bedchamber when the hot towels were being tested for poison. If Catherine noticed her unwarranted and unorthodox presence, she did not make an issue of it. Probably the day ahead was too important. The queen-mother and her entire household must be present and waiting when the king arrived. All must be a picture of harmony, to be carried over the course of the whole day, before the night's feasting could begin.

When the queen-mother was ready – a process which took several hours, beginning before dawn – she finally acknowledged Amy's presence, waving away some scandalised ladies and beckoning her forward. Amy looked at the other women – a little apprehensively. 'Leave us. We are guarded.' When they had gone, she said 'You have broken with all good sense, girl, to come into my presence thus.'

'I'm sorry, your Majesty. I thought I must bring you news. Others might not.'

'You presume much. And against my honour. What news?'

Amy, on her knees, looked up into Catherine's face. Her eyes rested on the receding chin, half-buried in a gold-edged, ruffled collar. 'There is a rumour going around amongst the ladies, your Majesty.'

'This is no news.' The older woman's voice was accompanied by the rasp of skin on lace.

'About … the duke of Guise.' When Catherine did not respond, Amy dared a glance up towards the old woman's face. The pale eyes were drilling into her. She presumed that was her signal to continue. The words tumbled. 'There is a vicious and cruel rumour. False, of course, I've no doubt. That the duke of Guise is planning to force himself upon a Protestant lady. A guest of the king. An attendant of my lady of Bourbon.'

'My grandson's betrothed?'

'I believe so, your Majesty.'

'What nonsense news is this you bring me?' Amy felt she had scored a victory; the old woman sounded genuinely bewildered.

'It is nonsense indeed. Yet ...' She swallowed and took the plunge. 'Yet the news might get around the court. And on such a day.'

'If it does, I shall find the speakers and have their tongues.'

'But,' said Amy, fear threatening to give the game away, 'it might be to your advantage, your Majesty. And the king's. And the new queen's, too.' Silence again. Amy went on before Catherine could speak. 'The diamond plotters – their goal is to bring the church into infamy. To ... um ... besmirch it. This rumour – it is so dangerous – it will bring out our plotter. They will seek to draw attention to the duke's ... to the duke. Whoever follows him – brings men who might be angry at such a ...'

'A liaison?'

'Yes. A liaison. Well, whoever does that – they are exposed.'

'But this is foolishness. It is a rumour. There is no liaison.'

'No, your Majesty. I'm sure there isn't. Yet you could order the duke to go somewhere. Tell him ahead of the feast tonight that at a certain time, he must leave the palace and go to ... well, I think the rumour is to our own ladies' bedchamber yonder. But others might be here to protect his honour already. And then, when our plotter comes, with a group of aggrieved Protestants hoping to find a liaison, they will find ...'

'They will find the duke and a number of guards reading the bible. A picture of innocence and peace. At worse a friendly jest on our Protestant friends.' said Catherine. 'I will think on it, girl.' She waved a dismissive hand.

Amy grinned before using her hands to get up off her knees. Before she could leave, Catherine spoke again 'You have a great knowledge of these plotters. One might almost think you had been putting your pretty little head together with some man of strategy and cunning. I warn you, if this is some English plot to embarrass the duke ... I warn you.'

***

Rather than lapsing into grinning, incessant, unwanted chatter, Jack found that the morning of the royal festival made him pensive. It had been half a year since Amy had seen him, and in that time he had grown thin. His hair, which always fell in an untidy fringe, was wild, and a sandy beard stuck out like a duck's tail. Thankfully, Walsingham insisted that his barber attend to him, to prevent embarrassment to the English contingent.

When both men were suitably attired, the master in an austere black suit and the servant in a similar one of lower quality, they set off from the house. Before leaving, Walsingham had warned him not to make a scene. Amy would likely be sitting with the dowager queen's ladies at a quite separate stand from that on which the king's honoured foreign guests were invited to sit.

The streets and rooftops of the city were packed. People stood gathered in clumps: most were in bright colours, but others were in black. The Huguenots were present, and they even waved white banners in the air, but it was evident from the clusters of black that they were not mingling with the Catholics.

The king was scheduled to enter the city through the Porte Sainte-Denis, over which had been erected an arch topped on either side by two enormous, painted stucco figures: the Trojan Francus, the legendary founder of the nation, and Pharamond, the greatest of the early kings. People were fighting around the giant statues – men and women eager to be the amongst the first to welcome the young king to his capital. Further along the route was another painted decoration, this one representing Gallia. It showed a figure vaguely in the shape of Queen Catherine, holding a map of the country. It was carved with hieroglyphics celebrating the queen-mother's efforts at securing peace. It was to the guarded wooden stands erected hard by this edifice that the dowager and her ladies were to sit. Walsingham led Jack to it.

'She will be brought here. You may have a moment's conversation with her, no more. My presence is required at my own seat.' As he was talking, a singing man rolled between them, burping to punctuate each verse of his bawdy song as he went on his way. Walsingham tilted his head back, disgust

184

carved on his face, and brushed his shining black doublet where the fellow's arm had touched it. 'Fripperies,' he mumbled. Then he shielded his eyes from the sun and looked upwards. 'No lessons learnt from the death of the Scottish regent last year. Any rooftop might house a madman, and yet see how the houses cry out under the weight of men.'

Jack said nothing. He took no interest in the torrents of people moving to and fro about the streets, jostling for the best position. As time passed, conversation would have been pointless in any case. The chorus of shouting and singing, the music coming from dozens of street entertainers, and the shouts of aldermen and soldiers attempting to keep order rose to a deafening cacophony.

Suddenly, the crowd quietened, and people fell to their knees. A small troupe of hautboys appeared from the direction of Les Innocents, their instruments tooting. They were leading the queen-mother and her ladies, some guards in glittering metal at their sides.

Jack's mouth ran dry. Walsingham took him by the arm, hard, and pulled him into the shadows. He did not protest, but he craned his neck.

At the back of the little procession was Amy.

Jack fought free of Walsingham's grasp, but he only succeeded in tightening it. 'I warned you,' hissed the secretary, close to his ear. The ladies at the front were helping Queen Catherine ascend the stand, and the junior, less important ladies fell into a line behind them. Amy stood at the back, a little apart from the women who were not her peers. Her arms were folded, and she had a curious little look of determination on her face. When the queue of women had made progress, Walsingham jerked Jack out of the shadows and moved towards them. A guard stepped in front of them. The secretary lifted his chin and said something which seemed to cause the nervous young blonde man to step aside. 'Mrs Cole,' he said, his voice tight.

'Hm?' Amy began to turn.

'Amy!' cried Jack.

She stood for a second, looking at him, disbelieving, he thought. And then she was on him.

'You're hurting me,' he croaked. 'You're choking me.'

'You're alive!' She squealed. 'I knew it – by God's truth I knew it.'

'You look like a lady, a real lady.'

She laughed, before throwing a look of thanks to Walsingham. Jack noticed he did not return warmth. Instead, he said, 'I have fulfilled my pledge to you. Your husband is alive. You must be satisfied with that. Now go, girl, before the queen hears of this … this scene.'

Jack kissed her forehead, and realised she was not going to let go. Gently, he had to pry her arms from around his neck. 'But wait! Have you been hurt? You've lost weight – are you well?'

'I've missed you, Amy. But I'm well. And soon all this will be over.'

'Soon,' she echoed. 'I'm not going up there. To hell with it.'

'You are going up there, girl,' said Walsingham. 'Or I will arrest your husband. It might interest you to know that he has uncovered one of the diamond plotters. A disgusting papist living in York. You have work yet. Get on and get up there, in the name of her Majesty of England.' Jack turned to him, and felt Amy stiffen beside him. He realised that she was on the brink of saying things, shouting them probably, that could not be undone.

'I have something to do here,' he promised. 'So that we're free forever.' He leant over and kissed her again. 'You have to get through today.'

She opened her mouth as if to object and then closed it. Tears had sprung in the corner of her eyes. 'Today. And tonight.' She turned her attention to Walsingham. 'Then our business is over, you said? Then he's mine again, not yours.' The secretary did not respond. Jack sensed that the old man had a grudging respect for his wife. But he suspected also that Walsingham was not planning on allowing them to escape his charge.

'Er … I think it's you who're mine, Amy,' Jack grinned. 'Again.' It was her possessive, protective attitude towards him, he knew, that routinely got her called a shrew and a termagant. Never having had anyone else who cared about him, he did not mind it.

The noise of the crowd, which had resumed, changed in pitch. From deep within it, from down towards the Porte Sainte-Denis, cheers had begun. 'Vive le roi' rose from hundreds, thousands, of throats.

'It begins,' said Walsingham, in the tone of a physician speculating on a particularly unpleasant patient's bowel movements. He pulled Jack away, leaving Amy standing by the base of the wooden staircase, her hand at her mouth.

Quickly, Walsingham led Jack through the crowd, resolutely trying to shout his authority that the way be made for England's ambassador. Eventually, he reached another stand somewhere near the middle of the parade route. Jack, who had kept his head turned to watch Amy until she and the queen-mother's party were swallowed by the colourful multitude, looked up. Seated amongst the orderly rows were a number of distinguished gentlemen, some conversing and others with their backs ostentatiously turned to one another. 'My fellow ambassadors,' said Walsingham with distaste.

'Do I go up there with you?'

'Certainly not.'

'I'll wait here then.' Jack kicked at the ground.

'You shall not. I see no reason why a foolish festival should prevent your business. It shall rather aid it, I think.' When Jack only stared dumbly, he sighed. When he spoke, he had shifted from physician to schoolmaster. 'The goldsmiths and silversmiths will have their own place by the road – their own welcoming offer to his Majesty. Seek them out. When you have finished, return to my house and do not leave it. I shall try and escape the supper that is to follow as soon as I might.' Discreetly, he produced a small purse and handed it over. 'Spend as sparingly as you can to loosen their tongues.' Jack nodded and Walsingham turned and, heavily, began trudging up to take his place. When he had gained it, he stood stiff and uncomfortable, a raven in an unfamiliar and uncomfortable nest.

Jack lost no time. Every step forward was a step closer to Amy – a step closer to regaining his life. He pressed himself into the crowd packed against the houses, the roads themselves having been cleared. Something hit his hat, running off the edges in a liquid rush. Bloody.

With a start, he realised what it was. Houses overhung the streets, and people, he knew, were using the tiled roofs as viewing platforms. Someone had spilled a jug of wine from a window or a roof above and it had come raining down. Others were gaily urinating over the edge onto the crowd below. He chanced a look up. The fellow who had spilled the wine held up the jug in salute. Jack hurried on.

He did not get far. The closely packed people prevented it. Suddenly the screeching cheers went up around him, as though explosions were going off in the crowd. The king was riding by. Dressed entirely in white and riding a white stallion, he had his right hand raised as he turned in either direction. A large white ruff framed his face, which was forgettable: even the wispy brown beard could not hide the receding chin. Guards in golden armour flanked him. Jack ignored the king and hurried on, pleading from those that would listen to him for news of the goldsmiths' stall.

***

At first, Acre believed he was imagining things. He had pushed his way through the Parisian crowds with the skill of the violent. As he had approached the queen-mother's stand, he saw Jack Cole, alive, and well, and embracing a little whore in a cream-coloured gown who must have been the wife. He stared until they parted, never blinking. It was certainly Cole, albeit he was a little better groomed than before.

Initial anger turned into laughter, and Acre swiped a mug of ale from an old man, shoving him back into the crowd. Mr and Mrs Cole were somehow both alive. The fellow he had slain in the lodging house in York was some other waste of skin.

When Cole went hurrying off with a crow-like man, Acre followed. Through the people they had went, pursuer and pursued. Then his quarry had been abandoned at another stall and run off again into the seething masses. Again, Acre followed.

He had punished himself severely for letting passion overcome him in killing the creature he thought was Cole. That act had necessitated his flight to France and, as recompense, he had had a brief glimpse of his avenging angel in the city; he had found that Mrs Cole was alive; and, miracle of miracles, he had found that the man himself, the man who had killed his brother, still breathed.

The surprise was so sudden that he needed time to formulate a plan. The thousands of people on the street were both a blessing and a curse. He could easily stab the man in the back, leaving him to bleed and be trampled, probably only to be found the next morning by the poor folk looking for lost things. The victim of a robbery gone wrong is how it would appear. Probably he would be one of many.

Yet many people meant many pairs of eyes. It meant many soldiers and guards on the lookout for anything that might harm the important people gathered. It only took one curious onlooker to make a fuss and he would find it difficult to escape through the people. As a suspected thief, he might be torn to pieces.

Acre shook his head, his mind working rapidly. None of that mattered. He did not want to stab Jack Cole in a Parisian street. Now that the wretch was alive again, he wanted him to suffer, slowly, surely, and for as long as possible. He would take care of the wife, too, where the avenging angel had shown mercy. If possible, he would get them together, use one to draw the other. And when both were in his power, they would suffer together.

4

Jack stood back as the goldsmiths passed around the pin. 'Fine work, fine work,' was the assessment.

'Of course it's fine,' snapped a crotchety, elderly one. 'It's mine.' With surprising vigour, he grabbed it from the man who had been inspecting it. 'Away,' he cried. 'Let me see it.'

Jack had found the goldsmiths standing at a table set up at the roadside, above which were hung the usual painted signs and the insignia of their guild. A painted effigy of Philip the Fair stood on the table – a reminder, thought Jack, of the link between the French monarchy and the gold-workers.

'Please,' said Jack. 'Who bought it?' He had not released the purse from his grip, and his knuckles were still white around it.

'I can't tell you that.' The old man looked around at his fellows, and they all began nodding agreement and making supportive gestures.

'It's … I need to know – I must know.' He lifted the purse. Rather than elicit greed, it seemed to fan the flames of the goldsmiths' indignation.

'Keep your money, my Huguenot friend,' said the old man. Jack's eyebrow rose, and then he looked down at his black suit, and lowered it. 'I'll share no secrets with you, peace or no peace.'

'But … it concerns the safety of the king,' tried Jack.

'Yes, yes. I'm sure it does.' The old man held it back out to him.

Jack tried to think of a more detailed lie. Then he sighed. He put a hand to his forehead. 'The truth,' he began.

'Will do as well as a lie,' observed the goldsmith.

'The truth's that I need to discover who bought this. My wife won't be safe till I do. Nor will I. A man tried to kill me who owned this pin. Don't know where he went. He will still be after us.'

The old man looked at him with sharp green eyes, and then gave out a low whistle. 'Quite a story, son.' Jack leant forward, daring to hope. 'In all my years of people telling tales to get secrets from my lips, that is the biggest pile of horse shit yet.' As the goldsmith shook his head in wonderment, Jack's face crumpled. Then the fellow held up a veiny hand. 'I'm an old man. I don't know how much shit I'll see shovelled before God takes me. I think you've earned a little something by that nonsense.

'I'll tell you only this. It was a great person bought these pins. Three of them. Three pins for three diamonds. Tokens of love and honour. To be given as gifts. Now away, boy, and take your mad tongue elsewhere. Use your purse on some fine wine. Drink the king's health.'

Jack grinned his thanks and wandered away from the stall. Three pins, three agents, each working for a master. One was dead, one's face was known – familiar, but unfamiliar – and that left one remaining diamond plotter and the mastermind of it all. A great person, he thought. In Paris, that could mean anyone with money and position. Perhaps Walsingham knew who was great in Paris that might wish to see the wars of religion restarted, and that might have three willing agents to set to work. A chill ran through him. He turned on the spot. The crowds had thinned a little, some chasing after the king and his party, but the majority had remained to drink and make merry. If a spark of violence lit them, the scenes would be unimaginable. The joyful, drunken cries and jubilant singing would turn to screams of pain and fear.

Someone was watching him.

Jack recognised immediately that one figure was not in step with the rest of the crowd. It was a man. The fellow began stalking towards him. The gait was unmistakable, slow, and deliberate. Wolf-like, he thought. It was the man from York.

Without hesitating, he slipped between a couple, apologising as he went. He let their bodies mask him. Then he slipped along the street and into the first open door he came to. It was a house, the front of which operated as a shop. A middle-aged woman standing over a simmering pot looked up at him without surprise. 'It's not ready yet, my friend. I'll pass it out when it is.'

He skipped towards her and alarm changed her face. Before she could cry out, he kissed her. It shut her up. Rather than screaming, she laughed. 'You drunken fool,' she cried. 'I'll tell my husband. He'll force you to take me off with you.'

'You do that,' he said. 'I'm going to throw coins from the roof – largesse from the king!' He bounded away from her and up a staircase. He passed the second floor and went up further, where a window opened out onto the roof. Today, rather than having washing laid out on it, it bore what must be the woman's husband – a corpulent man, lying with a cap pulled over his face to shield him from the sun. He began to rise, slowly at first, and then jerked up when the woman downstairs began screaming. Jack took off, balancing himself on the red tiles. His pursuer must have found the house. 'Protect your wife, man,' he cried over his shoulder. 'A thief and a murderer is abroad!'

Jack began moving amongst the tiles. His boot slipped. He righted it. His arms went out for balance.

A sea of red stood before him, stretching out and interrupted only by those who remained standing up on the roofs to finish their drinks and enjoy the comparative peace. He turned and saw his pursuer's head emerging from the window. Jack's eyes locked with his, and there again was that strange feeling of familiarity in the killer's thin features. The man clambered out and stood where the fat man had been resting. To Jack's delight, the homeowner and his wife stuck their heads through, and began hurling abuse and throwing chunks of bread. The killer stumbled at the surprise but did not turn. Instead, he continued his pursuit.

Jack moved. Along the roof, careful of the gutter, he realised that he was passing over several attached houses and shops. He could see out over the crowds of people. Hundreds of hats moved about. A false step and he would hurtle towards them, breaking his neck. Then he realised that the he would shortly run out of roof. A narrow side street bisected the main road along which the royal party had travelled. He would have to leap it.

He allowed only a second to hesitance. Only a few steps of run-up were possible. Trying not to think, Jack leapt, his arms cartwheeling as he sailed over the street. A collective gasp went up from the people below. With a graceless crunch, he landed in a heap on the roof opposite and immediately began sliding. His fingers grasped at the tiles and he managed to grip them before he went sailing over the edge. Slowly, laboriously, he managed to get his right leg up, hooking his foot around the edge of a tile. He dared not turn around to see what was happening as he struggled to his feet.

The number of people on this section of roofing was thicker. He saw why. Someone had gotten several barrels of wine up, and a girl was doling out mugs of it to those who had remained topside after the king had passed. Jack grasped at the purse he had tied to his belt and jerked it free. 'I'll take one,' he cried, shoving it in the surprised girl's face. 'I'll take a barrel.' He pushed the purse into her hand and turned.

Polmear's killer was tensing to make the leap over the alley. As he left the first roof, Jack pushed the barrel of wine, still half-full, over the tiles behind him. It sloshed, and a chorus of aggrieved cries sounded behind him. From the ground, too, came shouts of rage from those who had suffered a sudden and vinous rainstorm. He ignored them. The shift in noise unbalanced his pursuer, and the sudden soaking of the tiles wrecked his landing. The man slid, cursing, from the edge of the roof. Jack watched as his head, and then his arms, and then hands disappeared.

And then he began running again.

***

Amy waited in the ladies' bedchamber, alone for the first time that day. She paced, her mind at war with itself. The sight of Jack – the knowledge that he was safe – had lightened her heart and her mood. If she had known it before, she would not have put such a reckless plan in train. It was the operation of that plan that stayed her happiness.

After the royal entry, a banquet was to take place at the Louvre. The grand palace was only a short walk past the gardens to the queen's house at the Tuileries. Before Amy had come to the ladies' bedchamber, Catherine had told her that the duke of Guise would arrive before eight o'clock. That, the rumour went, was the time at which he would sneak his innocent young Protestant conquest into the Tuileries and ravish her.

Of course, nothing might happen. Other people, Amy mused, panic building, were unpredictable. They had a knack for being stupid when you wished them to be clever, and clever when you required them to be stupid. She felt sweat run down her back. She put her fists to it and cracked it.

Bells rang out.

But then, bells had been ringing on and off all day, signifying nothing but celebration. Amy made to sit down, wishing for a clock, or a watch, or at the least a reliable church bell, when the door opened.

The duke of Guise entered the room, flanked by guards. He gave her an angry, suspicious look, before his mask of charm fell into place. She gulped. The greatest risk to her plan was that she had no way of telling how much the man knew about the rumour she had started, or about anything that was going on. Catherine had not deigned to tell her anything beyond the fact that he would arrive at the ladies' room before eight – and that Amy had best put the time until then to good use packing her things. She had done so, not needing Kat, whom she had released to enjoy the day of festivities. It had, after all, been her work once, and soon might be again.

'My dear English lady,' said Guise. 'This is all some game? I am a married man, as beautiful as you are.'

'Stay awhile, your Grace.'

'I can do nothing else. The king's mother has commanded it. After she has commanded that I spend the day and evening dancing with the Protestant ladies.' A bitter edge overtook him. 'And the last lady – the last lady ran from the room before the moment I was to leave. What is this?'

'I … I think there has been a grave injustice done your Grace.'

'Oh?'

'A foul plotter has been using you to try and attack the faith.'

'What? What plot?' Guise looked more angry than confused. 'Is this why the old queen had these men escort me? I – am I to be arrested, huh?' He put a hand on his hip, indignant.

Before Amy could think of a reasonable response, the door flew open. Into the room stepped a number of men she did not recognise. Each one of them was wearing black, and each had a short dagger drawn. They looked around the room – first at Guise, and then at Amy, and then at the guards. Not seeing what they expected, they put away their weapons and turned, grabbing at someone just outside Amy's line of vision.

When they had hold of the woman, they threw her into the room, where she went down on her knees. 'This? This is your great ravisher?' shouted the apparent leader of the Protestant gentlemen. 'What fool's errand have you brought us on, woman?'

'A foolish prank,' said a voice from the doorway. Catherine had arrived, ladies on either side of her. Everyone in the room joined Vittoria de Brieux in getting to their knees. 'And a cruel one. Pray, good friends, return to my son.' Walking on their knees, their faces crimson, the Protestants fled the room, leaving the queen-mother and her ladies, the duke and his guards, Amy, and Madame de Brieux. Looking down at the latter, Catherine said, 'those are fine diamonds you have chosen to wear tonight, my lady.'

5

'I have no knowledge of this woman,' said Guise. 'Nor of any strange thing here.'

'Of course not. Merely a small prank, as I said.'

'I may go, your Majesty?'

'You may.'

The duke of Guise moved to the door and put his hand on the handle. 'That creature there,' he said, inclining his head towards Brieux, 'she has been a constant pain to me. Ever trying to move me to violent courses, despite your policy of peace. Seeking privy talks with me whilst her slave girl entertained my men. I did not pursue them. I broke with her some time ago.'

'Thank you,' said Catherine. Guise stuck out his chin and swaggered from the room. 'Let us hope you did not,' she added when he had gone. The guards did not follow him. 'You may stand,' she smiled. 'All but you, my lady. So. It is you have been intriguing here.'

'She is the queen of diamonds, your Majesty,' Amy said, the words bursting out. 'I told you it was one within the household when it was just a small number. I told you, your Majesty.'

'Be silent. She is the queen of nothing. Explain yourself, woman.'

'I know nothing,' said Brieux, her painted face betraying as much.

'Yet you brought those hereti– those our friends here, hoping to incite their wrath against the duke.' Still, she said nothing. 'And I think you have done worse things in this place.' Catherine turned to Amy, finally.

'She poisoned me. It was her that told me to use that lotion. Put poison in it during the night, or had her maid to it.'

'The maid now dead,' said the queen-mother. 'The one beyond all earthly questions.'

'Dead because she knew too much! I reckon it was that girl that she had lock me in with the wolf. And you heard the duke – she had the maidservant … carry on … with his men so that she could speak with him. The diamond plot, your Majesty – it is to bring the church into disgrace.'

At this, Brieux finally looked up at Amy. Her eyes alone betrayed her fury.

'Yet this creature is a Catholic,' said Catherine. 'She has never shown herself to love the Huguenots. I have known her for a great many years.'

'The diamond leaguers, your Majesty, they are Catholic. But Catholics with a grudge against the Roman church.'

Catherine looked non-plussed, as though the concept of an enemy within was too much to deal with. 'Leaguers? There are many?'

'Four, perhaps. Well, less now. One is dead. My husband killed him in York.'

At this news, Madame de Brieux let out a single plaintive wail. 'You have murdered my child,' she cried. She began crawling along the floor towards her cot and threw herself on it. As soon as she began moving, the guards moved to protect Catherine.

'You have no children,' said the queen-mother, speaking over her protectors.

'My children,' the stricken woman repeated, banging her fists on the coffer by her bed. 'Ripped untimely from me. Sold to English filth to be reared savages. Whom have you killed? Whom?' She wiped her face, her hand coming away coated in dried paste. When no one answered, she said, 'my babies.' As though in shame, she turned again to her coffer and threw herself on it, scattering the lotions and potions that littered its surface.

'When did you have children, woman?' asked Catherine. 'You disclosed no children to me.'

'Not to you or anyone,' hissed Brieux. 'Thirteen I was, when I had my first, and fifteen at the last. Taken from me by their father, year after year, using me as he wished. A man of the corrupt church, a priest of Rome who brought shame on the faith. Curly blonde hair and the face of an angel. But not the manner nor the morals. It was me who discovered them when their filthy false parents died. Me who gave them purpose.

197

Which of my children have you murdered?'

'I don't know,' said Amy, her voice hardly audible.

'You think you have stopped them? I have set them on their path. They will have their revenge on Rome's corruptions. They will avenge my lost child. And me.'

'You will not die,' said Catherine, folding her arms. 'You will talk. You will tell me all that you have done. If you will not, your secrets will be drawn from your lips until all your friends are betrayed, children or no children. Guards, you will take this wretched creature and–'

Before anyone could do anything, Vittoria de Brieux began moaning. She slumped fully over the coffer and, as she did, her hands fell open. A pair of vials slipped to the carpet, empty. 'Jesus,' said Amy. 'The poison. She's eating it. She's *eaten* it.'

At the word 'poison', everyone in the room leapt back. Still, the woman's whimpers went on, turning to cries of pain and she folded to the ground, clutching at her stomach. Only Catherine did not move. Out of the corner of her eye, Amy saw the queen-mother staring in rapt, grim fascination as Brieux writhed and convulsed, now screaming in agony. 'It is a fast poison,' she said. 'Very fast when swallowed. It burns her. It burns her from the inside. Has she supped it all? Left none to be examined?'

'Physicians, your Majesty,' said one of the ladies, her hand wrapped around her throat. 'Shall I call for them?'

'The physicians are attending on the king,' said Catherine. 'My son has more value than this painted priest's whore. She is dead already. Her plot has failed.' The woman was still in her death throes when Catherine turned to face the room. 'May God be praised we are free from all threat of war. It must be given out that the lady has suffered some malady of the heart. See to it. Put it about the court that it was my lady's sudden illness which took me from the king's side. This disgusting affair must not be allowed to threaten the peace in any way. This dead and broken creature is a nothing, and her death must mean nothing. To anyone. You understand me?' The two women who had escorted the queen-mother to the ladies' chamber nodded, bowed, and fled the room in haste. Then the old woman turned to Amy.

'Alas, but when those Protestant fellows hear that she is dead, it shall be me has the blame of it. I can see the cruel rumours their false friendship will breed – that the king's mother poisons her own women for the playing out of jests.' She shook her head, her hooded eyes bitter, before returning her attention to Amy. 'Your own plot succeeded, girl. You have found your plotter.'

'One of them, your Majesty. She said 'children'.'

'Yet this was the creature you heard was about my person. That is all that concerns me.'

'You … your Majesty trusted her?' Amy let her eyes dart to the dead woman, but only briefly. Her face had contorted and swollen beneath its cosmetics.

'Hmph. I have known she had meetings with the duke of Guise. But their purpose and their design I could not divine.'

'The duke … might the duke have known of her plot?'

'No. Certainly not. The duke has faults, but he would have countenanced nothing that sought to hurt the Roman religion. This monstrous woman tried to use him to her own twisted purpose. To turn him to violence. God knows the violence of the last wars brought the censure of the world down on the heads of true Catholics. Speak no more of his grace.'

'You knew she was up to something?' gasped Amy. 'You knew, your Majesty? You might have told me. I mean – it might have helped me to discover her plotting.'

'I need tell you nothing, girl. You are nothing to me. You have done me good service. You shall be repaid for it.'

Amy bowed her head. Whatever the odd balance of personalities and politics between the queen-mother and the duke of Guise, she did not understand it. Nor did she want to. Yet an unpleasant premonition had suddenly come over her that Catherine was going to ask her to join the royal household on her own merit. The old woman's next words swiftly disabused her of the idea.

'The gratitude of my house is that these guards do not take you from the palace and whip you bloody through the streets of Paris. It is a foul and abominable crime to spread false slanders and rumours about your betters. As you did with the duke of

Guise.' She raised a hand to stop Amy before she could respond. 'A foul and treasonable crime also to have illicit traffic with a foreign ambassador when you were living at my table. Oh yes, I had you watched as you took yourself to that English Puritan's house.' Catherine smiled at Amy's look of angry surprise. The smile was not malicious. More softly, the old woman said, 'I am giving you your freedom from this wretched world. Take it, take your Scotch girl, and run. Run away this night. Get you gone to your sour English friend. I am sure you have much to tell him. And when you leave my realm, which I hope you shall do in all haste, you might have a royal escort to speed you to your lady of Northumberland or wherever you chance to go. Now pray get out of my sight and my house.'

***

Jack sat in the parlour of Walsingham's house in Saint-Marceau, waiting for his master to return. After he had lowered himself from a rooftop, he had run, not waiting to see how badly Polmear's killer had been hurt in the fall. It was unlikely to have done too much damage – a break of something vital was the best he could hope for. He found he could not sit still for any length of time, and he sprang up again and began worrying at a tablecloth. He was still at it when the click of the lock drew his attention. It might be the master, or any one of the senior servants, all of which had been given the festival day as a holiday. He put his hand to the dagger at his belt all the same.

Walsingham stepped into the parlour, locking the door behind him. 'I was attacked,' he said, feeling the rosiness in cheeks. The secretary wasted no words on sympathy.

'Who?'

'The same man from York. The one who must have killed Polmear, who tried to kill me before that. He's followed me here.'

'Or come in search of a higher master. Come. I will not discuss such things in this room. This …' Walsingham seemed to debate whether or not to speak openly. Eventually he sighed. 'This will be my family's room when my wife and daughter arrive later this month.' As though hoping to reclaim authority, he added, 'by which time I heartily desire you and your wife to be gone from my side and from my service. Come.'

As they trooped upstairs, Jack asked, 'it's a girl you have, isn't it, sir? A little girl?'

Walsingham stopped with his hand on the wall. He did not turn. 'Yes,' he said, tonelessly.

'That's a good thing. I'd like a girl. Not so much trouble from a girl, I don't reckon.' Jack was smiling stupidly at his master's back. 'Unless she marries a fool who gets her in trouble. Like Amy did. I hope your girl doesn't marry a man like me.'

Still without turning, Walsingham said, 'you're a strange young fellow, Jack Cole. Yet an honest one I think.' Then, barely above a whisper, 'a shame.'

In the office room upstairs, Jack relayed all that had happened, from the goldsmith's revelation to the chase across the rooftops. Walsingham even attempted to get him to trace out his journey on the map that hung on his wall, though to what purpose Jack could not understand.

'You should have stayed in the street, in faith,' said Walsingham. 'And listened for news of him. He could not have run after a fall. You should have arrested him.'

Jack reddened. 'This not England, sir. I could not arrest him.'

'Tsk. It were better you had kept him in your sight howsoever you did it. You are a poor pair of eyes to me if you run from danger.'

'I don't want to be eyes. I wish to be free of madmen trying to kill me,' said Jack, the nervous smile on his face.

'Which you shall not be,' said Walsingham, his tone dry, 'if you let the said madmen escape you.'

'It was I escaping him, sir.'

'Enough!' Walsingham collapsed in his chair, gesturing over the desk for Jack to sit. Before he could, a knock came at the door, and the pair locked eyes. 'Answer it. My man is not yet returned. Perhaps it is himself, or one of the other servants forgotten their backdoor key. I am sure you have experience in acting the servant. Go.'

Jack put his hand on his dagger hilt and crept downstairs. The knocking repeated. He considered asking who it was. Despising the cowardly thought, he opened it.

'Jack!' Amy screeched it as she threw her arms around his neck. She was out of her borrowed finery, wearing instead her usual old grey dress. Behind her was a girl he recognised but took a few seconds to place. She was, he realised, the countess of Northumberland's little Scottish maid, a travelling chest at her feet. He managed to flash a smile at the sullen-looking girl before Amy began chattering.

'We found one of the diamond plotters. Brieux – Vittoria de Brieux. She's dead. By her own hand. Would rather die than be forced to talk, I think. A woman in Queen Catherine's household, a right odd and crazed old wench, painted face and, and she tried to kill me, and … oh Jack. Things have been mad without you. Madder than ever before.'

'Come in,' he said, looking out over their heads. When they were inside, he closed the door, turning the key in the lock. 'Did anyone follow you?'

'No. I don't think so. We came here straight from the palace. The queen-mother, she threw us out, really – though I think she meant it kindly. I think. But that woman, Jack, the diamond woman. I've been living with her. She spoke of children.'

'He'll want to hear this,' said Jack, jerking a thumb upstairs. Amy gave a tight, resentful nod, before gesturing to Kat to remain in the parlour.

'Good evening to you, Mrs Cole. I heard that it was you.' A note of gentle mockery wavered in Walsingham's voice. 'What news?'

When Amy had finished telling him all about Vittoria de Brieux, the secretary stood and crossed to his map of Paris. Even in the candlelight, it looked indistinct to Jack, but he did not think that Walsingham was really studying it. Instead he seemed to be thinking.

'So,' he said, not turning to look at them. 'This plot concerned a French woman who had three children by a corrupt priest. They were given into the care of an English man and wife. When that man and wife died, the woman reclaimed them. Together, this fiend and her children plotted revenge on their faith. She sent them out into the world hoping to bring the corruptions of the Romish religion – of which there are many – into the general hatred of the people. The goal was to provoke the Christian world into discontent. Into wars of religion.' He paused, but neither Jack or Amy spoke, sensing that he was still thinking. 'Now two plotters are dead. One is here in Paris, possibly injured. Another remains abroad somewhere.'

'Can we leave this, sir?' asked Amy. 'Can we be free of it?'

Walsingham crossed his arms. 'No. No. I regret to say it, Mrs Cole, but you are both entangled very deeply in this. You have witnessed the death of a son in one country and his mother in the other – the mother who set this thing in motion. Another son – for I think we can assume he is her son – has even tonight tried to kill your husband.' Amy turned to Jack in alarm.

'I'm well enough,' he grinned.

'So,' continued Walsingham, 'I regret that neither of you can run from this plot whilst two dangerous agents remain abroad.'

'He's right,' said Jack. 'This man … he's tried to kill me twice now. And failed. He'll try again. And when he finds out that the mother's dead …'

'I will make enquiries tomorrow about this man. I have business to attend to in the city. If he fell from a roof and was hurt, there must be people who nursed him. Or at least who know what became of him. If the people of this city are in any state to talk tomorrow, I shall find out.'

'You don't want me to ask?' asked Jack. Before Walsingham could speak, Amy did.

'He won't. He can't. This man's after his blood.'

'Peace.' The secretary pointedly put a finger to his lips, staring at Amy. 'No. I suggest you leave Paris tomorrow. As soon as you can get gone.'

'Please, sir – the queen-mother said we should have an escort out of Paris. To speed us, she said.'

'Speed,' said Walsingham, stroking his chin. 'Yes. Good. Mr Cole, you have rid us of one of these vile men, the false priest in York. That dead man might yet answer questions. You know where he sprang from?'

'Douai,' said Jack. 'Where he came from, him and the other

203

Jesuits. We'll go to Douai.'

'Jesu, that dread place. If it must be, let it be. For security's sake, these people must be stopped. But you go, Mr Cole. Alone.'

'No,' cried Amy, before Jack could speak. 'We go together.'

'Control your wife, boy.'

'He's right, Amy.'

'What?' she wheeled around.

'Your husband sees that it is too dangerous for a woman. You will only slow him, you and your little wench. And you, Cole – do you wish your wife to swim in dangerous waters?'

'Dangerous … I've been near eaten by a wolf. Poisoned. I've lived in the most dangerous place in the world – with a crazed woman near my head at night. I'm going and you can't stop me. There's no law can keep me here, I'll break open the doors.'

'Amy,' said Jack. 'You can't come if I don't take you. It's as simple as that.' He let his old smile touch his features and then steeled it away, all in a flash. It would have to serve better than a wink.

'I … this is not the end of the matter.'

'There, do you see?' said Walsingham. 'Here you can be granted protection. And I am sure that you have learnt these past months that you can live without your husband at your elbow.'

'I can, sir. I can, but that doesn't mean I wish to.'

'What you wish does not signify in this matter. Your husband might go to Douai, which is in any case no friend to women. Then he might visit that devilish lady of Northumberland. Whilst he does so, I imagine this house will be a place of greater safety.'

Jack frowned. Clearly, the old man still hoped to have eyes on the countess. That was probably why he had shown his friendly face these past days. His ostensible desire to protect Amy was his old form of insurance – a cosseted hostage to ensure his charge did as he was bid, returning with news. Having a man with news of the English Jesuit college and the countess of Northumberland's household would be a coup. Queen Elizabeth and Sir William Cecil would kiss his hands in gratitude.

When the discussion was closed, and the drunken servants

returned, the house in Saint-Marceau was locked up. For the first time in months, Jack and Amy Cole slept sound in each other's arms, in a dank closet under the staircase. 'He was right about one thing,' said Jack, cradling her head. 'They won't let you in Douai. It's a priests' world. A world of men.'

'Hmph,' she grumbled. 'Then what – where do I go?'

'Out of France. To the countess, I guess, with that girl. As soon as he goes to his business on the morrow.'

'Hmph. Well, I'll see you on the road out of Paris first. You'll need me to get the royal escort.'

They slept soundly - that night.

***

Acre lay with his ankle tightly bandaged on a cot in a widow's house not far from where he had fallen. The old woman spoke to him from the kitchen. She had a look about her of the woman he had pushed into the flames, he thought. A pulse of pain banded his ankle and he winced.

'Don't even know how many have taken tumbles yesterday and last night. You young fools, drinking up on roofs. Asking for trouble. Asking for it!' She brought a tumbler to him and he sipped at the ale. 'There'll be more than just you being nursed this morning.' He swallowed. Mechanically, he thanked her.

'I wouldn't trouble you longer,' he said. His French came easily. It was the benefit of being raised in a town that had become more French than it ever was English.

'No trouble, son. But I tell you, I'm glad this royal entry is over. If you've seen one king you've seen all of them. Rotten pack. The things that go on in their courts.' He began to tune out her chatter. '… painted face about the city a lot, de Brieux, probably a lover of–'

'What? What did you say?'

'The woman they're saying took ill and died last night. At the palace. It'll be poison by a rival or else they stuff themselves to death with rich food.'

'A woman died?'

'Yes,' she said, smacking her lips, enjoying the scandal.

205

'Heard it as I swept the vomit from the front step this morning. Name of Vittoria de Brieux – one of the queen-mother's painted ladies. It's all over the city, they say – that she was probably done to death. But the story going out that her heart failed her. Well, they always say that, don't they? I've seen her myself, lots of times, going about on her horse. You know what I think? That those fancy powders they wear make them mad.'

Acre pushed away the ale. His voice, when he spoke, seemed to come from far away. 'Who else is at home?'

'None but yourself. If you'd like to help in payment for the bed, you'd better wait until you can put weight on that foot.'

Acre leant on the wall and got to his feet, putting the pressure on his good ankle. The old woman opened her mouth to speak and he cuffed her across the face, knocking her to the floor in a stunned heap. Before she could cry out, he began kicking her with his sore foot, blooming pain shooting through his entire leg each time he made contact. He was scarcely aware of what he was doing.

When he came to, he stuffed her broken body under the mattress on which she had nursed him. He then found her key and left the house, locking the door behind him. Within the hour, he had managed to walk to the Tuileries, where he ascertained that his mother was truly dead. Asking about the whereabouts of a friend, he found that the English lady had gone to live with that realm's ambassador. As he took the road to Saint-Marceau, he nearly collapsed in pain. Realising he would be unable to take Amy Cole and her husband without resting, he sat in the shade of a tavern. He had only just done so when the filth-strewn street clattered with the sound of riders.

There, as though they were continually trying to escape him, went the Coles, man and wife and a little servant girl, a pair of royal guards riding before them in tandem.

Rest would have to wait. He would find a horse and follow them at a distance, asking about their passage at every gate out of Paris, at every town, at every village, at every tavern on the road they were taking. It would not be difficult to find news of a group of people with a royal escort – the countryside would be full of speculation. There was nowhere they could run.

Nowhere they could disappear.

He would not stop until they were dead at his hand, one forced to drink the blood of the other before spilling his own.

6

The English college at Douai, in the Spanish Netherlands, was notorious in England as the breeding ground for Catholic priests. Jack had heard it spoken darkly of even before he had become entangled with Francis Walsingham. Even though he had embraced Catholicism, in his mind the place was still shadowy and frightening. Words alone had had the power to make it so, and once a picture had been painted in words, it was hard to erase.

Rather than a brooding, black-walled fastness, he was surprised and delighted to instead find a compound of new, neat brick buildings set in leafy, clipped parklands. It had the look, indeed, of an English college. Young trainee seminary priests walked the grounds, discussing their faith and reading to one another.

Much as Walsingham had predicted, women were not permitted. Although Amy had protested that she could remain in the town outside whilst he did his work, he had eventually convinced her to go on ahead to the countess of Northumberland, to return Kat safely and inform the countess that she would be leaving her service, the mission to the French court having concluded. Walsingham did not prove a problem. When he went off to the city in the morning, he had simply accepted that Amy was required to go with Jack as far as the city limits, directing the royal guard to accompany him. The fact that she had left her chest of fine clothes in his house seemed enough to convince him that she could not go far. Mr Francis Walsingham, Jack had mused, had some lessons to learn if he wanted to become a true master of intelligence.

Amy took with her the royal escort, the two agreeing that they might as well make the most of them. Only men in French royal livery could commandeer horses and ensure speed. Journeys that might take a week on one set of horses could be done in a couple of days with their help – and Amy and Kat would be well protected. There was a greater distance between Paris and

Bruges than between Paris and Douai, and the additional men would even out their trips.

In Douai, Jack found that he could not secure an appointment with anyone in authority for some days, being given assurance after assurance, and then politely put off. It was a bluff, of course. He was being discretely interrogated as each new priest enquired as to what business he brought and what urgency it had.

After several days of trying at Douai, the names of the countess of Northumberland and the Scottish queen, both women he had met and whom he could describe, got him an audience with Father William Allen, the college's middle-aged founder.

'You come from England, as I'm told,' said Allen, standing, and leaning over his desk to take Jack's hand as he entered. 'I understand you served the queen of the Scots. And have more lately come from the blessed lady of Northumberland.' He shook his head. 'Both good creatures, driven into infamy and scandal by the false tongue of the whore Elizabeth. Please, sit.'

Jack sat on a stool in the office, as Allen regained his own seat. The desk between them was covered in curled papers and inkpots. Sunlight fell in through diamond-paned windows, making the college's master glow. 'Do you know, Mr Cole, that being the master of a religious college is more writing than praying?' He chuckled softly. 'I apologise that I could not see you sooner. I am told you have news out of Paris.'

'Yes, father. But … I'm sorry that it's me who has come to beg news from you.' Allen said nothing but cocked his head to one side and began plucking at his neat beard. 'And I would be honest with you. I'm a true Catholic, father. I was brought to the faith when … when I served the Scottish queen.'

'Yet?'

'Yet … I've been forced to serve the English queen's man. Walsingham. Against my conscience.'

'You have come here to confess? Or to save your soul by telling us of this Walsingham's doings?'

'I … to confess, yes. But in faith I have protected your seminary priests.' Jack bit at his lips and then plunged in. 'Three

209

priests went to York late last year. Fathers Adam, Thomas, and Robin.' Allen's expression betrayed no flicker of surprise and he gave no denial or affirmation. 'Mr Walsingham – he had me set to watch for such men. And I did. But I didn't betray them. I gave them news of where to go in safety. Father Thomas, he didn't trust me. I don't know where he went. But Robin – with the red hair and the freckles – he went to Newcastle. If you know them both to be safe, you know I speak true.

'But it's not for them I'm here. The other, Adam. I have to know everything you can tell me about him. About his family.'

'Suppose,' said Allen, 'that I know of whom you speak. Why should I tell a turncoat man anything? By your own admission, young man, you are not to be trusted. You work for more than one master.'

'Because Adam is dead. I killed him.'

That got Allen's attention. The priest rose, sudden fear passing over his face. 'There has been no word from Adam,' he whispered, half to himself. 'Nothing to say he has been hunted down and butchered by the heretic queen or her dogs.'

'No,' said Jack, biting at his lower lip again. 'He was not … Adam was not a true Catholic. I mean, I know he studied here – the other two knew him. Trusted him. But the countess of Northumberland knew of a plot. The diamond plot. We discovered that Adam was a part of it.'

'You and Mr Walsingham?' frowned Allen.

'Me and my wife,' grinned Jack. He fought to return his face to more serious lines. 'We discovered that Adam was son to a woman called Vittoria de Brieux. A Frenchwoman. She … well, she claimed to have had him by a priest, who sold him and two other children to an English couple. And when she found them again, they made this plot to bring disgrace on the faith. Father, they killed people.'

'This is all hard to believe, Mr Cole. I … I knew this Adam.'

'What was his true name? Where did he come from? Did he have brothers?'

'Whom did he kill?'

'Well, it was he and another. His fellow plotter – a man who's been trying to kill me. I don't know who did what. But … two priests. Last year, two priests were killed. It was made to look like they'd died in sin, one killing the other. But it was Adam's fellow. Killed them so that Adam could be sent from here. And then there was a Protestant reverend and a poor old woman. Both Protestants. Both killed so that the English Catholics might be inspired to violent acts, or that others might be so disgusted they would rise up against their own faith. All to blacken the name of the Roman religion. To bring violence and hatred and war.'

'A strange tale. An ugly one. You know, Mr Cole, there are men of ambition in this world. Men who would invent plots … encourage them in order to stop them. If someone has embraced our faith in order to do evil … well, I should imagine the devil queen of England's disciples are behind it. One of them likely encouraged Adam in order to then *discover* the plot and crave favour at her cloven feet.' Allen sat back, scrutinising Jack's reaction. The scepticism must have been apparent. 'I know the two priests. I knew them, I should say,' said the priest, tugging again at his beard. 'And I heard about the nature of their deaths. I knew it could not be true, what was whispered about it. They were like father and son, not a catamite and a murderous pederast.'

'And Adam?'

'It is true, that young man was … he encouraged violence. Often. It was why I agreed to send him into England. Not to do it, of course, but to prevent his wild talk infecting his fellow priests here. Some were frightened of his talk. I worried it might discourage them from the faith – that it might make them think the lies told about us by heretics are true.'

'His family, sir. We know the mother. She's dead. We think her to have been the chief plotter – the queen of diamonds. Yet there is this other creature who's tried to kill me, and one other, we suspect.'

Allen did not respond for some time. The clouds shifted outside, and the room was thrown into sudden gloom. 'It was a sad case, as I recall' he said. 'We investigated Adam when he arrived. His parents died in a terrible accident, both of them. He had letters from Paris commending him for study. From a grand

French lady. Her word meant we had to do no more thorough searches into his past, into his friendships. She was attached to the royal court of France – and untainted by the heretics who were then at war with it. He was visited by no one, but he did speak of his siblings.'

'Who were they? Brothers? A brother and a sister?'

'I do not know. I had no reason to take note of them.'

'Might anyone else? Could you ask the other priests?'

'I will make enquiries. Visit me again in a day.' He gestured towards the door, a flick of his hand indicating dismissal. Deep lines were suddenly etched between his eyebrows. As Jack was standing up, Allen said, 'I do recall, Mr Cole, that before he left, Adam had a letter from Scotland. I do not read the letters of the seminary priests – this is not a gaol – but I note where letters come from and where they go. In case our investigations into our young men fail and we end up with some planted heretic, here to do mischief. Dark fellows, these creatures. They infect any good Catholic household they can under the guise of innocence and honest labour.'

Something clicked in Jack's mind.

Bowing to Allen, who still looked troubled, Jack nearly tripped over his feet in his hurry to flee the room. He left the building which housed Allen's office and went out into the gardens. He broke into a trot, slowing only when he was free of the college building and back at the little confluence of streets that marked the town. He stared at the ground, his mind racing as he walked.

As he passed a side street, he failed to see the dark apparition, hobbling but full of insane strength, leap at his back. Before he could cry out, a rope was around his neck, choking him and pulling him into the lane. He did not think. He simply ceased to feel at all.

7

The choker dug in, tight. The little triple string of pearls was the only thing Amy had taken from the stock of finery the countess had originally sent her into France with, and she considered it fair recompense for her labours. It looked odd, perhaps, glimmering above a plain servant's gown, but if people took her for a thief, that could not be helped.

The royal escort had got Amy and Kat across France and the Spanish Netherlands, from Paris to Bruges, in five days. Since the pair had been gone from the place, it seemed that the countess had returned to something approaching her former state – she was spoken of in the town as the English lady who lived under the Spanish king's protection. Rather than a small house on the main square, she occupied a great townhouse staffed with servants seemingly speaking every language. The place was on the outskirts, hard by the canal which embraced the city in an almost perfect circle. If the countess needed to flee at short notice, it would be an easy thing to take the water stairs to a small boat and go.

'A good place, my lady,' said Kat. 'Safe.'

'You don't need to call me that anymore, Kat. We're not doing that anymore, not pretending. Amy I was born and Amy I'll die.'

'Amy. Feels strange, after the last months.'

'Well, get used to it. Come, let's go. Your new home, eh?' In truth, Amy was nervous about seeing the countess again. Still, it had to be done. It could ensure a clean break with the past.

The usual train of access rooms was still in place, despite the change in surroundings. Amy had released the guards who had escorted them on the road, but here Spanish soldiers stood in a large, outer hall. Amy and Kat, in their service clothes, breezed past them, rightly assuming they were there to watch for suspicious gentlemen. A smaller hall lay inside, populated by clerks, accountants, and those gentlemen who were not deemed suspicious. Beyond this was the countess's private chamber.

213

'I'm one of the lady's servants,' said Kat. The guard at the door gave a military-style nod, not looking at her, and leaving Amy to push the door open.

The countess was sitting on a carved wooden chair with gilt arms, dictating something to her secretary, the unpleasant, sallow-faced Cottam, who sat on a stool with a portable desk before him. Both looked up in surprise.

'What in God's name are you doing here?' asked the countess when Amy strode into the room and took a theatrical bow.

'I bring news of the French court, my lady,' said Amy. 'And the diamond plot.'

'Not you,' said the countess, giving her an exasperated look. 'You, girl.' Amy spun, confused. Kat stepped nimbly past her with only the briefest of apologetic looks.

'I'd no reason to stay, what with her going,' she said. 'I couldn't stay her, my lady. Couldn't think of a reason, with her playing the mistress.'

'What is this?' Astonishment had fallen over Amy's face, her mouth hanging open. She looked at Kat as if seeing her for the first time. 'You,' she said, feeling as though she had been punched in the gut.

'I'm sorry, Mrs Cole. The countess is my mistress. For now and forever.'

'You – you were watching me? The whole time ...' Amy put a hand to her mouth. Dropped it. Laughed. 'You cunning little bitch.' She reddened. 'I'm sorry, my lady. I ... I ... you sent her with me to watch me?'

'Yes,' said Lady Northumberland. 'It was you who gave me the idea, Mrs Cole, with your tales of watching the Scottish queen whilst cleaning her sheets. I did not trust you. Why should I? Yet I trusted my little Kat. She would not betray me. She has kept me informed of all your news. All that has passed at the French court. You were never intended to be my eyes or my ears. My clever Kat was always to be those. You were merely a mask for her. Yet I commend you on playing the lady.'

'Queen Catherine saw I was no lady on the day we met. She let me stay as long as the king and his bride were from Paris. As long as she might use me to spy on a lady she didn't trust.'

'I see.' Turning her attention again to Kat, the countess asked, 'stand matters where they did?'

'The woman who poisoned us is dead. And I heard on the road out of Paris from Mrs Cole and her husband that one of the diamond men is dead. I'd have written that sooner if I'd known.' Kat's intelligence was interrupted by the clatter of Cottam's inkpot falling to the floor.

'Poison,' said Amy to herself, her wits beginning to return. 'The Frenchwoman, Brieux – she was the mother of the diamond plot. Its queen. A dark, painted lady. Dead. By her own hand. And one of her sons dead too. Adam. What was he … the knave? The ace? And an attempt was made at poisoning here, in the old house – the ale-seller. It wasn't an attack on the countess at all. It was aimed at me.' Realisation dawned on her face as she spoke. 'You,' she breathed, pointing at Cottam. You were there, in Aberdeen. In the old house here.' The realisation blossomed into wild excitement. 'Madam, it's him. He's the king of the diamond plotters, the eldest son!'

'What nonsense is this?' spat Cottam.

'It's you! You! You're how they knew who we were – how men in York and a woman in France knew who we were. Kat?' She turned to the girl. 'Kat, you were writing to the countess, right? Weren't you? Writing all you saw me do, heard me say?' Kat gave an embarrassed nod.

'Aye – yes – I wrote. In your name, but my lady knew it was me.'

'And so all that you wrote went through his hands. For him to pass on to his brothers in England and his mother in France.'

'Enough,' said the countess. There was neither anger nor surprise in her voice. 'I have heard enough of your accusations, Mrs Cole.' She raised her voice and called for the Spanish soldier stationed outside. The man entered, a hand at the hilt of his sword. Amy backed towards the corner of the room.

'Take her – she is a madwoman,' Cottam spluttered. The guard made a move towards her.

'Arrest Mr Cottam immediately,' said the countess. Momentary confusion crossed the soldier's face and was quickly gone. He moved towards Cottam and took hold of his arms, twisting them behind his back.

'Don't believe her, my lady! She is a liar – a madwoman! Please, my lady, I have served–'

'Wait,' cried Amy. 'Search him – search about him for a jewel.' Roughly, the soldier began tearing at Cottam's clothing, ripping open his secretarial robes and pawing at his doublet. 'There, there!' The soldier withdrew a diamond-headed pin, identical to the one Jack had shown her on the road out of France as having come from the York priest.

'A token bought with my money?' asked the countess. Cottam did not reply.

'It's a proof of his guilt, my lady. The diamond plotters each wore one.'

'I see. Well it is his no longer. Lock him up securely. Bind him. Have two men guard any means in and out of his chamber,' Lady Northumberland said. Still, her voice remained entirely calm. The guard passed the pin to her, still holding Cottam with the other hand. She looked down and began rolling it between her thumb and forefinger as her secretary was hauled away. The movement shook him out of his silence and again he began protesting and screaming.

'You knew?' asked Amy when he was gone. 'You knew?'

'Mind your tone, Mrs Cole. You are a feigned lady no longer.' The two women locked eyes, and the moment drew out until Amy, scowling, dropped her head. 'I own,' said the countess, 'that I made careful and secret enquiries into all my people when you turned out not to be as you appeared. I owe you a debt of gratitude. You have given me the gift of suspicion. Thereafter I found that Mr Cottam was a man of cunning in his letters. Much more correspondence came in and went out than I heard tell of. Monies, too, have been strangely handled. As you can see, I have met with generosity. Gifts from the Holy Father and my friends abroad have been depleted before reaching me, the excess gone astray. More, I discovered from Dr Prestall – you remember Dr Prestall? – that the fellow had purchased certain admixtures from him the day the ale-seller was killed. He claimed to buy them as a means of creating some potion to send the supposed English queen.' Amy remembered the strange, mystical-looking conjurer who had visited the countess that day. 'And in my suspicion, I instructed dear Kat, bless her, to write me in your name. Even Cottam did not know that intelligence from Paris came from her and not you. I did not know the nature of this diamond plot, not precisely. You say you have discovered it – that it was a family affair?'

Amy took a deep breath and explained all she knew to the countess.

'A most horrible conspiracy,' was Lady Northumberland's assessment. 'Catholics turning on their own true faith. Yet you say one of these creatures is still at large.'

'Yes, my lady. If Cottam was the king, and Brieux the queen, then the priest, Adam, was the ace or the knave. Whichever one he wasn't is still out there. And he's the one who has been trying to kill my husband.'

'Trying and failing,' corrected the countess. 'Yes. And he is abroad somewhere. As is your husband. Well, perhaps we shall have something by Cottam. I understand that Spanish soldiers are very skilled in interrogation. They can make it last many days.' Her smile sent icy fingers down Amy's spine.

***

Acre rode unmolested through the Belgian countryside, making all the haste he could towards Bruges, where his surviving brother dwelt. The eldest of the three had always been the most reluctant of the diamond league. His interest was money, and it was the chance to raise great sums of it that the angel, their true mother, had promised him. War, especially religious war, always provided the chance to become rich. She had pulled herself up to great wealth during the last wars, investing the monies she had inherited from her merchant father on foodstuffs and supplies and then doubling, sometimes trebling, the price when the fighting got hot and the people were starving. That had been enough to convince William.

Acre did not have any strong feeling for brother William, but he was the only remaining link he had with the past now. More importantly, he had a shrewd mind. If the diamond plot was to continue, or any part of it, it would be for him to decide.

A groan drew him from his thoughts.

Bound and gagged on a small, low cart behind him was Jack Cole, lying next to a large shovel, a good length of rope, and a cheap wooden clothes chest – each purchased from different sellers on the road. The creature's neck was still swollen and red. It had taken a good deal of self-restraint not to simply kill him outright, but he had learnt from the first time he thought he had done that that it would be unsatisfying. Jack Cole was bait. He would draw his wife out, and only when both were in thrall would their pains begin.

Acre reined his horse in, dismounted, and looked around. They were not far from Bruges. The road passed through a dense, swampy forest called the Bulskampveld – a hunting ground for the local gentry. As good a place as any. Acre withdrew some bread he had purchased on the road and, pulling away the strip of his old bandage that went around Jack's head, he stuffed the food in. 'Don't choke,' he said, replacing the binding. He had tried to talk to the man as little as possible. It might bring on rage. As he was watching to make sure his captive swallowed, the sound of hooves turned him to the road behind.

'What is this?' asked a soldier, drawing his horse to a halt. His French was seasoned with Spanish.

'Prisoner, sir,' said Acre. 'Dutch rebel. Heretic. Taking him to the city governors.'

'A prisoner … do you need an escort?' He looked down as Jack began to thrash against his bindings.

'No, sir. Orders from the duke of Alba's men that he's to talk to no one and go straight to Bruges.'

The Spanish soldier looked momentarily flummoxed. Acre waited. Alba's was a name few in the Low Countries cared to meddle with. The lie had worked all the way from Douai. It worked again. 'Yes. Good. Get him there.' The soldier gave one hard nod and rode on towards the city. He did, Acre noticed, turn his head a few times to look behind him. Then he was gone.

Acre tethered the horse to a tree and detached the low cart from it. Before anyone else could come to or from the city, he pulled the contraption into the woods, going as deep as he dared. Before the ground turned marshy, he halted and took out the shovel. With the pleasant sounds of Jack Cole's frightened mumbling, he began digging a grave that he would be sure the man filled. His wife, though, would go first. If all worked out as he hoped, she would go in still breathing, her husband watching as she was buried alive, every limb broken first.

When the grave was dug – the perfect width to accommodate the clothes coffer, and deep enough that no one could climb out unaided – he hauled himself out using the rope he had tied to a tree before setting to work. He removed the heavy lid and slid the box to the edge of the grave, carefully lowering it in. He then checked and double-checked Jack's bindings.

That done, he left his prey on the forest floor with his hands and feet tied together and returned to the road. No one, thankfully, had stolen the horse. He ripped a shred from his shirt and, using the diamond pin, he affixed it to tree. A fitting marker, he thought. An end and a beginning. He rode for the city as the the flat spring daylight gave its last gasp, and the sweet air turned musky.

It took some asking around, but eventually he found his way to the grand house in which the countess of Northumberland was apparently living like an exiled queen. Acre hovered around the servants' entrance at the back. No one paid him any attention, except for a singing maidservant who was laying what looked like a baby's garments on a hedge to dry. He ignored her and continued to wait. When twilight had come on, he managed to gain the attention of a clerk as he stepped out to piss into the canal. 'Whatever you're selling, man, we'll have none of it.'

'Not selling,' said Acre. Bullishness rather than charm, he had decided, was key. 'Looking for a man. Owes me money. Name of Cottam.'

Acre thought a change came over the clerk, but the man's voice, when he spoke, was perfectly normal. 'I'm afraid you won't see that money, and you've no use waiting around here begging it.'

'He's not here?'

'He's … he's indisposed.'

Acre's mask slipped, the contained rage of the previous days bursting free. He grabbed the man by the collar and lifted him from his feet. 'Where is he?'

'He's in prison – he's locked up – a thief, a plotter! Let me go.'

'Here? He's locked up here?'

'Yes! Yes! Let me go!' Acre continued to hold the man, who tried to kick him. Without thinking about it, he returned the favour, kneeing the struggling clerk hard in the groin. So, he thought, Jack Cole's wife had brought her poison here. That complicated matters. He might continue as planned, luring her out, or demand that his brother go free in exchange for Jack Cole's life.

He did not give it much thought. The diamond plot was dead – it was exposed. Adam was dead and their mother was dead. William was a greedy man, and he had never shown the same kind of love and understanding towards him as they had, not when they were lads and not since. Acre found he did not much care if his eldest brother went the same way as the Cottam couple who had burned in their beds. 'Find a woman in that house,' he growled, close to the man's face. 'A woman called Cole. Tell her that her husband is alive. Ride out on the road through the Bulskampveld, tell her. Alone. I'll be waiting. If she doesn't come, he dies. If she brings anyone, he dies.' He let the clerk slide to the ground, gibbering. 'And then,' he added, 'change your clothes. You've pissed yourself, you filthy beast.' The clerk began half-crawling, half-bounding, back into the house.

He watched the house from the front awhile, hoping to see the tumult as horses were raised and the woman sent. Probably, he thought, they were debating what to do – how to try and trick him. They would fail. If they organised some mounted force and he ended up having to kill Cole and leave the wife to breathe another day, so be it. She could not last long, a foolish woman in a foreign country. As he watched, irritated and, he was loth to admit, unnerved by the lack of activity, a cold voice inside his head reminded him that the woman had somehow evaded his mother, and the husband had evaded him. As much to silence the voice as anything else, he took his horse and took the road back out of town.

The turning was hard to find in the dark and made more difficult by the fact that his marker had been stolen. He had half-expected it, of course – he had been lucky enough that the horse had not been taken when he was digging the grave. This time he took the beast part of the way into the brush before tying it to a felled stump and going in to check that nothing had happened to Jack Cole in his absence. Sure enough, the fellow was lying there by the edge of the grave; the most he had managed was to roll over onto his side.

Acre moved over to him. 'If your wife wants you, she will come. And when she comes, you will watch her beg for mercy. You will watch her–'

His words became a high-pitched scream as pain shot through his leg – the same leg that still throbbed occasionally from its turned ankle. But Cole was still on the floor, he thought, confused. He looked down. An arrowhead was protruding through his burst breeches. Someone had shot him. As he stared dumbly at the unexpected wound, he heard a woman's voice. 'Now, Jack!'

The prone man suddenly stretched out an arm – unbound – and yanked hard at Acre's bad ankle. He stumbled, tripped, and fell headlong into the clothes chest at the bottom of the grave.

8

'Is he dead? I was aiming for his head,' cried Amy. 'Can you see, Jack – is he dead?'

They had barely had time to speak since Amy had found him. He had heard the crackling of footsteps as he lay with his face buried in greenery and assumed that his insane captor had returned. Hope had risen when he heard her voice, to be replaced by confusion when she said, 'lie still, sweetheart – I'll untie you. Pretend you're still down. And throw him down when I say.'

Amy came stepping across the forest floor from where she had concealed herself, wraithlike in the gloom. 'I'm no shot even in good light. Is he dead?' Together, they peered over the edge of the grave. The man who had been calling himself Acre was very much alive, though on his backside, pulling the arrow from his leg. He made no noise as he did so.

'Alive,' gasped Jack. Speaking was still painful. 'How did you … what happened?'

'Later, I'll tell you later. We have to bury him.'

'But he's … still alive.'

'That's too bad.' She had picked up the discarded shovel. Below them, the man tried to stand and fell back. Instead, he began scratching weakly at the sides of the wooden chest, reaching up to the earth walls above him.

'Shouldn't … shouldn't we kill him first?'

'I'm not climbing down there. He's tried to kill you – would have killed us both. And God knows how many others.'

'But we can't … it's not …' Jack was too dazed to think properly. In his mind, there seemed something wrong about burying the man alive, even though that was probably what he had intended for them. There was something inhuman about it. Killing him outright, in self-defence – that would have been fine. Necessary, even. To have him at their mercy and then slowly pile earth on him as he lay wounded, though … what did that make them?

'Would stabbing him in the heart first make him any less dead, in the end?' asked Amy. 'Or giving him to the hangman?'

'But … for honour's sake, shouldn't we …'

'Hell with honour. What honour would he have shown you? Or me? If I'd got him in the eye would that have been honourable?'

'Give me the shovel,' said Jack.

Together, husband and wife began scooping and pouring dirt over the scowling creature who lay on his back, choking and gasping as it rained down on him, in the grave he had dug himself. 'He's saying something,' said Jack. 'Shut up, shut up, shut up!'

From the bottom of the grave, the wounded man was hissing. 'Demons. Monsters. Look at me. Look at what you do.'

'Ignore him,' said Amy. 'Don't listen.' Lacking a shovel, she was dropping and kicking mounds of dirt down into the grave. 'Where's the lid? Of the chest, where's the lid?'

Jack began scrabbling in the undergrowth until he found it. With him taking one end and Amy the other, they stood at either end of the grave and dropped it down. 'No!' cried the stricken man from below. 'Not the dark!'

The lid did not strike home perfectly, but it covered the fallen man well enough. 'Dirt'll do the rest,' said Amy. 'Weight it, I mean.' They fell again to filling in the hole with mud and stones.

When they had finished, they stood staring at the mound. 'How … how long can he be alive down there?' Jack asked, wiping sweat from his forehead and leaving a dark stain.

'I don't know. Not long. Probably dead already. I hope. I keep thinking his hand is going to pop out of the ground.'

Jack could not see her face in the dark, but he put an arm around her. 'He's dead. A bad way to go.'

'What are we, Jack? What are we to have done this?' She shook her head, not waiting for a response. Instead, she provided her own. 'We had to. We had to do it. He deserved it.'

He did not answer. Instead, he kissed her hard on the top of the head, and then took her by the lips. They trudged out of the forest and took the dead man's horse back towards the city.

***

Amy explained what had happened on the weary, moonlit ride.

A Spanish soldier visiting the countess reported that he had seen a strange man carrying a bound prisoner by the side of the road. The news had spread like wildfire through the household – especially because the soldier had himself come from the duke of Alba and knew of no Dutch prisoner.

'I was all in a panic,' she said, her hands clasped around his waist. The evening's events seemed to have taken something out of her. 'I forced myself in, begged the countess for information. Offended her, I think.' She paused to yawn. 'And confused the Spaniard. You should have seen his face. But he said he'd take me to where he'd seen the man. He was leaving tonight anyway. Had only come to say that she had promise of a house in Malines if she wanted it.

'We were all ready to leave. Then Kat came in and said there was a man outside who looked like Cottam.'

Jack gave a hoarse laugh. 'Yeah. Cottam. That's who he reminded me of. I knew the face looked familiar. I was coming to warn you all of him when that mad dog got me.'

'But he was alone. So we went anyway, right away. The soldier, he let me down when he saw there was no one about and I told him to go his way. I thought if he had you somewhere out there, I could get you before he got back.' It was her turn to laugh. 'And I remembered that bow, the one the countess made me practice with last year when she wanted me to look a lady. Never was any good at it. But I thought if I saw him coming on the road, I could get him before he could touch us. Then … well, you know.'

'I know you saved me. You saved me again. Whenever I get into a scrape, Amy Cole comes and … gets me out of it.' He had nearly said 'digs' and bit his tongue. The damp, earthy scent of turned soil had got into his nostrils. He doubted he would ever be able to walk in a forest again without the smell reminding him of that night's dark work.

'And if you keep getting in scrapes … I'll have to keep doing it. Promise. You know I will.'

Jack did. Amy had only just beaten the madman, sending the soldier on his way and tearing down the diamond pin and marker before he arrived. And then they had buried a man alive. 'It's this way,' said Amy. She directed him through the city and together they went in through the servants' entrance to the countess's house.

They ignored the barrage of questions and made directly for her private rooms. She received them.

'You are alive,' she cried. 'And … begrimed. This fellow you warned of, Mrs Cole, this last diamond plotter – he was here. Looking for you. He attacked one of my clerks. He wished you to ride out to meet him for your husband's life. I … I was worried. Worried that it was some kind of trap. Bless you, both.'

'It was,' said Amy dully. 'But it snared him, not us.'

'You mean he is …'

'Gone,' said Jack. 'There wasn't any other way.'

The countess nodded and gave a thin-lipped smile. 'Cottam has spoken. I did not have time to tell you before, Mrs Cole.' Jack and Amy said nothing, but they looked at her expectantly. 'He has confessed to everything. Rather a sad tale.' She bit her lower lip and looked down. In her hand was the diamond pin. Amy's hand went to the one she had torn down. Seeing them both, Jack reached inside his mud-spattered coat and drew out his. 'It was like this. A little girl had three sons by a corrupt priest. He sold them away from her to a family living in Calais. Back then it was an English town, before Queen Mary lost it to the French.

'When Calais was lost, the couple and their charges remained. Only the poor and the titled were expelled. The rest kept money flowing. One of the boys, William, the eldest, loved money. The nature of the man he had thought to be his father was passed on to him, I suppose. The other loved religion. Adam, who trained as a seminary priest. The third … he was a troubled child. And becoming a vicious brute, rather frightening to his eldest brother – and certainly to his parents.'

'What was his name?' Jack whispered.

'It doesn't matter,' snapped Amy. 'Sorry, my lady. But truly it doesn't. We don't need to know what his name was. Please, continue.'

'I … quite. Yes. I understand. Of no importance.' She cleared her throat. 'Well, when this boy learned of his true parentage, he burnt down his house. He and his brothers were then sought out by their real mother, by then a creature overblown in pomp and wealth, and driven half-mad by the years of waiting and watching. She embraced her sons, and together this group formed plans. They would bring shame on the church that had given the boys life and then taken them from their mother. They would see the whole of Europe brought low by war. The eldest boy would profit by it. The next would see corrupt Catholics and their enemies, the false Protestants, cut each other down, allowing a true Roman church to be reborn from the blood of the sinners. The last boy – troublesome boy – he loved his brothers, but he was a dangerous madman. He would be given purpose. They took the name of the suit of diamonds. The rest, Cottam says, were just numbers – nothings, nobodies used as couriers.'

'And now only the eldest remains,' said Amy.

'What happens to him?' asked Jack.

'He begs mercy. He says he has killed none by his own hand.'

'But the ale-seller in this town,' Amy began.

'Mr Cottam claims that that was an accident. He does not understand poisons. He acted only to scare you, my dear, from meddling.'

'Liar – that man is dead and –' The countess held up a hand before continuing herself.

'He says also that he believes you have taken more from him than he has taken from you.' Jack and Amy looked at one another but said nothing. 'He has constructed of you quite terrible monsters.'

'He and his family were the monsters,' said Jack. Amy nodded. 'Will he get mercy?'

'That is not for me to decide. I shall send him to the Holy Father. With a written report of all that he has done. If he deserves mercy, a higher power than I shall give it. If not, then … it will be divine judgement. At any rate, the faith is unharmed. The diamond plot is broken. Its worst agents are in their graves.' Jack shivered at the word, and the countess gave him a sidelong look. 'I wish to hear no more of the matter. The question remains, of course, what to do with you. And your wife. Mr Cole?'

'I'd like to go in peace,' said Jack. 'Somewhere ... holy. To confess and be shriven.' He could sense Amy rolling her eyes.

'Then that is for your conscience to decide. Tell me, does Cecil's man still court you? Walsingham? Never mind. Kat has already informed me that he waxes soft towards you both. Allowed you to lay your heads in his house. It is just ... those who are loyal Catholics and yet who have friends amongst the back-biting heretics ... especially friends who are trusted by the supposed English queen ... might be of use to me.'

'Madam, we would be out –'

'Pray let us think on it,' said Jack, putting a hand on Amy's arm to quiet her. He did not look down, although he could feel her startled eyes on him. The countess smiled. 'Very well. Go and think.' Her baby began to whine. 'Send Kat to me. You may lodge here tonight, after you have bathed in the waters behind the house. My hospitality is no less than Mr Walsingham's.'

Jack and Amy left as Kat, presumably alerted by the sound, entered. They passed through the clerks' room, into the outer hall, down the stairs, and outside via the front door. As soon as they were out of the countess's presence, Amy began an angry tirade. 'It's not right if Cottam gets to live. He's a killer – he killed that old man. Whether he meant to or not. And he was up to his balls in all the rest, whatever he says.' Jack did not respond, letting her run herself dry as they passed around the house towards its rear. 'And you! You don't want to stay, do you? Passed back and forth between them as they claw lumps from each other? Her, the French dowager, Walsingham – they only ever mean to use us. It's just all a more dangerous kind of service. Sure, they might pay us, but they'll never care for us, these lot. Not secretaries or queens or ladies or any of them. You can't want to be tangled with them, not again.'

'No. No, of course not. You'd have to be mad.' They had come to the edge of the canal, and the sound of gently lapping water caressed them.

'Then why did you tell her that? For a bed for the night?'

'No. Well, not only that. To temporise.'

'What's that?' Suspicion sharpened her words.

'Something a friend taught me. Say yes, if you have to. To keep going.'

'What friend? When?'

'It doesn't matter.'

'Well, we can't go back to Paris. Leastways not for a while. That old goat Walsingham won't be happy with us, me running off like that. I … What's wrong, Jack?' She licked her finger and wiped away dirt from his forehead, brushing away the stray lock of hair. 'This thing we've done tonight … it troubles you.'

'Doesn't it trouble you? I mean, shouldn't it trouble us? Jesus, Amy, what have these people made of us? Her, and Walsingham, and all of them? Are we bad people – are we monsters?'

'No,' she said, shaking her head. 'It's a monstrous world. Good people have to do bad sometimes because there are such monsters.' She sighed, and a tear cut a path through the muck on her cheek. 'It's a rotten business, this always thinking of what you're doing. It makes your teeth itch.'

To his surprise, Jack laughed. 'What? It makes what?'

She shrugged. 'Something my mam used to say. Let's get out of here tomorrow.'

'To where?'

'Calais. Put the pins down where those people were murdered. To remind us who the real monsters are.'

They laced their fingers together and kissed, grave-dirt flaking, as the calm, glassy surface of the canal bathed them in reflected moonlight.

Author's Note

Anne Percy, nee Somerset, the countess of Northumberland, has long been credited as a driving force behind her husband and the earl of Westmorland's Northern Rebellion of 1569. She fled to Scotland in the wake of the rebellion and thereafter had a chequered stay in that kingdom, eventually giving birth to her daughter, Mary, and leaving for Bruges in August 1570 'with neither penny nor halfpenny'. The ship was called *The Port of Leith*, as depicted, but having it taking shelter in Bridlington Bay is my own invention (this being a regular retreat for ships hoping to ride out North Sea storms in the period). Also fictional is the portrayal of the flight from Old Aberdeen taking place against a backdrop of an assault by Morton's soldiers. All we know is that the journey is recorded as having taken place from the 23rd of August to the 31st. Morton's men certainly had her husband, the earl of Northumberland, and would undoubtedly have liked to get their hands on Anne; yet escape with Lord Seton she did. Her husband, imprisoned at Lochleven (a castle on an island from which Mary Queen of Scots once made a daring escape), would be less fortunate. He was sold to the English government in 1572, taken to York, and beheaded.

Anne remained in exile in Europe for the rest of her life, attracting much interest from Catholic sympathisers and Protestant enemies. In the English state papers, she is reported as having called Elizabeth a 'supposed' queen, and, on arriving in Bruges, engaging with one John Prestall, a shadowy necromancer (and chancer) who sought to place Mary Queen of Scots on the English throne. Anne was in Malines by 1572, Brussels in 1574, and at Liège from 1575. She died in 1596. What became of her last child, variously identified as Mary, Maria, and Marie, is something of a mystery.

Astonishingly, no full-length biographical study of Anne Percy exists. However, I am deeply indebted to Dr Jade Scott for providing me with her ODNB entry and the biographical chapter of her doctoral thesis, 'The letters of Lady Anne Percy, countess of Northumberland (1536-91): gender, exile and early modern cultures of correspondence' (2017: University of Glasgow). It is to be hoped that this excellent piece of work is available to a wider readership soon. In a similar vein, I discovered John Prestall through Michael Devine's 'John Prestall: A Complex Relationship with the Elizabethan Regime' (2012: University of Victoria). Although he only appears fleetingly in the novel, readers might be interested in learning more about a man the thesis describes as 'an unsavoury, nefarious, spendthrift, Catholic gentleman from Elizabethan England. A conspirator, opportunist informer, occult conjurer, conman and alchemist'.

Although he became king of France in 1560, Charles IX (born in 1550) did not reach his majority until much later, and he lived very much under the influence of his mother, Catherine de Medici. The first decade of his reign was plagued by the wars of religion fought between Huguenots and Catholics, which were temporarily halted by the Peace of Saint-Germain-en-Laye, a treaty concluded in early August 1570. In November of that year, the king married Elisabeth of Austria, and the queen-mother busily raised money for and set the Parisian aldermen to plan his much-delayed royal entry. These royal entries were fabulous spectacles designed to introduce monarchs to the cities over which (and, in this case, from which) they would rule. A description of the tableaux and decorations used in Charles IX's entry can be found in Francis A. Yates' *Astraea: The Imperial Theme in the Sixteenth Century* (1975: Routledge and Kegan Paul) and *Epic Arts in Renaissance France* by Phillip John Usher (2014: Oxford University Press).

The most enjoyable and informative biography of Catherine de Medici is Leonie Frieda's *Catherine de Medici: A Biography* (2005: W&N). The queen-mother's reputation has suffered over the centuries, with the image of a malignant, calculating murderess holding sway. Frieda does not sugar-coat or gloss over the famous 'Madame le Serpent's' occasionally sinister behaviours (such as her very necessary skill in political intrigue), but she does present a more realistic, rounded woman. Catherine was not a scheming poisoner, and her much-criticised interest in horoscopes and the occult was entirely normal for people of her class (of either gender). For an enthralling overview of the structure and dramas of Catherine's household, Dr Una McIlvenna's *Scandal and Reputation at the Court of Catherine de Medici* (2016: Routledge) is a must-read.

In researching the effects of poisons, both ingested and cutaneous, I was continually delighted by Eleanor Herman's *The Royal Art of Poison: Filthy Palaces, Fatal Cosmetics, Deadly Medicine, and Murder Most Foul* (2018: St Martin's Press). Of especial interest is the section on remedies and amulets used at royal courts in the period to ward off poisons: from disgusting-sounding theriac mixtures to jewels with supposedly magical properties to the much-famed unicorn horns. These were actually narwhal tusks found washed up on beaches in the northern hemisphere and sold at eye-watering prices thanks to the belief that they belonged to unicorns and could reveal the presence of poison. Interestingly, the French royal physician Ambroise Paré rejected the power of these horns in the 1570s (though certainly not because one was used in a murder).

Catherine de Medici ordered construction of the Tuileries Palace begun in 1564. This palace stood at the west side of an as-yet unconnected range that included the existing Louvre on the east. Between them stood a courtyard filled with gardens. The two buildings would be connected later in the century by the Seine-facing Great Gallery, which today forms part of the magnificent art gallery. Construction was still underway during the period of the novel. Sadly, the Tuileries was destroyed in 1871.

Catherine was much credited with helping broker the Peace of Saint-Germain-en-Laye, but it was unlikely that she thought it would last. One of the obvious losers from it was Henry, duke of Guise, later known as 'Le Balafré', or 'Scarface'. Guise enjoyed a love affair with Catherine's daughter, Margaret, in 1570, and was drawn rather unwillingly into the peace and all but forced to marry Catherine of Cleves in order to restore his good name. Peace never sat well with him. In 1572 he became a suspect in the assassination of the Huguenot Admiral Gaspard

Coligny, whom Guise held responsible for his father's death. The result of Coligny's death was the eruption of hideous violence known to history as the St Bartholomew's Day Massacre. The kind of widespread bloodshed the villains of this novel hoped to spark really did happen. Although it was not for the reasons they hoped, the result was the same: the massacre became a stain on Catholicism, and it led to the fourth war of religion in France (1572-3). Those interested in the Guises will enjoy Stuart Carroll's *Martyrs & Murderers: The Guise Family and the Making of Europe* (2009: Oxford University Press).

Guise did not gift the royal family an African hyena, but such creatures were known in Europe. Menageries existed, although the word itself was not coined until the seventeenth century, and exotic animals were housed in royal courts from Scotland (which boasted a lion and, under James VI, a camel) to England (where the Tower of London was, over the centuries, home to jackals, tigers, pumas, leopards, and a polar bear). The idea of a nobleman owning a vicious hyena is borrowed from a later chapter in France's history. In the 1700s, the French countryside was the hunting ground of the mysterious 'beast of Gevaudan'. This animal supposedly slaughtered dozens, favouring women and children. Its reign of terror ended when it was shot dead by one Jean Chastel, Rumours have since grown that the monstrous creature was trained by Chastel, who was said to be able to control its behaviour. Though unverified, eighteenth-century museum records supposedly show that the animal shot, skinned, and then publicly displayed as the beast was a striped hyena – one of which Chastel's father is said to have housed in his private menagerie. It is a story so intriguing it has been made into a film: *Brotherhood of the Wolf* (2001: Dir: Christophe Gans). In the picture, 'La Bête' is depicted as a trained, armoured lion. Other theories hold that it was a deformed wolf, or a wolf-dog hybrid.

If Guise was unhappy with peace in France, Francis Walsingham was rightly proud of his work in helping to achieve it. In the autumn of 1570, he was sent as a special ambassador to France to help consolidate it after the previous ambassador, Sir Henry Norris, was recalled. Walsingham returned briefly to

England before being dispatched to Paris as the new resident ambassador in January 1571. He had the unenviable task during this second sojourn, which lasted until 1573, of negotiating marriage between Elizabeth and the duke of Anjou. During his time in Paris, he lived at a modest house in Saint-Marceau, and at this period he was years away from acquiring the reputation of the all-powerful spymaster that he would enjoy in later years. He was, if anything, far too trusting and eager to prove his worth, as evidenced by the fact that he trusted in the Florentine agent, Roberto Ridolfi, who would later be found to be behind a plot to put Mary Queen of Scots on the throne. I thoroughly enjoyed John Cooper's *The Queen's Agent: Francis Walsingham at the Court of Elizabeth I* (2012: Faber & Faber); Stephen Budiansky's *Her Majesty's Spymaster: Elizabeth I, Sir Francis Walsingham, and the Birth of Modern Espionage* (2006: Penguin); and Robert Hutchinson's *Elizabeth's Spy Master: Francis Walsingham and the Secret War that Saved England* (2007: W&N). Useful as ever was Stephen Alford's *The Watchers: A Secret History of the Reign of Elizabeth I* (2013: Penguin), and critical in providing a perspective on the role of women as early modern spies was Nadine Akkerman's *Invisible Agents: Women and Espionage in Seventeenth-Century Britain* (2018: Oxford University Press).

France was far from alone in suffering religious tensions in the late sixteenth century. The failure of the northern rebellion saw the north of England hideously scarred by a wave of brutal punishments for those found guilty of having been part of it. As it was the first (and would be the only) major rebellion against Elizabeth's government, the reprisals were swift and brutal. Hundreds of men were hanged. Although the clergyman killed in East Gilling was fictional, the death toll for rebels in that town is recorded as 225. When combined with Pope Pius V's infamous bull, *Regnans in Excelsis*, which declared Elizabeth a heretic and released all English Catholics from their allegiance to her, the government crackdown on the north ensured that it was an unsettled place throughout the period. It was from 1570 onwards that the English government really began to treat Catholics as enemies of the state rather than nuisances who could be ignored or cowed with the occasional show of barbarity. Similarly, Catholics were suddenly empowered to dispatch Elizabeth with any means that came to them. Jack's experiences in the north were supported by Krista Kesselring's *The Northern Rebellion of 1569: Faith, Politics, and Protest in Elizabethan England* (2007: Palgrave Macmillan) and George Thornton's *The Rising in the North* (2010: Ergo Press).

The Jesuit college at Douai, then in the Spanish Netherlands, was founded by William Allen in 1568, and became a production factory for Jesuits: missionary priests, usually called seminary priests, whose goal it was to infiltrate England and build support for a return to the Roman religion. Allen would go on to be a vituperative opponent of the Elizabethan regime and would pen a number of tracts and treatises condemning Protestant England and its leaders. The old 1909 biography, *William Cardinal Allen: Founder of the Seminaries*, by Bede Camm, has been recently reissued and paints an interesting picture of one of Elizabeth I's bêtes noires.

Although it is only visited briefly in this outing, London will always be an interesting place to write about. I strongly recommend Ian Mortimer's *The Time Traveller's Guide to Elizabethan England* (2013: Vintage Books) and Liza Picard's *Elizabeth's London: Everyday Life in Elizabethan London* (2004: Phoenix). The latter contains the finest modern map of Elizabethan London that I've ever come across.

Jack and Amy Cole are reluctant spies. Whether or not they will be dragged into any other plots remains to be seen. Yet the times in which they lived were fast-moving, complex, and endlessly involving for people possessed of intimate knowledge of events and public figures – even if they would rather forget them. As Jack seeks a greater sense of absolution, Rome would seem the natural choice. Amy will go where Jack goes, because he might need rescuing. In 1572, the eternal city would be the site of one of Europe's most splendid spectacles, and one which drew together any number of diplomats, watchers, and cunning cardinals: a papal conclave...

If you've made it this far, thank you. Whether you enjoyed this book or threw it aside with great force, Dorothy Parkerstyle, feel free to let me know on Twitter @ScrutinEye or on Instagram: steven.veerapen.3

*

Printed in Great Britain
by Amazon